FOLLOW ME
ALL THE
WAY
DOWN

For the wanderers...

author's note

Hey everyone! You're here! And that's so cool! (I really appreciate you.)

Just before you start, I wanted to put a little content warning beforehand, because as a fellow human person, (and also a queer human person), I know we all have things that make us uncomfortable or aren't awesome for us to read about. This book contains heavy themes, including death, memory loss, a kind of psychological torture, and abusive relationships. Those are the major ones, but if anything makes you start to feel a bit weird, take a break, put down the book, drink some tea, throw the book at a wall... whatever helps.

Don't hesitate to skim or skip sections you don't really vibe with, and above all, please take care of your wonderful selves.

Thank you :)

Zoe

prologue

July 13th, 6:35pm

Location: East Harlem, Manhattan

Ezra Colton

The teeth are the very least of my problems at the moment. The fire blowing goat with four chicken legs and a rat head isn't even my biggest problem. The biggest problem is that I'm alone. I can't protect myself. (I'd expect *some people* to be out here. There were people outside a few moments ago. And now the street is empty. They probably ran inside, screaming, like a normal person would if teeth started falling from the sky.) (*How* can no one be out here? Everyone's always trying to stick their noses into places they don't belong.) (So it only takes some teeth falling from the sky to get people to leave you alone. Great.)

The broken glass crunches as I run. I'm sweating, not only from all the running, but from the copious amounts of fire being blown at me by the rat–chicken–goat. The teeth are still falling.

I don't really care about the bloody little nicks the teeth make on my skin. The lenses of my glasses are smudged with sweat. And I don't care about that either. What I do care about is not getting incinerated by said rat–chicken–goat. I'm absolutely terrified. I've never seen anything like this before. I was just wandering through the streets when it started raining teeth (really messed up), but I didn't have time to even acknowledge the awfulness before this abomination decided I was going to be its next... meal? But now, I'm getting tired. So tired. I'm just kind of done. Though, my death is now almost guaranteed ... a tooth hits me right above my brow. A trickle of blood leaks down, stinging my eye.

"Shoot," I mumble, (because, even in mortal danger, I refuse to swear. Apparently.)

In that moment of distraction, I stumble and fall. *What a cliché*, I think. *Tripping while being chased by some stupid monster.* There are shards of glass and teeth stuck in my palms. I turn around to see that horrible *thing* catching up.

Suddenly, the fight in me is just ... gone. (It's not like I had much fight in me to begin with.) I rest my head on the pavement, not caring at all anymore. I make eye contact with the creature. It rears up on two of its scaly legs. I almost feel bad for it, because... well, I don't actually know why I feel bad for the thing that's going to kill me. I close my eyes, ignoring the crunch of glass. I'm honestly fine going like this. No one will even care and it'll... be over.

The silence is deafening. The teeth make a steady clinking as they hit metal or empty window frames. The monstrosity's feet grind into the tiny shards on the ground, making sickening screechy noises as it approaches. My throat gets all tight, as the sound is kind of like nails on a chalkboard. I breathe deeply. All I notice is the acrid smell of smoke and blood. *I'm* probably bleeding. The abomination sneezes. I open my eyes and laugh a little. It bares its teeth, standing over me now.

I know it's the end.

It opens its mouth.

I see the fire a second before it hits me.

There's so much pain. The burning. Agony.

Nothing.

CHAPTER 1

chapter 1

July 13th, 5:30pm

Location: East Harlem, Manhattan

(San)Tiago Grey

As we're being evacuated, I find myself looking over the crowd. Always scanning. I see her alone. Alone as she can be, in a mob of panicking children and teenagers. Her curly red hair and pale, freckled skin stick out, making her easy to find. I still can't see him. *Where is Ezra?* Just like him, though, to disappear before a crisis.

Something hits my shoulder, but when I turn, no one's there. I'm absolutely sure someone ran into me, but it's chaos in here. Whatever.

In the metal evac tunnel, it's dark. Tiny plinking noises sound above me. I don't really care. I need to know where Ezra is. Ever since I was seven, I've needed to know where Ezra is. I don't know *why*, but I've been in this dump since I was three. I don't remember my parents at all. Ezra's been here for just as long. Seeing him is sort of... a sadistic form of reassuring. Yeah.

Ezra's almost always with Rosemary. She's his guardian or something, because he's normal.

Faint shrieks come from outside. I look at Rosemary again. She catches me looking and glares. I smirk and wink. She pretends to vomit and flips me off. She hates me enough for both of them. Her and Ezra, I mean. Ezra knows I hate him, but he doesn't really care. Maybe it comes easier after being hated for your entire life.

"Shhhh," the caregiver (jailer) says as she halts us. "We will be going to our muster points in groups. You will be numbered off and we will let groups out at two minute intervals. Do not resist, or—" she sniffs disdainfully, "use your gifts." She walks down the crowded passage. I'm not sure why we need to evacuate, but they're telling us to. I've learned it's better to listen to the guards, even though I can't remember ever being evacuated like this. I've snuck out of this place more than once, and was locked in an actual jail cell that I couldn't get out of no matter what I tried, for almost three weeks as a punishment. So, yeah. Rather not do that again.

"One, two, three, four, five, six—oh shut up—seven, eight, nine, ten, eleven, twelve..." She's on her fourth round of counting to twenty when she reaches me. "Eight," she snarls.

I don't think she likes me. None of the guards like me. Or anyone here.

"Please hold up your number on your—"

"I don't have twenty fingers," a little boy interrupts.

"Shut *up*," the jailer (caregiver) yells. "Just find your groups."

Chaos erupts again. Everyone's screaming their numbers. I lean against the wall, holding up eight fingers. This is ridiculous. An anxious looking, snivelly teenage girl comes and stands beside me. So does a tall guy with a black hoodie. I don't know what's happening. Things eventually quiet down. We have a group of six. Looking around, I notice that all the other groups have seven. We're missing one. Rosemary sulks over, taking her sweet time. Shit. Why *her* of all people? I swear she's the personification of annoying. She hates me, she's Ezra's best friend, she's favoured by the jailers... it just never ends. *Why does Ezra like her?*

I scowl. The seven of us sit in miserable half silence as the first five groups go to god knows where. The screaming outside is gone now. Just the tapping on the roof. I shudder. It's odd that after so much time being trapped in this place that they're just sending us into whatever's outside on our own. A twinge of anxiety creeps into my stomach. This is really weird. After the fifth group, we have to wait an extra ten minutes. Emeline leaves Group Six to come sit beside me. She's tall, slender, with light pink hair that goes down to her waist. (Coloured with dye I stole for her when I snuck out.) I grab her hand. She smiles her lazy half–smile, and rests her head on my shoulder. I discreetly kiss the top of her head (because this place doesn't tolerate romance), while making eye contact with Rosemary. I don't know why. Rosemary just looks away.

A few minutes later, Emeline has to go back to her group. My shoulder is oddly cold, apparently missing the warmth of her. Actually, I'm just oddly cold in general. It must be this stupid tunnel. Why are we even *here?*

Group Eight (my group) soon gets ushered to the exit. An intimidating guard with ridiculously thick penciled–on eyebrows forcefully hands me a slip of paper. I turn my violent burst of laughter at the bad makeup job into a (convincing?) cough.

"Your muster point location," Eyebrows says gruffly. "Go there now. You're to return here at eighteen hundred hours unless otherwise notified."

"Thank you." Rosemary's too nice to any adult. She's somehow completely unfazed by the caterpillar brows. But these people think we're dangerous. They don't care if we live or die. I guess I could say the same about them. I hate them. I hate this *place.*

I'm thinking this as we walk out, but my thoughts stop mid–rant. It's the strangest thing I've ever seen. It's raining teeth. Human teeth, coming from the clear sky in a downpour of awfulness. I stare up for a second, shuddering and trying to see where they're coming from. Then, a tooth hits me in the forehead. I flinch, bringing my hand to my face. My fingers come away sticky. Red. I glance backwards in time to see Rosemary step outside, stop, gasp, look slightly sick, gag, then swallow thickly. I walk over to her. She tries to stumble away, but she's a little wobbly. Lucky for me, I have long legs.

"Hey," I say softly.

"What do you want, Santiago?" she says flatly, without looking at me.

I'll cut to the chase then, I think. "Where's Ezra?"

"I don't have the faintest clue." She pauses. "But I wouldn't tell you even if I knew."

"Jesus christ," I mutter. "You're impossible." She really is.

"Thank you." She smirks, glancing back at me briefly.

This time, when she tries to walk away, I let her speed up. The teeth *really* hurt when they hit me. I want to get to our muster point as fast as possible. We're stumbling down a narrow alleyway, about ten minutes later when the boy at the front of our group stops.

"What's wrong?" I ask him.

He just points. The teeth are falling faster now. There's a burning, over-turned car in the middle of the street. It's surrounded by strange creatures. I can't quite see what they are, but I've never seen anything move like them. Jerkily animalistic, taller than an average person and shrouded in white feathers. The road is covered in glass, teeth, and chunks of random broken things. A loud, invasive beating noise fills the air, and when I squint up, there's a big machine circling above us. Like a plane but with like. Spinning blades. What is it? Sirens are blaring, far away. Far away.

Rosemary and I make eye contact. There's panic shadowing her dark brown irises. She picks up a crying little girl, whose skin is now steaming. She hands the girl to another teenager in our group. Mason. Dark hair and ivory skin. Emeline's friend. *My* friend. I didn't even realize she was here.

"Stay with them," Rosemary says, glaring as she stumbles over to me. "I need to find Ezra," she hisses, mostly to herself.

"Are you crazy?" I demand, leaping in her path. I need to go with her.

She shoos the other five members of group eight in the opposite direction of the ravaged street. She gives me a stern, yet frightened look. "Go."

I hand the slip of paper to Hoodie Dude, shooing them away as well, while returning Rosemary's pointed look. "No way. I'm coming with you," I say stubbornly.

She sighs, then walks towards the creatures.

"Wait. Do you want protection?"

"No," she says and then resumes walking. I want to say something along the lines of, '*Well that's your loss, sweetheart,*' but I keep my mouth shut. I take a deep breath and imagine safety; a shield of sorts. I can feel the air around me come alive with popping magnetic energy, like a forcefield. And then it's done. Simple as that. No one else can do the stuff I can. (I can manipulate atoms and particles into doing what I want.) I can especially do more than *Ezra*. He can't do anything. Rosemary can heal. Emeline can move things with her mind. I can just. Be better than everyone.

I have to run to catch up to Rosemary. She's determined; I'll give her that. The only reason I reach her is because she stops at the end of the alley. When the creatures take off running, out of my view, Rosemary gasps, abruptly bolting away and stopping just as quickly.

What? Is it Ezra? What's happening?

"It's group twelve!" She's panicking. "Those... things are chasing them!"

"I'll save them." I'm confident I can. There's a twisted piece of metal on the ground, like a lightning struck branch.

She keeps staring in confused horror while I focus. I can *feel* the singing atoms in the debris. They vibrate, rising from the ground as they come apart. Previously bound to each other, the pieces of shrapnel practically laugh as they speed through the air, towards the creatures as I run out of the alley's mouth, ready to hurl the metal shards.

As soon as I release the pieces, I crumble, a gasp of pain escaping my dry mouth. The metal tinkles to the ground around me, hitting the teeth with little pings and clangs. It feels like someone stabbed me in the stomach. What? That only happens when I've tried to hurt people. (Humans have a way of resisting my gift. I have no idea why. Maybe their particles are more intelligent.) But those things *are not* human. My hands hit the ground. Panting, I struggle to my feet. There are teeth sticking out of my palms. I've lost contact with the particles. *Fuck.*

"Santiago, you have to keep try—" The screams of group twelve cut her off. We both jerk our heads up, just in time to see... She covers her mouth. I'm shaking. Frozen. I *failed.*

"Where are they?" Rosemary gasps again. "Jesus Christ, they're just *gone.*"

She's right. Group twelve is gone. The creatures are too. We run into the now dead street. We're both spinning around, looking for any signs or clues or... anything that could be a living human named Ezra. The teeth bouncing off the broken glass from the streetlamps and windows make the creepiest noises. Everything is feels off kilter. Rosemary is almost hysterical. Her face is dusty from who knows what, and the dust is streaked with tears. That yanks on something in my gut. I have no idea how to comfort her. Or if I even need to?

"We need. To find him," she says, twice, pulling me out of my head.

She grabs my wrist, dragging me through another alleyway, to check the next street. It looks the same as the one we were just on. I stare at the back of Rosemary's wild hair. There are so many teeth caught in it. This is starting to get... awful. Grotesque.

Fighting back a sudden wave of nausea, I let out a slow breath. And that's when I hear it.

Footsteps. She hears it too. We stop. Someone runs past. He's tall, slender, with messy, brown curls. Light brown skin. He's wearing jeans and that stupid T–shirt with the stupid typewriter font that says: *Daydreamer*. He has super long eyelashes that I can see, even from here. His jaw is clenched. Pink lips hanging open, breathing heavily, glancing over his shoulder, panic in his green green eyes. His clear framed glasses are smudged with dirt and spattered with bits of blood.

He's running. Alone.

It's Ezra Colton. He's completely useless. Rosemary is about to dart out after him, when a jet of fire appears, followed by a humongous ... thing. It has the body of a goat, four chicken legs, and the face of some weird rodent.

"Oh no, oh no! We have to do something!" Rosemary's frantic. She darts forward before I can stop her but then Colton trips and falls. His hands scrape along the glass and teeth and pavement. He slides a little bit. Winces. Rolls onto his back.

Everything stops, including Rosemary. Including my heart.

The only sounds are of chicken feet on broken glass. Ezra's heavy breathing.

"No." Rosemary's whisper breaks the trance.

I still don't move. Ezra needs to fight it. I'm yelling at him in my head. He needs to get up. He needs to keep running. Ne needs to do *something*. But he doesn't. The thing sneezes. Ezra barely reacts. Is he *laughing*? He's bleeding from a small cut over his eyebrow. Probably the teeth. And he's literally laughing, in that soft, half desperate way of his. He's giving up. That fucker is giving *up*.

Rosemary screams. The air smells like smoke.

Ezra screams too. He's burning. He screams pure agony.

She's running. And crying.

I stumble after her, my feet moving on their own. The flames, though. They're not quite right. They come out of the beast's mouth, but it's burning *itself*. Not Ezra. I stop about seven feet away. Rosemary's right in front of me. She must have noticed it too.

Then, the beast shrieks.

And simply turns to dust.

We both run to the smoking body on the ground. Ezra. He has to be alive. He has to be. He always survives. He *always* survives.

Ezra Colton

"Ezra."

Everything is burning.

"Ezra." More urgent this time.

I don't want to get up. There's no point.

"Ezra." Yelling now.

My head hurts. So do my neck, and legs, and arms, and feet, and—

"Oh God." The voice is panicked. "Ezra!"

I should be dead.

"Colton, you *dumbass*." Different voice. Softer, less afraid. Tiago.

Why is he worried? Why is he *here*?

"Come on."

Someone touches my face. Cool knuckles brush my forehead. It feels nice.

"*Goddammit*." Tiago again. "Colton."

I twitch. Not what I meant to do.

"Ezra?" the first voice whispers.

I twitch again, and open my eyes a little. Two people are crouching over me, blocking the late afternoon sun. It's still too bright. I can't see their faces, but I know Tiago is here.

Slowly, my eyes adjust, and I see Rosemary. She covers her mouth with a filthy hand.

"I knew it was an act." Tiago rolls his eyes. They're blue. A really cold blue. His pale skin is a light orange in the sunset as he stands up, crossing his arms. I watch him pace a little ways away, and run a hand through his wavy blonde hair. It ends around the ropey muscles that connect his shoulders to his neck. I swallow, letting my aching eyes drift back to Rosemary.

She's crying. I'm still lying on the decimated road. One of the teeth is embedded in my shoulder. My skin feels like it's on fire. Blistering. Burning.

"I thought you were..." Rosemary can't finish, which is kind of surprising, because I've almost died at least eight times. Normally, it's my fault. I've gotten electrocuted four times (you'd think after playing with live wires once, I'd have learned my lesson...), burned twice, now three times, fallen, (or got pushed, depends on who you ask,) off a roof, and other stuff along those lines.

"Ezra ..." She gently lifts me up to sitting.

It's excruciating. I grit my teeth, so she doesn't worry. Too much.

"Ezra. I—" She looks really scared, and her face is stained with tear–streaked dirt.

Tiago's standing a few feet away from us. Rosemary grips my arm. Her hands are warm against my already scalding skin.

"Where's the monster?" I ask. My voice is weird. Scratchy.

"Always the questions," Tiago mumbles under his breath, pausing to look down at me with a disgusted grimace.

He goes back to pacing. The teeth have stopped falling. And the monster is gone. Rosemary shares a look with him, except it's not really sharing, because he doesn't even look at her. Somehow, he's mostly clean. His hair is lit from behind, giving him a kind of halo. Rosemary's dark eyes are intense when she looks back at me.

"Ezra, you—you—" She's stuttering.

"You killed it, Colton," Tiago says, stopping again. "Like. You burned it. Unless it was *supposed* to self–destruct."

I squeeze my eyes shut. "What?"

"You heard me, idiot."

Rosemary's glaring at him.

"You were getting burned. Then the fire just, well, turned inside out and burned it. Like it disintegrated. Just poof," he says, miming *poof* sarcastically with his hands. "Just in case you didn't get that, I was talking about the monster." Tiago doesn't usually ramble like this. He looks at me for the first time since I sat up. His eyes are hard. He hates me.

Rosemary's wild red hair is matted. She sticks with me, no matter what. She's my best friend. Why is Tiago even *here.* I don't understand what's happening.

Rosemary always has to help me get out of these situations. I don't have a gift. A lot of the time, I wonder why I'm in a home for kids with powers. I'm *normal.* So I used to get bullied a lot. Not really anymore though. I got taller. People stopped caring about me and started caring about things like friends. Partners. Books. Dreams. Gossip. Whatever. It's easier now, I guess.

Rosemary, Tiago, and I pretty much live in a prison. It's called Ester Myrtle Kellwether's Home for Unusually Gifted Youth and Children. Kids get taken to the 'home' if they're strange. Like if they have magic, of sorts.

I don't know if the government is really involved, but they must endorse the home. Or home*s*. Some of the guards have medals pinned to their chests. A man who worked at the home told me they were under so many gag orders from the 'higher ups,' but he's gone now. Sometimes parents find the home themselves, and sometimes the guards find the gifted kids and bring them to Ester. But I'm not gifted. I can do nothing out of the ordinary. And yet, I've lived around gifted kids like this my whole life. I've come to the conclusion that my parents just hated me, and there was nowhere else for me to go. I used to think Madame Ester was my mother, but only because I can't actually remember my real one.

Rosemary's still gripping my arm, which is starting to feel less burn–y. Her gift is healing me. "Ezra?"

"Yeah." I rub my eyes with my palms. She lets go.

She puts her head in her hands. We've all seen strange things before. We breathe, eat, and live strange, but we've never seen something as strange as this.

Tiago's back to pacing. I don't know why he's here.

Rosemary Mae–Anderson

I swear. I swear if he ever disappears like that again and almost dies, I will have to kill him myself. (It's a wonder his glasses haven't melted to his face.)

Why Santiago followed me? I have no idea.

How Ezra killed the... thing? I have even less of an idea about that. But Ezra's okay. I grab his arm. Pathetic, hopeful, happy–go–lucky Ezra lives again. Or. He lives *still*. He's fine.

He's burned really badly though.

The spot on his arm I was holding is almost back to its normal light brown. It looks really strange, how his whole arm is an angry red except for my handprint. Pus filled blisters spatter his angry skin. I push down the pity that twists my insides.

Santiago won't look at us. He keeps pacing. Ezra's shivering. His favourite T–shirt is mostly incinerated. There are teeth everywhere. The ones in his mouth are chattering. The sound is echoing down the empty streets. The sirens are louder now. *Much* louder. The helicopter that was circling before is still there. If any first responders find us, we're gonna be well and truly *fucked*.

"Tiago, why—why are you here?" Despite everything, Ezra's smiling. Santiago stops and looks down. He runs his hand through his wavy hair.

"I couldn't miss a chance to see you die, Colton," he says, in the least convincing way possible.

Ezra just laughs. He was laughing when he almost died. (I can't decide if that's terrifying or reassuring.) I can't help but smile. He's the kind of guy who cares about everyone. It's so hard to understand why he's nice to all the people who hate him. When he laughs, it's hard not to laugh along. *Hmm*. I see that even Santiago is smiling slightly.

"Rosemary..."

I whip around, looking for whoever said my name. Police officer maybe? It wasn't Santiago or Ezra. How would an officer know my name? I glance at them both. Neither one seems to have heard. Taking a rattling breath, I shove down the uneasiness. Ezra needs me right now. It's probably just stress. And trauma. I have enough of that to go around. It'll be fine. So fine. One hundred and *one* percent fine.

"Okay. I'm going to fix your face," I say to Ezra, trying my best to sound like everything's fine. (Voices? What voices? I'm *not* hearing voices.)

"Yes, ma'am."

I put my hands on his face. I focus on the heat I feel and take it away. Slowly but surely, the swelling and redness and blisters disappear. They disappear, just like group twelve. They're gone. Just gone. I... don't know what to think about that. (More trauma. We are *winning* today.) I decide not to tell him about them yet. He's still shivering. Even worse now than before. Ezra tries not to show when he's in pain, but I can see it behind his eyes. I can *feel* it.

He's struggling to keep smiling. Santiago isn't. Smiling anymore, that is. He's still looking down, massaging his neck, the glimmer of happiness now gone. When I look back, Ezra's face is contorted in a strange smile–grimace, which would make anyone else look ugly, but not him. I touch his arm again. He's freezing under his burning skin. I don't have a coat to give him. Or a sweater. I also can't lift him alone.

He grabs my sleeve. "Rosemary. Don't worry. I can get up."

His eyes are pleading with me not to feel sorry for him. When we were young, he didn't have a gift. (He still doesn't.) He pretty much had a target painted on his back. He was so small. He would always sit alone at meals while people twice his size threw things at him and laughed. Right now, he's reminding me of the first time I talked to him. Tiny and inadequate. Except, that time, he was crying in a dark corner of the stairwell.

He glances at Santiago, who's scornfully upturned lips are taunting us. "Please."

I shrug, stand, and walk slowly towards Santiago. How Ezra doesn't hate him is a mystery to me. Santiago Grey has been cruel to Ezra for more years than I want to know about. Not once, not twice, but three times, he convinced Ezra to play with live wires. The wires set Ezra on fire once. And that's just the beginning of it. So, I've made it my duty to hate Santiago enough for the both of us.

Santiago glances back and starts pacing again. Ezra grits his teeth and tries to push himself up. I shouldn't have let him do it alone. He's on his feet, but he's swaying dangerously. I lurch forward at the same time that he falls, but I'm too slow.

Santiago catches him.

CHAPTER 2

chapter 2

July 13th, 7:00pm

Location: East Harlem, Manhattan, Ester Myrtle Kettwether's Home for Unusually Gifted Youth and Children

Genevieve Legend

This evacuation business is so fucking stupid. Useless. I wish I were somewhere else, doing anything else. I wouldn't have even evacuated at all if I hadn't been dragged out of the library by an aggressive guard who made me go to that nasty tunnel.

There is no way I'm going to go running around outside in the falling teeth. Dear god, does this sort of stuff happen here all the time? Because if it does, then screw all the paperwork my parents did (to legally give up their responsibility, obligations and custody of me so I could live in this place) and promises I made to them (that I wouldn't escape, and that I wouldn't tell people about my mind reading). I'd at least keep the second one. I'm not telling people I can read their minds. Generally, thoughts aren't something people express out loud unless they've decided to talk. Never again will I expose someone's personal thoughts. Questionable choices are what got me here in the first place.

I need to be rational. But, that tunnel was crazy. And loud. I'm usually super good at avoiding people when I'm invisible, but I was running into people left, right, and centre.

I waited in the storage closet as people left in small groups. The roar of internal chatter got quieter and quieter, until the last guard locked the evacuation tunnel.

I sigh. My head is pounding a little, which is normal when there's a billion people around. The more humans there are, the louder the thoughts get. I slide down the wall in the storage closet. The guard who's searching the halls for any stragglers has tiny, almost inaudible thoughts that are just a whisper in the back of my head. I can ignore that.

Some of the things I hear are crazy. Today, it was mostly people's fears. The most common one, unsurprisingly, was death. So many people's minds were like *Am I gonna die? Is this a life threatening situation? Why are we evacuating?! What if I die. What if I die. What if I die.* That was fun. I make a list in my head. Of their fears. Death, confusion, drowning (a strangely high number of people were concerned about drowning... even though there's no water anywhere near us), annoyance, anxiety, dragons, dental floss... and this one guy I ran into was really worked up about a whole dramatic situation, with a girlfriend and some other girl and a guy. I can't even pretend I want to understand *that.*

I don't really want to be involved in that kind of drama here. I prefer to do things on my own, especially after getting... hurt. At my school. I made some strange, emotion fueled decisions, in a strange emotion fueled situation. A girl can only take so much. I'm currently reading, even though I can hardly see. A copy of The Hobbit. It's super worn, the pages soft with wear. All my books are at home. I was lucky to find this one in the home's library. Most of the books here are just bad.

Rosemary

Santiago caught him. Thank god. The two of them are awkwardly standing in the middle of the road, leaning against each other, Santiago's arms wrapped around Ezra's waist. Neither of them are breathing. I frown, inching closer to them.

Ezra tries again to move forward. Santiago steps back tentatively, but his hands are doing a weird little dance, like he's debating whether or not he should reach forward again. Ezra's still swaying. This time, he takes a wobbly step before falling sideways into me. I push him back up. His shivering is worse. I wish we could find him a jacket or a sweater... or a shirt. Goosebumps prickle along his trembling shoulders. He stumbles. Again. Santiago's closer. I assume he'll catch Ezra, but he's not ready this time. Ezra struggles for balance for a moment, then his legs give out. His knees crunch against the glass and he curls into a ball, head in his hands.

"Shit," Santiago mutters.

I immediately drop to my knees next to him, putting a hand on his shoulder. "Ezra..."

"Stop," he whispers. "Don't say my name like that." The whispers seem so loud in this empty, echoing space, backed by sirens that get closer and closer. Someone's talking. Giving orders. We need to get out of here before someone sees us.

I'm about to wrap my hand around his arm and try to drag him to his feet but... he's shivering and his shoulders are quivering harder now. Is he... oh. He's crying. My throat tightens. I put a hand on his warm shoulder.

Ezra's whispering into his hands. "I'm not weak. I swear I'm not. I'm not—" He breaks down. "I'm not weak," he pleads, trying to convince himself in a broken whisper, it seems. Trying to convince the voices in his head. (Voices. Hah. There are *no* voices.)

I haven't seen him cry in years. My eyes well up. Santiago kneels down beside Ezra. He unzips his light down jacket and lamely offers it to Ezra, who doesn't even notice. (That fucker had a coat this whole time... I'm gonna throw hands.) (I would, with no hesitation, but then. Ezra's more important.) He's crying really hard now. I wrap my arms around him and press my cheek into his back as he struggles for breath.

"I'm sorry," I whisper.

Santiago's still kneeling, looking lost and a little bit cold. The sun's setting for real now. There are footfalls crunching against the teeth. People are coming. The windows that aren't broken are casting golden light everywhere. I let go of Ezra and make eye contact with Santiago. He looks upset as his gaze drifts down to Ezra.

"Colton. Come on," Santiago urges, out of the blue. "We really need to get moving. Everyone else is probably back by now, and if we're not there soon we'll be stuck outside all night and in the morning, they may lock us up. Or normal people will find us and then we're so screwed. I'll help you walk. I really don't want to be stuck outside all night again."

How many times *has* he been stuck outside? I lift my eyebrows at him, but he's not paying attention to me. Ezra inhales stuffily and looks up at Santiago with his big green eyes.

"Okay." He stays on the ground.

Santiago offers him a hand. Ezra doesn't take it. He's still shaking. Santiago hovers for a moment, then picks up his jacket, gently placing it across Ezra's shoulders. Ezra stiffens, then exhales, getting slowly to his feet. He wipes his face with his palms.

"Okay?" I ask.

Ezra nods, looking absolutely miserable. He puts his arms over our shoulders and we slowly pull him into the nearest alleyway. He keeps shivering. His feet drag.

Having Santiago here is bizarre. Although, now that I think of it, he's almost always here when this stuff happens. Ezra just seems to attract this kind of disaster. Not ever in the form of falling teeth and chicken-goat-rats, but yeah, I think it's him. He just has *really* bad luck. (Bad luck with wavy blonde hair and blue eyes, that is.)

This is only the second time something awful happened to him without Santiago's direct help and influence. The first time was when we were eight. Ezra had been missing for a few weeks, which just happened a lot when we were younger. And still now sometimes, though it's usually only a few hours. I don't ask him where he goes. He needs time in the real world and no one stops him. The world doesn't need to be protected from him, because he's just a boy. (Sometimes he lets me sneak out with him to go to restaurants or the park.)

But when we were eight, he came back one day from who knows where, his neck, and arms covered in tiny punctures, his face swollen, maybe burned. He wouldn't tell me what they were from. We had just become friends. That was the only other time he got hurt without the assistance of Bad Luck (aka Santiago Grey).

This is the way Ezra and I work. We each have our secrets, places where the other knows not to prod. And we're good with that. If it weren't for Ezra, I'd have no one.

Tiago

About halfway back to our home (prison), I'm definitely certain that Ezra's miserable. I hate it when he's miserable. I also love it. It's hard to decide how I feel about his feelings.

"You're full of mysteries, Colton," I whisper. *Wow*. What a great attempt at cheering him up.

A hint of a smile spreads across his face, but it doesn't reach his eyes. "That's what they call me. Full of Mystery Man," he mutters, sarcasm dripping from his hoarse voice.

"Okay, but really, did that monster thing just combust on its own? I don't think so," I pause for a second, but he doesn't say anything.

Rosemary butts in, "Ezra, that was crazy weird... you're like a hero. I thought you were done for."

Ezra isn't having it. "Yeah, because they praise heroes for saving themselves *all* the time." The eyeroll is apparent in his tone.

"Colton, what if..." Do I say the thing percolating in my mind? "What if you have a gift?" It came out on its own. Alrighty then.

"And what if it starts raining teeth?" He actually rolls his eyes this time. It's such a big eye roll that I see it in my peripheral. "Oh, wait, that already happened."

Rosemary glances at him, her eyes full of pitying concern. "Ezra, if you were trying to imply that you don't have a gift, you should say something that *hasn't* happened."

"Yeah, I know. I was just trying to point out how outlandish today's been, because it doesn't normally rain teeth..." He looks at both of us, as if trying to prove a point, then huffs, "Okay fine, maybe Tiago will..." he trails off. "Actually, never mind. It doesn't matter. I don't have a gift. That's that. Period. End of story."

Maybe I'll what? Maybe I'll what? Maybe I'll *what*? But I don't ask what I might do. I just sigh. "Fine. You don't have a gift. You just have magically good luck where demented monsters about to kill you just spontaneously combust."

Ezra grins for real this time as his eyes dart to me. "Aah, yes. That must be it."

Rosemary scoffs. Ezra playfully glares at her, the smile still on his lips as he pushes up his glasses with his shoulder.

I stumble on a piece of broken concrete. Surprisingly, Ezra pulls me back up.

"What," he hisses in my ear, "are you doing here?"

His question shocks me. I purse my lips, looking straight ahead. We're getting close to the home. We wait in an alley as a police car zooms past. Ezra keeps watching me, his eyes glinting in the dying light. I don't know why I'm here. How am I supposed to answer that?

"Uhh, because... because I..."

"You're kind of awful at hating me, you know," he cuts me off quietly. "I must be a positive influence on you..."

I roll my eyes, but can't help smiling a little (sometimes he talks like a fifty-year-old). One side of his mouth is quirked. He laughs softly.

"You think you're so funny, you dumbass."

He laughs harder and snorts. All three of us really start laughing now. His laugh is contagious. It makes me wonder why I decided to be a jerk. I shove that down quickly. No time to worry about my (possibly stupid) decisions.

"Maybe I do," he says wistfully.

We're almost back to our prison (home) when he stops.

"Okay, Tiago," he says while unzipping my jacket. "You have a reputation to uphold. Go in now and you won't have to be seen with us."

"Keep the jacket. You can't go in there looking"—I give him a once over—"like that."

He isn't wearing a shirt and his jeans are singed down to threads around the cuffs. (How does he kind of have abs? That's... what. *I* don't have that good of kind of abs. That's not fair. And *how* is his skin so smooth? I have freckles and little moles all over my shoulders—)

Rosemary clears her throat. I swallow, darting my gaze back up to his face. He's biting his bottom lip, trying to hide a weird little smile. Blood crawls into my face. Hot and itchy. Good thing it's almost dark?

"Um. Sorry. I—," I bluster, for *no reason what the fuck.* "I will go. Now."

Ezra wrinkles his nose at me. "It's fine. I walk in *like this* at least twice a year. Give or take a couple."

"Haha."

He throws the jacket. I snag it out of the air with one hand.

"Come on." He nods his chin towards the door to the home. When I don't move, he raises his eyebrows. "Go, Tiago."

"Please, just go," Rosemary says, exasperated when I hesitate.

I run my hand through my hair and turn away from them. I don't understand. I've done nothing but torment Ezra Colton, yet he's still so nice. The wrought iron gate isn't locked. I guess we got lucky. I don't even know what time it is, but I'm sure it isn't 6:00 pm, when we were supposed to be back. I slip through, then open the door. Hopefully no one notices me.

The room goes silent. They noticed me. Drat. Everyone got back. Almost everyone. The picnic benches are full of kids. Who are now all looking at me. But there's a couple of empty spots where some of those people who disappeared on the street used to sit. Group twelve. I shudder, swallowing thickly. A Black girl with coils of hair tipped with light blue dye smirks at me. Have I seen her before? I don't know.

I realize I'm still holding my jacket in one hand like a moron. (Because that's the first thing *I* use to tell if someone's a moron. Holding a *jacket?* They *must* be an idiot.) My hair is also a mess. Emeline stands up—my girlfriend, *right,* I have a girlfriend—but before she can move, a guard with a scary amount of facial hair grabs my arm and drags me down one of the many hallways leading off the common room.

I couldn't stop him if I wanted to, but they don't need to know that. I can't hurt people with my gift. Some sort of weird moral compass. So I don't resist—they'll lock me away if I do.

I end up in the dark office at the end of the hall. I've definitely been here before.

Too many times for me to count.

Shit.

Genevieve

When this guy walks in, I can't help but laugh. He's the same guy I ran into earlier (Drama Man), and the look on his face! Priceless.

His mind is racing: *Why did I give Ezra my stupid jacket? Woah, everyone's back already?! Everyone's looking. Shit this is bad we're all gonna get in so much trouble. But where's group twelve? Gone. They're gone. Who's that girl over there sitting alone? There's Emeline and holy crap I look like an idiot holding this jacket. People who hold jackets are morons. I should go over there*—A guard grabs him by the arm *not* holding the jacket, and drags him down a dark hallway.

I look down at my plate and the guy's thoughts fade into the general chatter. I glance over at Emeline who's on her feet, gaping at the spot the boy was. She's about to have a screaming or crying fit because her boyfriend (because he is her boyfriend) didn't say hello. Unfortunately, no one gets to see that fit because one of her friends pulls her down onto the bench again, comforting her about her *nasty, inconsiderate, jerk* of a boyfriend who I now know is *the famous Santiago Grey.* People think about him a lot.

He's not actually famous. He's just popular in this place. He's a conventionally attractive so called alpha male who could possibly be a really mean guy without a personality. I haven't talked to him, so I wouldn't know, but. I did go to high school. I've seen people like Santiago Grey. Sometimes they surprise you, but sometimes... well. They suck. His girlfriend reminds me of this girl named Lucy. They don't look similar, but from the way she acts... I think they'd get along. I could be wrong. I thought *I'd* get along with Lucy, but it didn't work out so well.

The last few months have been rough. I'm so lonely, but I'm scared. In the blink of an eye, I lost my life as I knew it. Some people here would probably sympathize with me, to be honest, because I've overheard snippets of stories like mine, where guards showed up at people's houses to take them away. Because of our gifts. (Bullshit, in my opinion. They should have a better name. One that tells you how much of a burden they are.) My parents didn't have a choice. I didn't have a choice. But I try not to think about life before. Because it just. Hurts too much.

I'm done with people. For a little while at least. I need to make sure I'm comfortable in the world again. I'll find someone who isn't going to hurt me like that, but not right now. I'm tired. But I also kind of feel like I'm waking up. Like I've been in a coma for seventy days, and the colours are just starting to come back. I can breathe a bit again. I've been around this place for three months, and today was the first time I became visible in the common area. I like to eat in the library, because it's empty at mealtimes, and being surrounded by books, no matter how bad they are, is more comforting than being surrounded by lost souls patched up with off brand duct tape. I'm usually invisible when I get food (if I touch an object, or am wearing clothes, they become invisible too.) Today, I felt like eating around other people for some reason. People's minds are so worked up tonight. At least I don't have to pretend I'm completely normal here. No one really cares about anything unless it's made up gossip or contraband. One guy's got a computer he won't share with anyone. Some people are hooking up in the attic, because apparently there's a secret passageway the guards don't know about. And also it was raining teeth today. Apparently people went missing, too.

Where's Evander? It's not like him to be late.

How are we gonna be okay if group twelve went missing with no fucking explanation?

Why is the salad so gross tonight? (I agree with that wholeheartedly.)

Teeth were falling from the sky.

I let go of my focus on the minds. It become chatter, like a bunch of chirping birds. Doesn't make sense, but it's kind of comforting. There was a coffee shop by my house, and they had a little hedge where there always seemed to be a convention of happy sparrows.

Madame Ester noticed me at first, which wasn't attention I wanted. Another reason I don't want to become super known here. Her iron gaze and slightly vacant glare remind me of... fear. Everyone's scared of her. I haven't ever had a conversation with her, but every now and then, I see her in the common area, pacing around, staring at people with her lips pursed. She's an old white woman who just. Looks like she'd support the Republicans. I don't know. I don't like her and I don't want her in my life more than she needs to be. I'm biding my time I guess, but the biding feels like it's coming to an end. Maybe I thought Ester would forget who I am if I stayed invisible. That's getting kind of isolating. The pain I felt before is lessening to a dull ache. But the idea of Ester not knowing me is so appealing. And then I can run away. I'll go to England or something, and build a cottage in the woods. Or I'll go home to my family. (I miss them so much. We're so close. I wish they would come find me, but I understand why they haven't. It's too dangerous for us all.) Maybe I'll find someone in my small town. Who knows? I'll find comfort. I'll find people whose love isn't conditional. One day, someone will take care of me.

Another plus about eating in the library is that I don't pay attention to what I'm eating. I pick up my fork and poke the limp spinach salad doused in way too much raspberry vinaigrette. It's that cheap dressing you buy at a grocery store that's pretty much corn syrup with some oil. What I wouldn't give for a decent vegetarian meal.

CHAPTER 3

chapter 3

July 13th, 8:35pm

    Location: Ester Myrtle Kellwether's Home for Unusually Gifted Youth and Children

Tiago

I came here–to this office–that time I 'pushed' Ezra off the roof. I also came here the three times I got caught sneaking out of the home, because I ended up getting stuck outside all night. At least now, hopefully, Ezra and Rosemary will be able to get in without too much of a fuss. They probably will. The guards have always liked Ezra. Not openly, but, since we thought he didn't have a gift (I really don't know what happened today with the fire and the rat–goat–chicken), they've always sided with him, because they're like him. Ordinary. Giftless.

I sit down in an old office–type chair. It squeaks. I think it used to spin, but now it seems jammed. Too bad. This room is always cold. The guard who could probably lose a full sandwich in his beard is standing at the door. I put on my jacket. It smells like smoke. Go figure. It also smells faintly of cloves.

"Mr. Grey."

Well, golly gee! It's Madam Ester Myrtle Kellwether! She runs this place with an iron fist. I swallow.

"Yes, ma'am," I answer without turning around (because I can't in this chair).

I must be in a decent amount of trouble for her to make the journey down the hallway. Her private quarters are to the right of her dusty office. No one I know has ever been in Ester's rooms. She sits across from me at the heavy mahogany desk, and pivots in her seat. (Why does she get the spinny chair?)

"This is your sixth offence in fifteen years," she says sternly.

"Yes, ma'am." I try to sound bored.

She's so strict. I mess up once every two years or so and this is what I get. I think not being wanted by your parents is a bad enough punishment. My gift showed up when I was three. I think I disassembled a toy or something. Made it disappear before their very eyes. I bet they didn't think twice before sending me here. (It's so funny. You wouldn't expect parents to just... notice something off about their kid and then dump them on the step of some sketchy home. I secretly think most parents don't *want* to give up their kids. I'm pretty certain that the guards are sent to kidnap them, and then Madame Ester pacifies them with legal contracts and money.)

"This is your last warning, Mr. Grey. If you offend again, you will be banned from contact with other humans for one year."

Fuck.

"Yes, ma'am." Suddenly, my jacket zipper is very interesting.

"Do you understand me?"

I nod carefully.

"Santiago Grey?" she demands.

I fidget with the zipper toggle, looking down. The guard (who's now become extremely intimidating) steps closer. He grabs my head, forcing me to look up at Ester. My heart is hammering against my ribs like it wants to break them. She's the only person who actually scares me.She has grey hair that's always in a tight bun. Her eyes are steel.

"Do you. Understand me." She purses her lips into something that could be considered a smile if you were... insane.

"Yes." It takes so much willpower not to show fear. My hands are shaking.

She doesn't take her eyes off me. "Good."

The guard lets go of my head. I rub my neck, but I don't take my eyes off Madam Ester Myrtle Kellwether. I can't let her win.

"Go and eat, Mr. Grey." Even *that* sounds scary when she says it.

I nod again, and stand. As soon as I'm out the door, I have to stop myself from running back to the common room. When I'm about to go in, I decide against it. I'm not hungry. The chatter is too loud, the gossip too daunting. I don't want to be questioned about being with Ezra or where group twelve is or being late. So, I go upstairs, to the boys' rooms. This hallway is dark, windowless, and narrow. Sketchy gas lanterns hang outside every room. I think it's probably ridiculously outdated, but I've hardly been in another building since I was three, so I wouldn't know. I lean over, putting my hands on my knees. I breathe in and hold it for a long second. When I get a bit dizzy, I let the air out and stand up.

For the first time, I notice Ezra, sitting outside his room with his head against the wall, eyes closed. My heart knocks against my chest again. What am I supposed to say? His knees are bunched up to his chest with his arms loosely draped on top. He looks better than earlier. He's wearing an intact and not incinerated shirt now, (another stupid one with *another* stupid quote).

Rosemary's nowhere to be seen. Strange. She's always with him. I keep walking, trying not to disturb him. My room's at the very end of the passage.

"Hey, Tiago."

I look back. He's smiling again.

"Why are you up here so early?" he teases, his eyebrows raised. "On a mission to kill me now that the Rodentface didn't do the job for you?"

"Colton," I retort. "You're such an idiot."

"Only to you." He looks so confused. I walk back over to him. His brow is furrowed and his mouth is open, ever so slightly.

"Tiago?" he says.

Why does he always say my name?

He looks up at me. "Why do you hate me so much?"

I can't keep looking at him and his curious eyes. I focus on the ground for the millionth time today. He tilts his head forward to make eye contact again. He always wants eye contact. I can't stand it. (His glasses are clean now.) I just shake my head and keep walking. I feel his gaze follow me all the way down the hall. I feel it on my neck as I lean back against the door, inside my room. Grinding my teeth together, I clench my hands into fists. Gently, I pound them against the thick metal door. The truth is, I hate Ezra because no one else does anymore. I hate him out of obligation. When we were young, everyone hated him. He was small, he always cried, and the adults said he was special, but he obviously wasn't.

Then, Ezra grew up. He's happy-go-lucky, joyful, everyone's friend, not to mention good looking. Girls love him. He talks to them, but he's only ever been close to Rosemary. She's the only kid who didn't hate him back then.

And another truth? I don't want to admit it, but when he made his dumb jokes, and smiled with half his mouth, and threw my jacket back at me... I kinda wish I could've been his friend instead.

Ezra

I've always wondered why he never stopped hating me. Or never stopped saying he hates me. I don't know if he actually does. I want to know. If he does hate me, why did he give me his coat? Or catch me when I fell? Or even come to find me at all?

The hallway is cold. I'm a little bit feverish. It's like I'm chilled under my skin. Tiago went into his room a few minutes ago. The guards were scared that if the gifted kids shared rooms, we'd plot and scheme and inevitably kill them, so we have our own rooms. They're small, dark, musty, and overall not a great place to be. That's why I'm in the hallway. I'm lonely. Alone. Rosemary's almost always around, but as soon as we got inside, she just slipped away without me even noticing. It wasn't like her at all. I'm cold under my burning skin. And Tiago didn't answer me.

I get up, and rub my arms in a vain attempt to warm up. I knock on Tiago's door.

"What do you want?" he yells, sounding tired. It's funny he knows it's me. Or not. Maybe I'm just annoying.

"Tiago," I say softly. "I want you to answer my question."

"Can you just... go away? Please?"

I don't move. The faint chatter of everyone downstairs mingles with the thoughts in my head that don't really exist.

Shaking myself out of that pointless reverie, I'm turning away when he yells, "Are you still there?"

I breathe out a laugh, looking down at the ground.

His footsteps come closer. He stops right at the door.

It creaks when he opens it. I glance up at him, still facing down the hallway. His hair's a mess. He looks exhausted. He's also at least four inches taller than me. I look up and meet his gaze. I didn't know humans could have such blue eyes. His are icy. I don't know that I actually want to hear what he's about to say. I could just walk away. I just need to take a step and another step and I'm down the hall and in my room—he takes a deep breath.

"I hate you because you're you," he whispers, stepping forwards and gripping the door frame with both hands. His knuckles are whiter than usual. White as new paper.

And I was right. I didn't want to hear that. But I hold his gaze.

He lets go of the door and takes a small step forwards. I don't know what he's going to do, so I just stare. He keeps going, an angry laugh bubbling in his throat, his words, his very being.

"You smile all the time. Your laugh is so goddamn contagious. You're powerless, but everyone loves you, Ezra. Can't you see it? If I don't hate you, who will? I can't stand your stupid poetic T-shirts and the way everyone takes your side. I hate the way you're looking up at me right now with your annoying, innocent, green eyes. That's why I hate you, Ezra. Because you're so..." He struggles for a moment, so close to me now I can feel his warmth on my arm, his breath on my face. "You're so... you."

Then he stares at me. It's silent, save for the faint chatter of the dining hall. I swallow, and his eyes flick to my throat. My mouth falls open a little, but he backs up, as if he's been shocked.

He slams the door in my face.

Rosemary

As soon as we walked in those doors, I slipped away to the girls' rooms. Ezra won't get in trouble. He never does, but I might.

I sit on my bed with my face in my hands. Just now, it occurs to me that I have no idea what Ezra was doing today. Before they told everyone to evacuate, he just disappeared. Honestly, Ezra seemed fine when we came in (though he was still stumbling over his feet a little...), but why am I fixating on him? I always worry. I'd throw myself in front of a bus for him. But he's right. He isn't a kid anymore, and he's clearly not weak. Jesus. I'm probably in shock.

Whenever something like this happens (using the term *like this* very very loosely), I try to stay with him as much as I can. I'm not sure why. Maybe it's an instinct left over from when we were young. I always wanted to stay near him because so many people hurt him, and they didn't usually do it in front of me. And if they did, I could heal him right away.

But today? I was scared. He didn't even try to fight. He just gave up. I thought he was dead. He didn't open his eyes when Santiago talked. When he cried, I almost broke. He's so good at hiding his pain. Until he isn't. When *he* breaks down, it reminds me how broken we *all* are.

The adults used to say he was special because he's ungifted. They like him because he's harmless. Santiago doesn't get that. He just assumes special means super powerful. Here, it means weak. One of the secrets Ezra doesn't know is that I can feel pain when I touch someone. Whether it's emotional or physical, I feel it. I know why he's so kind and carefree—it's because if he wasn't, he'd have nothing to disappear into. He's so lonely. He feels weak and unwanted. And he's almost always cold and I don't know why. He was warm today, even though he was shivering.

I have no idea what Ezra went through before I got here. Santiago got here fifteen years ago, when he was three, but Ezra's been around this place his entire life. My gift didn't show up until I was eight, so that's when my parents dumped me here, *after* I had a bunch of memories to stew over. Ezra refuses to talk about the five years he was here without me. Or he just avoids it when I ask. But something changed when he turned sixteen. He got taller and adapted. He suppressed the pain. He doesn't get bullied at all now.

When I touch him, I feel this great, crushing weight. Like thousands of blocks of ice, but behind that is this awful searing heat. Touching Ezra feels like sticking my hand into a fire so hot it's cold, or water so cold it's hot.

Of course, he doesn't know it hurts me to put my hand on his shoulder or to lean into him. I think that's one of the reasons why I'll never love him as more than a friend. He's my best friend and my only friend, but never more than that. I'm not sure many people here remember the old Ezra. He's just a memory you suppress. He was someone you'd laugh at or beat up, then move on. I wonder how many of them regret that now. I wish he'd tell me about his life before I saved him from the bullying and the people who hurt him. I think some of the weight would lift off his shoulders. My lock clicks.

"Emeline," I quip. "Please knock."

She barges in anyway. Two other girls follow her in. These rooms are not meant to accommodate more than two people. This whole situation makes my heart skip. She crosses her arms.

"Rosie, why'd you drag Tiago along with you to find your boyfriend?" she pouts. "You guys were gone for so long, and now he won't talk to me, even though he scared me to *death*."

"One, don't call me that, and two, he forced me to let him come. I'd rather he hadn't. And three, Ezra's not my boyfriend," I respond coolly.

"But Rosie's a cute name," she wines. Mason and Kenzie giggle. Emeline chews her lip.

"And if he's not your boyfriend, why wouldn't he kiss me last year when I asked him out? Before Tiago and I got together?" she demands. "He's always flirting..."

"With everyone," I finish her sentence and continue, "That's just who he is."

Last year, Emeline was obsessed with Ezra. She kept coming up with these stupid plans to get him alone so they could make out or whatever, but he really wasn't into her at all. He made excuses when she asked if he could find her a book, he asked me to sit in between them when she sat at our table and when she tried to kiss him in the hallway when there were no guards watching, he pretended to have a coughing fit, just so he could leave. Which is crazy, in my opinion, because what guy doesn't want to be with Emeline?

"I guess you would know." Emeline smirks.

"Do you really believe her, Em?" Mason whispers loudly. Kenzie rolls her eyes and blows a big pink bubble in her gum. Emeline ignores them both.

"That still doesn't explain why Gogo didn't talk to me." She's back to her sulky pout.

I look up at her, confused. "Who the hell is Gogo?"

She rolls her eyes at me, like it's obvious who Gogo is. "SantiaGO. Gogo. Come on, Rosie."

I just sigh.

"Unlike you, Emeline, I don't care to know everything about everybody."

She throws her straight (cheaply dyed, against the rules) silver–pink hair over her shoulder. "Unlike you Rosie," she snaps, "I have friends, a boyfriend, and a real gift."

"Look at you gogo," I mutter.

She makes an offended little growl and stomps out with her pretty cronies in tow. The door slams shut on its own. Emeline can move things by thinking about moving them. Exactly like I can feel pain and heal people by focusing.

Except, no matter what I've tried, I just can't ease Ezra's pain. Not even a tiny bit. He hardly ever lets me heal his injuries anymore. Today, though, I didn't ask if I could and he didn't resist. It was like we were kids again.

Minus *Gogo* and you'd have our childhood.

Tiago

I rest my forehead on the cool door. I said all of that, staring into his eyes. He did nothing to deserve that. He also didn't have to ask. I can blame it on him as much as I want, but it's really my fault. Isn't everything though? I hear him slide down the wall. He always sits on the floor. Another thing about him I can't stand.

I'm not sure why I start to cry, but I know I don't want him to hear me.

I lie on my bed, face down, tears staining the worn–out beige blanket. I don't remember the last time I let myself cry. I don't like crying. It hurts too much. Pretending it doesn't hurt is easier. I don't *like* crying. Especially over Ezra. Stupid Ezra. Why am I crying over *Ezra Colton*? Maybe I'll just lock my door and never leave. At least then I won't have to see the hurt in his eyes.

Why am I the one who makes the stupid mistakes? Ezra is literally perfect. Hate boils violently through me. I don't even know what it's for at this point. I roll over and stare at the ceiling for god knows how long, tears silently leaking from the corners of my eyes and into my hair. I don't move to wipe them away. They hurt. They're hot trails of pain and shame. But also release. Kind of. Why is everything—it's just... so hard. I don't know.

When I sit up, it's completely dark. I'm a bit dizzy, my eyes are dry, and my throat hurts. Whatever.

There aren't even streetlights because our prison-home is located in a remote New York alleyway, somewhere on the edge of inconsequential and forgotten. I don't know if the lights would be on tonight anyways, because of all the chaos and discord. I'm not entirely sure where I'm going when I get up and walk into the hall. (So much for never going out again.) It's bright in here at night. I almost scream when I see a person curled up in a ball outside my door, leaning against the wall. Then I realize. It's Ezra. Asleep. In the hallway.

I take a deep breath, letting my almost-scream go out silently as I exhale. His head is lolling to one side. He looks so peaceful. Except for the fact that he's shivering again. Just lightly, but still. I gently touch his forehead. He's burning hot. Touching him makes me cold. I... don't know what to do. What if he's sick?

He shifts, placing his head on his arms. His glasses are pressed into the side of his face, half off. It makes him look so young. I go back into my room and dig through drawers. I find a hoodie I haven't worn in a while. In the hall, I wrap it around his shoulders. He shifts again so he's facing me. Jesus, his eyelashes are long. I flick a piece of his unruly hair off his face, stare at him for a long moment, then go back into my room. I'm uneasy.

That's when I remember Em. She won't be happy I didn't show up at dinner. I can hear her now: *Gogo, why didn't you talk to me yesterday?*

I absolutely hate my name, but I hate Gogo even more. Em's got a thing for ridiculous nicknames. Rosemary wouldn't use a nickname for a million dollars. Although, when she was panicking I think I remember her calling me Tiago. But, I was *also* panicking, so I could've made that up completely.

God, I'm so tired. I want to crawl out of my skin.

I collapse onto my bed, again, and fall asleep.

Genevieve

After dinner, I sit in the library. I miss the public libraries with their cafes and little desks. There's only so many places to go here. I can't wander around outside, though, I did find a way up onto the roof. It's peaceful up there at night. I overheard a rumor the other day that the guards used to lock everyone in at night, but since the dorms have no washrooms, it quickly became a problem. I like showering in the middle of the night. It's less crowded.

My days are definitely emptier now. I have too much time to think, unfortunately. I used to be good at hiding my 'gifts'. But there was this girl at school, Lucy Evans, the Prom Queen Extraordinaire. Lucy. Goddamn Lucy. I kind of miss her sometimes. The squad I hung around with was Lucy, Audrey, Venus, Dakota, and Pat. And me, for a while. We had sleep-overs, went to parties together, and once I convinced them to go hiking. The mindreading wasn't too much of a problem. I just didn't talk very much. They talked enough for me anyways.

We were friends for a while. It was nice and fun and dandy until Lucy, drunk kissed *me*, then proceeded to tell me she wasn't like that *after* I told her I had feelings for her. She wasn't a *lesbian*. Which, definitely not a bad thing, but she didn't want to hang out with me anymore. That pissed *me* off, so I used my mind–reading to expose Lucy's secret. Which. Bad idea. I was hurt. Sometimes good choices, hormones, and pain don't mix well.

Before, I had friends, then I had a gang of tormentors who followed me wherever I went. Lucy told all the girls I was gay, even though she started it, which was so so *so* funny. (Not really.) My school was fine, but somehow Lucy made it seem like thinking girls were pretty was bad. I wanted to get back at her. She ruined everything. My everything. Before, I'd been able to have a conversation with people in the halls, but now, since Lucy hated me, everyone either agreed with her, or was too afraid of her to say anything. Even the teachers turned a blind eye to this because Lucy's parents donated a huge amount of money to the school.

A day or so after this happened, I walked past the cafeteria, saw Lucy there in her usual spot, and I heard a thought. I totally could've ignored it but. I told the entire school Lucy Evans' biggest secret.

People are coming into the library after supper now. Everything is loud again, reminding me of the cafeteria that day. The Ester–instigated evacuation is over, and has been for hours. She wanted all of us out of the building, so she could take some people somewhere. Steal them. I don't know what she wanted with them, but she wanted to make their disappearance seem like a coincidence. I pick up snatches of nervous gossip. Whatever Ester wanted to do must have worked, because people are worried about the group of kids who haven't returned.

I'm sitting in a worn velvet arm chair, pretending to read a book when a guard walks in. Some of their faces are hidden by a daunting helmet made of mirrored glass. A brave girl with blonde pigtails runs up to him.

"Excuse me, sir?" she asks.

"What can I do for you?" The guards, from what I've seen, can be very kind to small children who aren't rude. They don't like teenagers, like way too much of the adult population. I blame it on stereotypes. (And Tiago's friend group. They're so loud, always breaking rules…)

"Sir, my friends and I," she gestures back to a group of concerned look-ing girls sitting in a circle on the floor, "are worried about Julia and Eevie. They haven't come back from the evacuation yet."

Yep, Ester got her people. It makes my stomach squirm. We're supposed to be protected by the government, right? But that can't be, because no way would the government allow children to be removed from safe homes to come here. I… don't like this place.

"Don't you worry about that," the guard says. He then proceeds to walk out of the room.

The girl stands there for a moment, her face scrunched in worry. She walks back to her friends and shrugs. One of the other girls starts crying. I feel a twinge of pity for them, but I don't tell them that their friends are probably gone for good.

They shouldn't have to suffer like that. They've already been through so much.

CHAPTER 4

chapter 4

July 14th, 12:10 pm

Location: Ester Myrtle Kellwether's Home for Unusually Gifted Youth and Children

Ezra

Why is it so hot? I can't seem to cool down. Someone please tell me why it's so hot.

Ester Myrtle Kellwether

I jump awake. My blasted hearing aids are beeping. Then, I realize they are not out of batteries. That is the noise I set for a gift related emergency. *Not* a fabricated emergency, purely for the purpose of quietly taking some people as test subjects for an experiment. Though, I did not plan for the teeth. That was certainly a morbid addition to the day. And a good reason to call an evacuation, though no one questions me anyways. And no one can pin it on me. Yes, government officials will be contacting me in the later hours of tomorrow morning, blaming the disaster on me, but it is not my fault. Besides, the news will chalk the teeth up to a large, elaborate prank, and arrest some people they needed excuses to arrest. Solved.

I still think this is one of my better ideas, designing my hearing aids to act as communication devices as well as to assist with my declining hearing. I did not remember the emergency noise because we have not had one in fifteen years.

My computer screens are on, pulling up the camera feeds. I throw off the covers, and hop down. I am getting old, but that does not mean I am slow. One of the feeds has a red exclamation mark beside it. I click on it. It is the top boys' hallway and it is full of smoke. Zooming in, I see a boy, sitting against the wall. And he is on fire.

I cannot see his face, so I zoom in further. He is sleeping. I cover my mouth.

Ezra?

Rosemary

Click. Click. Click. Click. Click. Clack.

Deadbolts. Six of them. Locking slowly.

"Lockdown. Lockdown. Lockdown," a digital voice repeats.

What? I blink to get the sleep out of my eyes, and rake my fingers through my knotted hair.

Plink plink pl–plink. Plink.

Four teeth fall from my scalp, onto the floor.

"Lockdown. Lockdown. Lockdown."

Has this ever happened before? I think I would remember if it had.

Emeline screams. The walls are so thin.

"What?!" I yell in response, terrified.

"I can't unlock the door!" she shrieks.

I roll my eyes and lie back down. My heart is beating so fast. I turn over and try to ignore the sinking feeling in my gut. Guards rush past the door, stomping in unison. I'd forgotten that they've trained in the military.

Wait.

My eyes fly open. Is Ezra okay?

Ezra

Please. Someone. Make it stop.

Tiago

The smell of smoke wakes me. What the hell? Something's burning.

I jump up. What if the fire gets blamed on me? My heart's thumping. If I go out to see what's going on, I'll be the culprit but—oh. Oh God. Ezra's out there. I need to get him out of the hallway. I run at the door. Click. Click. Click.

I hit the door and turn the knob. It won't budge.

Click.

I slam my shoulder into the metal.

Click.

Again and again.

Click.

And again.

"Lockdown. Lockdown. Lockdown." Automated female voice.

I shake the knob. I bang on the door. I slam against it even though it hurts. Even though it's pointless. I could make it disappear. But what would Ester do to me if I did?

"Lockdown. Lockdown. Lockdown." She's mocking me.

The smoke gets thicker in here. I'm trembling. I try to unlock the bolts. I could dissolve the whole *door*. But I can't focus. I need to be able to *focus*. Ezra's right on the other side. (And Ester will kill me if I get out.)

I sit down. (More like, my legs give out.) I'd be back to back with Ezra if the wall wasn't here. I rest my head, only to pull it back and jump up. The door feels like it's seconds away from burning down. I try to calm down. It does *not* work.

"Lockdown. Lockdown. Lockdown."

Guards' loud feet march down the hallway. They stop at my door. I slowly back away. It's silent for a smoky, adrenaline filled eternity. I stop breathing. The marching resumes, fading down the hallway and into the staircase. Still shaking, I sit on the edge of my bed with my head in my hands. Why was the wall so hot? Was Ezra even out there anymore? Is he hurt? Is it my fault? I need to know.

"Lockdown. Lockdown. Lockdown," she repeats.

"Just shut up," I say into my hands.

The smoke is clearing a bit. I think. I hope everyone's okay. I shake my head and can't help but smile a little. He's right. After all these years of hating him, he really is influencing me. For better or for worse... well, who knows.

Ester

I do not go back to sleep. What happened should not have happened. He is not supposed to have any 'magic' left. There were five infants that I got, mere days after they had been born. I had a theory about how to rid them of their unusual powers. My somewhat unethical methods worked on all the other infants. I wanted to keep them here. Just to make sure.

But, in the end, every family wanted their children back. Except for Ezra Colton's parents. They wanted nothing to do with him. So he stayed. His gift was gone. Now, apparently, it is back. His ability to burn. To set on fire, like a torch. A phoenix child. Not a child anymore.

I must figure out how to make his gift go away and stay gone.

CHAPTER 5

chapter 5

July 14th, 7:15am

    Location: Ester Myrtle Kellwether's Home for Unusually Gifted Youth and Children

Rosemary

The lockdown voice played all the way until the sun rose. I tried to sleep but I was too worried.

In the morning, soon after the voice stops, I get up. I change out of my clothes from yesterday. The door unlocks. Thank God. I don't want to be in this room another minute.

When I get to the showers, I'm glad I got up early. It takes me half an hour to get the teeth out of my hair. When I'm done, I put my still dripping hair up in a bun after I'm dressed. I'm never this late to breakfast. I hope Ezra doesn't mind. The common room is quiet when I walk in. People glance at me and whisper to each other. I scan the room, and make eye contact with a girl I don't recognize. I feel like maybe I've seen her before, but I don't know where. She has dark skin and coily hair with light blue tips, tied back in a large ponytail. She's so. Gorgeous. And it feels like she's staring into my soul. Weird.

I don't see Ezra. Santiago's sitting alone at my usual table. Emeline keeps looking at him, from the table where he normally sits with her. She's pouting. I grab a bowl of cereal, then I get Ezra one too. I walk up behind Santiago.

"What are you doing?" I demand.

He actually jumps. "Don't do that ever again," he mutters under his breath.

"Do what?" I retort. "Talk to you?"

"Don't sneak up like that."

"Okay." Why's he even here?

I put down Ezra's bowl, then my own. I sit across from him.

"What are you doing?" I ask again, trying and failing to keep the venom out of my voice.

He runs his hands over his face and through his hair. Then he slams a singed piece of notepaper on the table. I give him a questioning glance. He just slides it towards me. I unfold it and immediately recognize the messy handwriting. I raise my eyebrows at Santiago. He's upset. It's practically radiating off of him. I read:

I don't know why

I even care if you hate me.

You always have.

It shouldn't matter,

But it does matter. It always will.

I hope you'll consider a quote from my stupid, poetic T-shirt:

Let it hurt

Until it can't hurt

Anymore.

–Liam Ryan

Haha fat chance...

If I were actually brave, I'd slide this under your door. BUT. I'm not brave. I'm still sitting in the hallway outside your room. I'm probably just making it all up. Tiago, I'd give this to you, but I'm weak. I'm scared and cold underneath burning skin. I know you meant to hurt me with your words, but it just made me sad. Did you really say my eyes were innocent or did I make that up? Okay, but that's reaching. We could've been friends if it weren't your job to hate me.

Thanks for the hoodie. Not that you'll see this, but, yeah.

"He's missing," Santiago whispers. "He must've woken up, put on my sweater, written this, and fallen back asleep."

"What do you mean?" I ask, panic rising in my throat.

"Shhh."

People are looking at us. The blue–haired girl is gone. (Umm what?) I take a bite of the sawdust–like cereal, trying to act normal. I fail miserably. Light floods out of the windows above the large oak doors behind me. The early morning sun glows across Tiago's milky skin. He has dark circles under his eyes.

"Okay," I sigh. "Tiago. He clearly didn't mean for you to have this." I wave the paper in his face. He tenses, eyes going wide, reaching for the paper but pulling his hand back at the last second. I wrinkle my lip at him as I put it down. He smooths the paper out, taking a deep breath.

"I know. That's when I knew something was wrong." He points to the last clump of uneven writing.

I look at him again. "Did you say his eyes were innocent?" I ask skeptically.

This is all so confusing. Maybe he doesn't hate Ezra? But that would be so... different! What if they were friends? What if *we* were friends? My brain can't wrap around that.

Santiago blinks a few times and bites his lip. "Um... among other things."

"Like what?" I blurt out, way too loudly.

He pinches the bridge of his nose with his eyes scrunched shut before looking over at Emeline's table. They make eye contact for a moment, then she gets to her feet dramatically and stomps out of the room with Mason and Kenzie in tow. Declan (I think that's his name) gets up from his table and casually strolls out after them. Santiago grabs the folded note. My mind is spinning.

"Come with me," he whispers, scanning the room.

Both of the cereal bowls sit untouched (other than my one bite for show). I don't clean them up. Santiago walks out of the room. He's acting so weird. This is all so messed up. I follow him up the stairs to the top boys' floor. Ezra's room is up here. That's why I know this floor. Girls aren't really allowed to be in the boys' dorms, but the guards let me sit in the hallway with Ezra every now and then. We get to Santiago's room. Beside his door is a huge, black burn mark.

"The paper was right here." He's still whispering as he drops the note in the center of the charred linoleum floor. "So was Ezra."

"What?" I'm confused.

"Ezra was sitting right there," he says, picking the note back up and shoving it in his pocket. "When I got mad at him, he sat out here. After I slammed the door in his face. He fell asleep, and I gave him a hoodie."

He keeps wincing, like he's in physical pain.

"You slammed the door in his face *and then* you gave him a hoodie?" I ask in disbelief. (I'm so confused. Aaaaaaaagh. Maybe I'm imagining this. But Santiago's acting so weird. I'm imagining things. Okay, we'll go with that. I'm fine. We're fine. I heard no voices. Proof. I'm just... making things up. Gaslighting myself. Healthy.)

He nods.

"He was so... feverish." He pauses. "During the lockdown, I tried to get out." He winces, rubbing his shoulder. "Obviously I couldn't, because the metal doors and all...but the wall he was sitting against got so hot."

I close my eyes, trying to make sense of it all. Why didn't he just use his gift?

"That still doesn't explain why he's gone," I point out.

I open my eyes. He glances up at me, with his eyebrows bunched together. "Rosemary. I think they took him."

"You think who took him?" I ask.

"I don't know. The guards? I just... I feel like someone did."

"Great." I put my face in my hands. "Perfect lead. *Someone* took him. Awesome."

Emeline Wiliams

I don't know what happened. It's like Tiago hates me now. The only thing Mason knows is that Gogo and Rosie ran away from their group to find Ezra. Mason was in group eight with them. Yesterday screwed everything up. What was with the teeth? Does no one else think that's purely disgusting?!

Everything was fine until I left for our muster point. Stupid little Rosie thinks she can waltz around and ignore all the damage she does. I don't know why Gogo even talks to her. It's no secret that she hates him. She's literally not pretty. He's only ever paid attention to *me*. Why is he so obsessed with her now? He's always been slightly obsessed with hating Ezra, but as long as he was with me, I didn't care what he talked about.

"Did you hear?" Kenzie asks me as we walk out of the dining hall.

"Hear what?" Mason demands.

"Mason!" Kenzie scolds. "You're so clueless!"

"What, Kenzie? I can't handle this anymore."

"Ezra Colton is missing!" she squeals.

I stop. "Wait, really?"

"Yesssss."

She's so pleased with herself. Kenzie's gift is actually eavesdropping. She can tune into any conversation from far away if she concentrates.

"Rosemary and Tiago looked so suspicious sitting at the same table," she says with a self satisfied smirk. "I just had to know what was going on. There's never any good drama." She pouts.

"This sounds like good drama..." Mason adds.

"Duh."

Sometimes, these two just get on my nerves. They're my friends, but why do they have to be so... annoying? I speed up.

"Em! Waaaaiiit!"

"Hurry up if you want to come with me!" I shout back. Someone who is not Mason or Kenzie catches up to me.

"Em, are you okay?"

It's that guy, Declan. He's tall, cute, and now he's following me around. I turn into the library. It's full of boring books, but it has a few old mismatched couches left over from decades ago. (They're just as gross as the teeth. Well... almost.)

"What do you want, Declan?" I ask wearily as I flop onto a faded, lime green, leather couch. (I don't know, maybe it's pleather. It shouldn't even exist.)

He sits beside me. "Well, Tiago wasn't with you at breakfast ..." He leaves the sentence hanging, so I finish it for him.

"Sooo, you thought you'd make your move?" I offer, smiling lazily.

He nods. "Something like that." At least he's honest.

I kiss him. I don't care that I'm possibly cheating. Tiago's probably cheating on me right now too. I wrap my arms around his neck and he beams, pulling me closer. I kiss him again.

CHAPTER 6

chapter 6

July 14th, 8:12am
Location: ???

Ezra

I'm cold again. I also can't move my arms or legs. I don't know where I am. I can't see, even though I can feel my glasses on my face. It's really dark. I'm definitely not in the hallway anymore.

Why is it smoky in here? I cough. A slit of light opens up over my face. Am I in a… box? I try to jerk my arm up to shield my eyes. It doesn't move. My wrist hurts. Someone peeks through the glass, then closes the little door. It's dark again. Maybe if I keep coughing they'll let me out. I do. My throat hurts now too. The person opens the sliding door again. This time, I don't stop coughing. I can't. They close the door. I hear muffled voices.

"He's not burning anymore," one replies.

"He also sounds like he's dying in there," says a different voice. I cough more. It tastes like blood and smoke.

"Let's open the—" I don't hear the rest.

The sound of locks clicking reassures me. The top of the box slides off with a mechanical grinding. I close my eyes tightly. The light kind of burns. I still have no idea where I am. I open my eyes, ignoring the ache, and the fact that I can't really see past the sides of the box. I look down at myself.

The first thing I notice is the sweater. It's not mine. It's Tiago's. I need to give it back. Why do I have it in the first place? Um... I actually have no memory of him giving it to me. I almost laugh. A giggle bubbles up through my nose. So weird. But then I notice I'm shackled down. What did I do? My wrists are bleeding. The half joy from seconds ago dies. What is this?

"Hello?" I call out.

My voice is rough. I don't think anyone will hear me, but two people in hazmat suits walk over. I smile, relieved. Not completely alone.

"Why am I here?" I ask. They look at each other. "I have no gift, so why the suits?"

No response.

"Guys?" my quiet voice echoes. "Guys. I'm bleeding." I sound so small. Scared. Maybe I am scared.

Tiago's going to be so mad when he sees the blood on the cuffs of his sweater. The two people look down at me, like they just remembered I was here. One guy takes a key out of a bin (or I think it's a bin) beside me. He unlocks all four of the shackles. I sit up. I'm so dizzy that I have to grab the sides of the box (so it is a box!). The hazmat people jump back.

"It's okay. I'm not going to explode." I laugh, which comes out as this horrible, forced barking sound.

I roll up the sleeves of Tiago's sweater. My wrists are purple, swollen and bloody. Shackles only do this to you if you're thrashing. (I don't know how I know that. That's creepy knowledge.) My ankles are in the same banged up state as my wrists. What is *happening*? I look around the room for the first time. It's a loading dock.

Uneasiness settles into my body like a fog. I feel like I know this place. I'm scared

July 14th, 8:15am, Ester Myrtle Kellwether's Home for Unusually Gifted Youth and Children

Tiago

After we talked for a few minutes, Rosemary said she had things to do. What, I don't know. Currently, I'm getting supplies. I needed to get away from her to prepare. Rosemary's not in the dining hall at lunch. Good. Why am I so concerned? I really shouldn't care this much.

Ezra. Ezra... Ezra. I hate him, don't I? Yes. Yes, I do. But if he's gone, then who will I bug? Oh, my God. That's a fucking stupid excuse if I ever heard one. Plenty of people would be easy to pick on. No one else is like Ezra, but *still*. There's no one here who everyone else is weirdly in love with. So that makes sense. Okay then, I'll do it for everyone who cares. But looking around the dining room, I don't see anybody who's acting like me. *Does* anyone else care? There isn't a single person plotting how they're going to rescue him. They're not even remotely concerned. Or maybe I'm overreacting? He does have a tendency to disappear every now and then... but not accompanied by a lockdown.

I don't know who took him or where he is, but I have to find him. I'm leaving tonight. I won't be able to come back. Rosemary won't know I'm leaving because I didn't tell her. Hopefully, she won't find out until I'm gone. And even then, she won't know where I went. Maybe the other shoe dropped and I just decided to coincidentally run away at the same time Ezra disappeared. Bet she'd never think of *that*. (Which is the problem. She wouldn't think of that.) I close my eyes, focusing on my backpack, buried in my closet. It comes out easily. I grab it, stuffing it with as much as I can fit inside. I have food from lunch. Sandwiches. No one saw me take the leftovers.

Rosemary

I saw Santiago taking the leftovers. He thinks he can leave without me. But Ezra's my best friend, so, no. I'll just have to do something to convince him to let me come. And I already know what.

I would just go on my own. But he's got a good gift. It might be easier with the two of us, even if I hate him.

Madam Ester Myrtle Kellwether doesn't favour me, but she also doesn't hate me. She knows I'm close to Ezra. I knock on her office door. Hopefully, she'll never find out what I'm doing because then she'd definitely lock me up until I die (or be the reason I die...). As always, there's no answer. The door's open a little. I push it all the way, step inside, close it and turn around to find Santiago already in here, hunched over the laptop on the desk. He looks up at me, like a deer caught in the headlights. Then, he realizes that it's *me,* not Madame Ester.

"What are you doing?" Santiago hisses.

"I'm coming with you." When he starts to disagree, I interrupt, "I know her passwords."

He's frustrated, and I'll use that to my advantage.

"Tell me," he demands quietly.

"Agree to let me come and find my only friend. Then I'll tell you." I cross my arms. I can't help but anxiously glance over my shoulder at the door.

He sighs. I take that as a yes. This office is dark. There are no windows. Just a single panel of buzzing yellow lights. Footsteps come slowly down the hall. I panic. So does he. He snatches the computer off the desk and ducks underneath it. (What an original hiding spot. He should seriously consider a career as a secret agent.) It's now clear that it's *my* job to get us out of this. What a partnership. This is going to be wonderful.

The handle turns. Now Madam Ester walks in. She looks mildly surprised to see me in her office.

"I, um, I was wondering if you could help me with something?" I ask. She looks questioningly at me. "I want to find a book in the library. Um, I think it was *Mythical Symbols and Stories from the West* or … it might have been the North?" I look down, holding my breath.

"Yes. Yes, I can help with that. Come along." She walks out of the office and I follow her. I let out a breath. God, that was too close.

July 14th, 8:25am, A Loading Dock **and** *A Tiny Room*

Ezra

The hazmat people walked with me out of the loading dock. I tried to make conversation. They ignored me. I tried to distract myself from my heartbeat, which makes me anxious, by asking questions. Since they wouldn't answer me, it didn't work. We walked down a sterile hallway, our footsteps swallowed by the deadness of the air. They opened a door and locked it behind me. Neither of them came in. The room is tiny, with a low ceiling. There's a bed pushed to the far wall. Being in here makes my breathing shallow.

What is this place? It's so small, so empty, so bleak. No colour. Just white and grey and linoleum. I sit on the bed and focus on breathing. In… out… in… out. Slowly, I calm myself. Sort of. It's a mediocre calm, but what more did I expect, really. I'm pretty sure I just got… kidnapped. And I can feel my heart pounding in my ears. I shiver. There's a piece of paper beside me. It's folded. Thinking it's the note I wrote last night, I pick it up. It's not my note. It's short, simple. It destroys my unstable calm in an instant.

Ezra Colton,

FlAmes IlLuminate yoUr fRozEn soul.

No. I can't be here. This can't be real.

I thought–I thought I made... it up.

Tiago

After the door shuts, I sit under the desk for another minute to let my heart slow down. I can't believe I'm doing this. The computer is cold against my skin. I hug it to my stomach and slip out into the hall. Thank goodness nobody's ever in this part of the compound. I run up the stairs to my room. There are never any guys in these rooms during the day. They hang out in other random places around the home. The burn mark on the wall has already been painted over. The melted linoleum tiles have been replaced with new ones. (Damn, they're efficient.) It's like it never even happened.

I didn't intend on stealing the computer, but I slip it into my backpack and zip it up using my gift. The bag slides under my bed. I go to the hallway to wait for the sun to set. It seems logical that we wouldn't leave until it got dark, so the guards would have less of a chance of catching us. But now, I'm starting to think that's stupid, because we stole Madame Ester's computer and we're just chilling out with it in the same building and that probably won't go well... all I can do is hope that she's busy all afternoon and wait for Rosemary to show up.

There's still adrenaline pumping through my body. I sit right next to where the burn was. I hope there's footage of what happened last night, but what I really want to know is where they took him. I wonder what it would've been like if I'd just sat down beside him. If I didn't blow up. Maybe I would be gone with him. He wouldn't have to go through whatever he's going through alone. If I had acted differently, would he still be here, laughing and making his stupid jokes, trying to get me not to hate him? Maybe he would.

I reach inside my pocket for the note, playing with the soft paper. The burn mark is gone. Ezra's gone. My fucking *certainty* is gone. Madam Ester had to eradicate all evidence of a flaw in her perfect machine. And now everything is gone, gone... gone. No matter what I do, I can't change the past. I don't think I've gone a day where I didn't wish I could.

(I have too much time to think about my definitely stupid decisions.)

Genevieve

Hoolllyy. It has been a morning.

So apparently, *the famous Ezra Colton* is missing; there's trouble in paradise, aka *the famous Santiago Grey* and *the famous Emeline Wiliams* are not speaking to each other; and I am currently watching *the not so famous Declan What's-His-Face* make out with the very same *famous Emeline Wiliams*. I seriously didn't intend to spy on him. I just ended up in the library a few minutes before them, and didn't want to interrupt their moment.

And this is where invisibility and mind reading become a curse. Emeline is thinking about Santiago. And Declan? Ugh. Well, Declan.

(I hate it here.)

Rosemary

When Ester and I walk into the library, we come across Emeline. And Declan? For a moment, it's hard to tell what's going on. They're tangled together in a passionate... something. I swallow thickly as Madame Ester inhales. I cross my arms, staring up at the ceiling because. Ew. I don't know. People are weird. And this is extremely awkward.

I hear Emeline simper, "I didn't do anything!"

Ester, shockingly, seems to believe her. I look at the grey haired woman as she disdainfully clears her throat, and turns to me. "I'm sorry, Rosemary," Madam Ester says. "The book should be ... over there." She gestures vaguely to the left.

And I take that opportunity to scamper behind a tall shelf. Peering through the books, I watch Ester haul Declan away. Emeline... is nowhere to be seen so I wait until I can't hear their footsteps anymore to dart out from behind the shelves. Emeline walks over to me. She was supposed to be *gone*. Agh. I'm screwed.

"How did you know, Rosie?" she asks sweetly. "How did you know I was here cheating on my boyfriend... because he was cheating on me with you?"

It takes me a few seconds to understand her question.

"What? No! I honestly didn't." I shake my head frantically. (Incriminatingly.) "He's not cheating either. There's no cheating happening on our... on his side. I'm not even *on* his side. There aren't even sides!"

"Exactly what a cheater would say," she coos, tapping her lips with a painted fingernail.

I try to push past her, but somehow, she blocks me.

"Do you even care about that guy at all?"

We both spin around to see the blue–haired girl.

"Who," Emeline demands, "are you?"

"Genevieve," she says, immune to Emeline's anger. "Never mind, don't answer me. I already know."

At this point, I'm slowly inching towards the door, away from this standoff.

"Why the hurry, Rosie?" Emeline turns to me with wide eyes. "Is my Gogo waiting for you?"

"If that makes you happy, then yes. Believe that. Like he'd ever even think about cheating on *you*"—I point at her—"with *me*." I point to myself.

She smirks, and my cheeks flush. I have no clue why I was expecting *Emeline* of all people to reassure me.

Genevieve clears her throat. "You really shouldn't use people like that Emeline."

"Excuse me?" Emeline's voice is deadly now. "I wasn't using him. Why are you sticking up for a random nobody? *You're* just a random nobody. Who even *are* you?"

I swallow nervously, rooted in place. Girls are scary. Genevieve's nostrils flare. Emeline turns to me, taking three long strides so she's standing about a foot away, looking down on me. "You'd better scurry along, Ratmary. Gogo doesn't like to be kept waiting."

And then... I punch her. My knuckles pop and her head jerks to the left. She grabs her cheek, tears and vengeance welling in her eyes. Genevieve stares at me. I cover my mouth and gasp. After that, I do the brave thing: I run for a very long time, and I don't even remember doing so until I end up having to slow down because of the crowd.

People are starting to file in for dinner, talking with their friends. I slip up to my room, breathing hard. What was I *thinking*? Clearly I wasn't. Hah. I rake my hands through my hair, trying to calm myself down. Now I absolutely have to leave. I'm going to get murdered in my sleep by one of Emeline's thousand admirers. My bag is still on my bed. I grab it and run across the common room with my hood pulled low over my face. I think I hear someone following me, but there's no one there. (Yay, paranoia!) Santiago's sitting with his legs out, next to where the burn was. They've already destroyed the evidence. They sure are quick around here.

He gets up when he sees me. His room is bigger than mine, I notice as he shuts the door. There's a bruise running from his elbow up into his t–shirt sleeve. I take off my hood.

"Is that from trying to get out during the lockdown?" I ask, pointing at the bruise. Which reminds me I just punched his girlfriend. I wince, deciding not to tell him about that.

He rubs it. "Yeah."

"Let me heal it." I reach out for his arm, but he pulls away.

"No. That's alright. Thanks."

He hasn't looked at me since I came in. He pulls a black hoodie over his head, messing up his hair. He runs his hand through it. He does that a lot.

"Oh," I respond simply, unsure of what else to say.

He opens his hand–me–down backpack (we never get new stuff in this place but I'm pretty sure he wouldn't have chosen a pink and green plaid bag), and slides the computer out. I take it and sit down on his bed. The welcome screen flashes. Then, the password box pops up. I'm not sure how Ezra knew her passwords. He told them all to me. Just in case, he had said. I thought he was delusional, saying that he knew them. We laughed together about it at the time. Now, all six are written on my arm. I don't know why I suddenly believe they're actually real. As I came up with this plan, I copied them there from a piece of paper Ezra gave me a long time ago. I don't know why there are so many. I take a deep breath. Santiago's watching over my shoulder, making the back of my neck prickle. I type: For nOthing i sLowly stoLe yOu aWay367

The screen stays the same. It flashes: 'Extended clearance, extended clearance' before going white. A crowded desktop opens. I look back at Santiago. He takes the laptop from me and looks through the open folders.

"There's nothing obvious here," he says, sighing. "We should wait 'til we get away to go through it all."

I take the computer back, close it, and shove it in his nightmarish carnival coloured bag. It's almost dark out.

"Rosemary, we have to go out Ezra's window."

I look up.

"What? Why?"

He looks down. "Um, there aren't any bars on his," he replies quietly, pointing at his own prison–esque window.

"Oh. Right." I say, ignoring the tightness in my throat as I get up.

I grab my bag. (I realize now that I'm very lucky to have a plain brown one.)

"I'll meet you on the street," he mumbles.

"Um, why don't we just leave together?" I ask. "That makes way more sense."

He fiddles with his sweater cuffs. "I just need a minute, okay?"

"Okay, fine."

Then I leave.

Ezra's window has no bars. Santiago's right about that. It's also three stories off the ground. I enter his empty room. Ezra has always hated how small it is. He hates small spaces in general. I open his window, look back to make sure nobody's watching, then jump.

It really, *really* hurts to land. The breath gets knocked out of me, into next week. It's like huge stakes are being shoved through my feet. My vision goes blurry for a moment. I sit on the pavement, focusing on the pain, focusing on warmth taking the pain. I heal myself, sitting in the crunchy alley gravel with my eyes closed. After a few moments, I feel completely fine. A little bit giddy, but fine. Now, I wait. His minute is taking a long time. I don't want to just stay here to be caught. I'm kinda tempted to yell for him to hurry up, but that would be counterproductive. Everything will be fine.

CHAPTER 7

chapter 7

July 14th, 5:39pm

Location: Ester Myrtle Kellwether's Home for Unusually Gifted Youth and Children

Genevieve

Emeline Williams is a self–centred egotistical jerk who deserved to be punched in the face. But coming from Rosemary? I didn't expect that. She didn't even *think* about punching her. I... am kind of inspired.

I'm going to leave. I never said I'd stay here, honestly. And Rosemary is interesting. She seems kind of meek, but apparently. Not. (Why is my type women that slightly scare me.) (I. Want to get to know her.)

Apparently, Rosemary and *the famous Santiago Grey who hates Ezra Colton with a passion* are breaking out of this hellish place to go rescue *the famous Ezra Colton who has supposedly been kidnapped*. Even though I don't know either of them, I'm going. At least I won't have to go alone. I'd be fine by myself (being invisible gives you a good sense of independence) but. I just feel right about this. If they don't want me along, I'll just go home. Either way is okay.

I followed Rosemary up to the top boys' floor, where she and Tiago went into a room, which I presumed is his. The walls are thin, so I just chill out in the hallway, eavesdropping invisibly. I packed my own bag, which

I brought from home. Sometimes, I kinda wish that my clothes and stuff didn't become invisible when I did. It would be hilarious to see peoples' faces if they saw a floating backpack. But I do wish that I could make people invisible with me. It's a real dilemma. Rosemary keeps thinking about how ugly Tiago's bag is and it's hilarious. Come on, babe. You're planning a rescue mission for your best friend and all you can think about is a hideous backpack? The door to the room cracks open. Rosemary slips out, runs across the hall, and into another dorm.

I'm confused for a moment, but then remember that they have to go out Ezra's window, because there are no bars. I love how the windows are barred here. It gives this place a really cozy, homey feeling. (Yeah–no. No homey feeling here.) I can't wait to be gone.

Taking a deep breath, I walk swiftly through the open door of Ezra Colton's room. It's small, and plain with absolutely no defining features, except for a notebook on a nightstand. The window is open, making the room chilled. There are curtains, though. I don't have those. They flutter eerily in the gentle wind. I cross the room and look down. Rosemary's just sitting there, on the ground. Her legs look... broken. She's thinking about healing them. Aah, I see. She *can* heal them. I'm about to climb onto the window sill when I notice the walls.

They're covered in writing, so light you can hardly see it up close. Each sentence is separated by a dot.

The sunset in your eyes. That's the only thing I remember, really. And the falling. And the wind. And the apologies that got me there in the first place. But still, it was worth it. Dot.

Huh. I read another one, lower down.

She acts like she doesn't know me. I don't know me. Dot. *Why am I such a nobody? Will anybody want me?* Dot. *I'm like a lightbulb, beside the sun, trying to outshine it.* Dot. *There are too many suns.* Dot. *I'm like a bird, trying to fly into the wind, but the wind is too strong. I'll get swept away.*

My throat hurts a little as I glance up. I spin in a slow circle, my eyes picking up on the faint writing. Every wall. Covered in letters. Stories. A lifetime spent in this place, hidden in plain sight. His soul is written on these walls. So honestly. So openly. It's such honest pain, made pretty. Poems of suffering. I... wonder if Ezra's okay. Whoever he is. I've seen him in passing, but not much more.

Will anyone else ever see this? Or will only the lonely girl have time for invisible poetry? A small, pitying sigh escapes my lips as my eyes trace the words. It looks like he... had no one to talk to. Not really.

Footsteps in the hall yank me from my thoughts. I shake my head and climb out the window. I think Rosemary jumped. But there's literally one of those metal ladders down the brick side of the building. So maybe she just. Wanted to jump? For the fun of it?

July 14th, 5:45pm, Ester Myrtle Kellwether's Home for Unusually Gifted Youth and Children** and **The Streets of Manhattan

Tiago

I run into Ezra's room. Rosemary left the window open. I look down. She's sitting on the gravel. Ezra's room is clean. His closet is open. Without really thinking, I pick up the little notebook on his scratched night table. I put it in my backpack with the laptop. I turn away, and climb out, onto the window ledge. It's a long drop, which. Doesn't matter. I focus on the pavement below me as I jump.

When I hit the ground, it absorbs my weight before springing me out onto solid road. Rosemary's already standing. She opens her mouth to say something, but I put my finger to my lips. I don't hear anything out of the ordinary. She looks up at the open window. Our feet crunch on gravel as we run down the alley. Something's wrong. Nothing's happening. No alarms or guards. Just our breathing and the sounds of late night traffic. I don't care. It'll be okay. We keep running until we get to a main road. Street lights cast beams of yellow over the clean pavement. A lot of people are out. Rosemary and I weave through the busy streets that were empty only a day before. I've always wondered if Madame Ester's home was a government operation. It would make sense to separate kids with unpredictable abilities from normal civilians. Rosemary laughs quietly.

"What?" I hiss.

"Normal people clean up so fast." She giggles. "Almost as fast as Madam Ester."

The lower windows of the skyscrapers are still broken, patched over with plywood and cardboard, but the glass and teeth are gone without a trace. People are going on as normal. It's not funny at all. I'm still looking up at one of the buildings when one of the higher windows lights up. A silhouette of a man paces back and forth. I think he may be talking to someone on the other side of the room. I squint at Rosemary. *Why* is she laughing?

"How did you get down from the window, Rosemary?" I ask, grabbing her arm. A man glances at us, brows furrowed. I flash him an anxious smile.

"I jumped!" Rosemary nearly screams. This draws more looks. She's being so loud. I put my arm around her shoulders, and pull her down the sidewalk again. Loud angry music is playing somewhere,

"Look at me," I say quietly, eyes darting to all the people we pass. "I think you're in shock. I need you to be quiet, Rosemary. We need to get out of the city. Or even just downtown."

She goes silent. Eerily so. I almost (almost being the key word here) wish that she would talk again. We start to walk. I hold her tightly, to remind her we're in the middle of an escape. We walk down the (clean) sidewalk. The vehicles speed past. Police cars and ambulances sometimes blast through the traffic, sirens blaring. I keep tensing at the sound. What if they're after *us*? I don't know what time it is. It's either very late or very early. There are no stars in the city. I've never seen a clear starry sky. When I was seven, I found a book in the library about stars. I loved it until some jerk saw me reading. He nicknamed me Lunaboy. It was worse than Gogo.

Eventually, I notice that Rosemary has slipped my arm off her shoulders. The streets and buildings all look the same. I think we're lost. I am at least.

"We should find somewhere with Wi–Fi to look through the computer," Rosemary finally says.

I nod, agreeing, though I'm not entirely sure what Wi–Fi is. We're quiet again. The horizon is starting to lighten. She points to a fast food joint.

"There's a free Wi–Fi sign on the door."

"We have to free who?" I ask, confused and a little concerned.

"Never mind." She shakes her head, exasperated.

She walks over and holds the door open for me. Buttery light spills onto the dark street as something makes a loud jangling noise. I jump, looking around. Rosemary snorts and points to the cat shaped bell over the door. I roll my eyes, trying to cover up my moment of terror. It's warm inside. The smell of deep fried goodness overwhelms me.

"Do you have any money?" My lack of foresight hits me like a book over the head.

"Mhm."

Huh. I wonder where she got it.

She points at a plastic booth at the back. I walk over and sit down, pulling out the computer. A free Wi-Fi thing pops up on the screen. Wi-Fi. Mysterious. I guess that's what she was talking about. Also, I was right. The gas lamps back at the home are definitely outdated. (Though now that I think about it, they were probably just lightbulbs in gas lantern… containers, because Madame Ester's office had fluorescent lights.) I agree to the terms and conditions on the Wi-Fi page without a second thought. I don't know what it's asking me anyways. Rosemary comes back with a muffin. It's probably deep fried. She sits beside me and enters the first password. It makes me kind of uncomfortable for no reason. (It's a weird password, okay?)

While she types, I realize that I left my jacket at the home. I'm cold. Weirdly, my sweater smells just like the jacket did. Smoke and cloves.

"I'm going to check her email," Rosemary mumbles.

I look at the computer screen. Then I take the greasy muffin.

July 15th, 2:59am, Ester Myrtle Kellwether's Home for Unusually Gifted Youth and Children

Ester

Sometimes, from what I have observed, a gift comes from a lack of fear. It comes from a child raised without trauma. Other times, a gift is caused by an excess of trauma. A coping mechanism, sometimes. Or a response to love. In the rarest cases, a child is born with a gift. Ezra's case.

Fear and pain caused his gift to go dormant. But now, I believe he has suppressed those troublesome memories enough for it to come back. I am always learning about these gifts. Recently, Ezra has been happy. It was making me worried. Clearly, I was right to be.

He went out by himself before we evacuated the building. I let him go, as I always do. There is no harm in letting a normal boy go out into the world. Though, I was hoping he would go conveniently missing like group twelve. He nearly did. Until his gift came back and his meddling friends showed up.

They left a few hours ago. Right out of Ezra's window. I knew they would. I knew the girl would go. Rosemary. Santiago surprised me, though. I did not think he would care. If anything, I thought he would be happy.

July 15th, 3:07am, Unknown Fast Food Joint

Rosemary

He's about to take a bite of that greasy excuse for a muffin. I don't look away from the computer, but I can sense it. For some reason, I'm momentarily distracted by intense fear for Santiago's health. *Get a hold of yourself, Rosemary. If he gets muffin poisoning, you can just find Ezra on your own. Come on. Focus.*

Strangely, the email account doesn't need a password. It just opens. The first email is unread. I open it, and see Ezra's name. Santiago puts the muffin down (thank God), looking over my shoulder again. Nobody comes into the restaurant. I turn back to the computer. I read quietly to him.

"'He went out three hours after arriving.'"

"What's that supposed to mean?" he asks, leaning on the table.

"I don't know," I huff. "Let me keep reading,"

"'We have successfully gotten parts of the facility running again. The other tests went quite well. He panicked and ignited once more when we put him in his room. He was satisfactorily extinguished. He has not lit again since his first session,'" I finish.

The whole message makes me sick with anxiety. Attached are two files. Santiago reaches over my arm. He clicks the first one. It's a video. I look at him for reassurance. He clicks the play button without reassuring me. (Rat bastard.) The video has no sound and the camera quality leaves much to be desired. But it's definitely Ezra. I force myself to watch. First, Ezra reads something on a slip of paper. It falls from his hands, drifting to the floor. The video glitches. Ezra's in the middle of jumping up when the video starts up again. He slams into the door, silently screaming. I can't. Watch this anymore. I'm about to stop it when Ezra catches on fire. Santiago pauses the video at that same moment. He squints at the screen. I press play again. Ezra realizes he's flaming. He drops to the floor when something comes across his face. It's like he's remembering.

The door opens, and the clip ends. We sit in tense silence before Santiago puts his hands over his eyes, rubbing his temples. (I've never seen anyone do that before. Weird.)

"Colton has a gift," he whispers, amazed, staring at the picture of Ezra through his fingers. He moves his hands to his chin. I'm a little bit shell-shocked. I mean, I've always thought Ezra had a gift, but I never actually thought he had a *gift*. My head is a jumble. Full of confusion.

"This doesn't make sense," I groan.

"But, Rosemary!" Santiago's eyes light up. "It *does* make sense. That's why they took him! Because he has a gift!"

"Okay, but why didn't they take everyone then?"

He thinks for a moment, the light fading. "Because... because he didn't have a gift before? Or... has he been *hiding* this from everyone?"

A burst of disbelieving laughter escapes my lips. "Ezra could *not* have kept that a secret. And besides, why would he? Do you think he *likes* being tormented?"

He opens his mouth, then closes it again and I remember who I'm talking to.

"Oh, wait," I say drily, "I'm talking to you. You *do* think he likes being tormented."

"Shut up." Is he blushing?

I change the topic. "But who came in at the end of the clip?" I ask. "Were they coming to put him out?" The message said they put him out. Anxiety starts creeping back into my tone. "What does it mean to put him out?"

"Calm down," Santiago says. "Let's look at the other attachment."

I push the computer towards him, exhaling shortly.

"I don't want to see it if it's that awful," I reply.

He clicks on the second one.

"Shit," he grumbles. "We need a password."

"Remember? I have all her passwords written on my arm." I show him.

"We just have to try them all, I guess."

"Well at least we have a start. What's the first one?"

"We already used it. The second one is: *it was as siMple as can bE367.*" I spell it out. He raises one eyebrow. (I so wish I could do that.)

"Doesn't that seem like an odd password?"

He enters it anyway. It doesn't work.

"Here's the next one," I say, reading from my arm. "Capital A, although it's over, capital L, lowercase I, remember your, capital L, light."

"So that spells?" Santiago asks sheepishly.

"*Although it's over iLl remember your Light*," I say, rolling my eyes. It works. (On the second try because of the random capital letters and Santiago's inability to understand anything.) I look away, but then look back because I hate suspense. It's just a profile on Ezra.

Last name: Colton   First name: Ezra   Middle name: Levi   Age: 18   Eye colour: Green   Birthdate: March 3   Height: 5'11"   Hair colour: Brown   Care facility: Dr. Charlie Dallas Observatory (now Madam Kellwether's research institute.)

This information was updated on Wednesday July 15th.

"Don't you think this is a little too easy?" Santiago asks after a long moment.

I have to admit, I agree with him. We got the computer too easily, we snuck out of the building too easily, we found Ezra's location too easily. But we have to keep going with it—it's the only chance we have. And they *probably* don't know we have the passwords.

"Santiago." Panic hits me again all of a sudden. "Did you close the window when we left?"

"*Shit.*"

"I did."

Our heads snap up from the computer so fast and perfectly in sync. (Which is kind of scary.) It's Genevieve. She's standing right beside our booth, wearing cargo pants and a grey hoodie, arms crossed, her coily, blue tipped hair in a bun on top of her head. Santiago looks at me, confused. I shake my head quickly, to let him know I had no idea she was here.

"Okay guys," she says nervously, looking over her shoulder. "I know this is weird, but I need to come with you."

Santiago looks between me and her, his jaw clenched.

"Look," she continues. "There's nothing for me at the home, if we can even call it that. My family was happy, but I ended up there. I might have screwed up a little but. That doesn't matter now. I just. Can't stay there."

I'm a bit surprised, but there's nothing wrong with her coming along as far as I can see. Santiago looks at her, a crease between his eyebrows.

She looks at me with her piercing, soul staring eyes. One is blue and one is brown. That's so *cool*. "And just so you know, there was a ladder outside Ezra's window, so you really didn't need to jump," she adds.

I blink at her dumbly, my mouth hanging open a little. In the back of my mind, I know we have to get out of the city before they discover we're missing, but I just. What?

"So can I come or not?" she asks. "I have my own stuff."

Santiago nods slowly, confused, but starting to get it now.

I'm about to close the computer.

"Wait." He stops me. "Shouldn't we see where the observatory is?"

"Oh. Good idea."

Genevieve sits down on the opposite side of the booth, her face unreadable. I grab my bag and run to the washroom. When I come back, Tiago's looking at a map.

"It's in the middle of nowhere," he says without looking up, "but if we follow exit 207 off the highway, we should find it at some point."

I nod, closing the computer. Genevieve bites her lip.

"We should leave that here," I suggest.

"Why?" asks Tiago.

I don't know much about technology, but clearly I know more than him.

"When they find out we have it, they'll track it," Genevieve explains. "If it's sitting in a cheap fast food place, that'll give us some time to get away."

"Yeah," I agree, looking over at her. She shrugs.

"Okay," Tiago replies. "Sounds good to me."

I leave the computer and (thankfully) the friendless muffin, which, in my opinion, is unfit for human consumption. We walk outside. It's still chilly. Ester and the guards will realize we've left soon. Emeline will have a fit. (I wish I could be there to see that.) Funny that at the exact moment I think this, Genevieve smirks to herself. If she were Ezra, I'd ask what made her laugh, but she isn't him. And I really don't know where we stand. Like, are we friends? Can I talk to her?

She bites her lower lip again. The streetlights are on now, and they cast beams across Genevieve's dark skin. Tiago starts briskly away without saying anything.

"Santiago? I think you should know that Emeline cheated on you with Declan," I blurt out.

He stops, hands tucked in his pockets. Someone yelps and darts out of Santiago's way.

Genevieve winces. I cover my mouth and look at her. She shakes her head, smiling a bit. We both jog to catch up to him. Santiago glares at gum spotted pavement.

Genevieve nods towards me. "And this badass here punched her in the face."

Santiago looks up at me. He smirks, then frowns, then runs his hand through his hair. He eventually shakes his head.

"I figured she would," he says, taking a deep breath. "Cheat on me. Not specifically with him. But with someone." He pauses, then looks at me with a strange expression on his face. "You punched my gir—Emeline in the face?"

I nod carefully, expecting him to say more, but then he drops the subject.

CHAPTER 8

chapter 8

July 15th, 6:15am

  Location: Ester Myrtle Kellwether's Home for Unusually Gifted Youth and Children

Ester

I did not expect them to steal my computer. I thought I had accounted for everything. I assumed that they were idiots.

They have probably hacked into my accounts. I suspect they are on their way to find Mr. Colton at this very moment. I am guessing that such clever individuals thought this was all too easy. I specifically turned off the window alarms everywhere last night so they could escape. They were very smart to go out of Ezra's window, because there is no alarm there in the first place. Though, leaving the window open was... a rather foolish mistake. But, since the lovely invisible girl closed it for them, I know she is with them as well. How odd.

Emeline

The two of them are just gone. Rosemary and Santiago. I don't get how they did it. No alarms went off. No lockdown (thank god for that; I don't think I could handle another one). Worst of all, no Declan or Gogo. Madam Ester put Declan in confinement or something. He definitely hates me now, though. So what? I lied a little and said I wasn't doing anything with Declan. Ester came in at a good time for a bit of a show. See, if I had been on top of him at the moment she entered the room, then I'd be out of luck, but I wasn't. It shouldn't be such a problem. He's the one who wanted me to cheat on Tiago. Whatever.

What's really a problem is that my Santiago ran away with *Rosemary*. Why couldn't he have taken me?

Maybe him running away has something to do with Ezra Colton. But he hates Ezra. Why did he run away? I don't know the answer, and it's driving me crazy.

July 14th, 6:32am, The streets of Manhattan

Tiago

Of course I knew that Em would cheat on me one day. She's too pretty and shallow to stay with one guy. And I guess I did just leave without telling her. Or talking to her at all. This one is definitely my fault. A little guilt knots in my chest, but that's it. (I should feel more about this, shouldn't I? Shouldn't I be upset? Sad? Anything?) I should go back.

What am I even doing? Maybe it would've been better to think this through. Spontaneous action is always an awful idea. If I could go back, I would. But they'll probably (quite literally) kill me. So I have to run, no matter what.

Why did I let Rosemary come? My companions are a curly haired demon and a blue haired mystery demon that I didn't even know existed. Actually, I don't think it's fair for me to group her with the demons yet. I don't know her.

"Do you hear that?" Rosemary's (annoying) voice drags me out of my head.

"Hear what?"

"Oh my god," she says, already frustrated with me. "The sirens!"

"Rosemary. The sirens have been going all night."

She grabs my arm. "These ones are different," she whispers intensely.

Genevieve nods. "They've been going for a long time. I... think they're following us."

I pause, actually listening. There are the normal, distant wailing of first responders, but on top of that is a louder, discordant kind of wail. And it's getting closer. Genevieve raises her eyebrows and tilts her head.

"I'm sure they're for something else..." I trail off as three black cars pull around the corner. The cars on the street veer over to the sides as they speed down the road. I grab Rosemary's hand, dragging her into the closest alley. Genevieve follows us.

"Yeah," Rosemary retorts sarcastically. "I'm sure they're for something else."

"No, they're definitely after us," Genevieve says under her breath.

We run into the next street, scattering people dressed for a day of work with a few confused gasps and scattered swears. Definitely after us? How does she know that? The cars screech down the alley we were just in. I have to shove someone out of the way. Rosemary trips on a grate and Genevieve grabs her arm, hauling her along. Business people and teenagers yell at us as we run. The cars turn into the street. I look over my shoulder, seeing them going against the traffic. *Fuck.*

"There's no way," Rosemary puffs as we sprint down the sidewalk, "to outrun these cars."

"C'mon," I yell, swerving towards an office building. I don't see Genevieve anywhere. Rosemary and I blast through the revolving doors. I get slightly dizzy. We (metaphorically) fly into the lobby. Several professional–looking people gasp. I hear footsteps pounding ahead of us. *What?* The receptionist glances up at us through her tortoiseshell glasses. A man in a suit by the elevator falls to the floor like he's been pushed. Papers fly into the air. He yells. Genevieve. She can turn invisible.

"Sorry," Rosemary squeaks to no one in particular.

We run past the now empty secretary's desk, as she's currently helping the man on the ground pick up his papers, which we run through, messing up the stack again. Rosemary slides on the polished marble floor. I'm about to catch her but she rights herself at the last second. Guards, like the ones from the home, slam through all the doors (including the scary revolving ones).

An elevator is opening to our right. We bolt for it and the door slides shut as we slip in. Someone inside grabs my wrist and it must be Genevieve, because the only other occupants are two businessmen in suits, giving us questioning looks. Rosemary grimaces. I avoid their curious gazes altogether. My legs start to cramp when the door opens again. I wave awkwardly while she pulls me out, Genevieve still holding onto my wrist. There aren't any guards on this floor yet. Rosemary tugs me towards the emergency exit. No warning sign says an alarm will go off, so we burst through the door. A stairwell lit by harsh white lights opens up in front of us. I look at Rosemary, but she's already halfway down. I follow after shutting the door as quietly as possible. She isn't paying attention to the steep steps.

"Rosem—" I say as she starts to fall.

"*Christ,*" Genevieve whispers, becoming visible again.

She tumbles forward, face first. I sprint down, skipping three stairs at a time.

"Oh my—fuck. Rosemary? Are you okay?" I shake her shoulder at the bottom. She rolls over. Genevieve and I crouch over Rosemary, concerned.

"Yeah. I'm fine." She sounds dazed. "We have to go." Then to Genevieve, "Where the hell did you come from?"

Genevieve shakes her head. "Been here the whole time, dude."

There's a huge cut over Rosemary's eyebrow. It's bleeding pretty heavily.

"Um, your head." I point.

"Yeah. It'll be fine. It should heal in a few minutes."

Oh right. I nod curtly, offering her my hand, which is awkward, because Genevieve offers hers at the same time. Rosemary takes Genevieve's hand, stumbles up, and opens the door leading on to the street. Someone walking by inhales sharply, staring at Rosemary's face. Rosemary pulls a twenty dollar bill out of her pocket. (Seriously, where is she getting all this money?)

"Get a taxi," she says to me.

"Oh... okay. Um, how exactly?" I ask, embarrassed.

"Just wave into the street," she responds drily.

Genevieve snorts, then looks at me. "Open the trunk when the taxi gets here," she whispers. "And please please please remember to let me out."

"Uh..." I start to answer, but then she actually disappears before my eyes. Rosemary looks at me. Neither of us know what to do. Then, I hear Genevieve snickering.

"I'm still here, guys. You *know* this. I can invisible."

I laugh uncomfortably. Rosemary looks jealous.

"Yeah... uh, okay, that's good. I'll um, open the trunk for you when I, um, finish waving at this street."

(I feel ridiculous waving into the street.) A taxi, which is one of many aggressively yellow cars, pulls up next to us. I guess it's that simple. Rosemary opens the door and gets in. I go around to the back and open the trunk. The driver looks at me through the mirror. He's a late middle aged man with greying curly hair. He looks like maybe he's from Mexico? I don't know. There's something about the shape of his face that's familiar. I shake my head and mime putting something into the trunk. I keep looking over my shoulder, waiting for the sirens to start again. Or for guards to burst through the doors.

"All good," Genevieve whispers. She's grinning. "Please don't forget me."

"Yup," I reply nervously. "Won't do that."

Shutting the trunk quickly, I rush around the car to the side Rosemary isn't in and slip into the seat.

"Can you take us to Exit 207 off the 287, please?" she asks politely.

How can she pull herself together so quickly? She definitely doesn't sound like someone running for her life, though it's quite possible that she and Ezra have done things like this before. (Plus, she didn't just shut some girl in the trunk of a vehicle...)

"Are you sure you don't wanna go to the hospital?" the driver responds.

"Yes."

"Alrighty," he says skeptically.

July 15th, 6:46am, The Trunk of a Cab

Genevieve

This trunk is freaking tiny. There was no real reason for me to go in here, except that I've always wondered what it would feel like to ride in the trunk of a car. So far, it's a bit bumpy, but generally kind of nice. Warm, dark... oddly comforting. I feel kinda bad for knocking that guy over in the building, but I heard what those guards in the speeding cars were thinking. They want to sedate us, lock us in boxes, and take us back to hell. To Madame Ester. Who will apparently try to take our gifts away. (How can she even do that?)

Not gonna happen. Not if I have anything to do with it. And the secretary in that building was thinking that the three of us were on hard drugs. Which. Is actually hilarious. I guess we did burst into their calm, normal day, knock people over, got some military trained operatives to tear through their building, and possibly ruined some important documents. Except the documents are definitely backed up online somewhere, so there's no *huge* problems. They'll get over it.

Now, I'm a little worried about the cab driver. He's freaking out about the gash on Rosemary's face. And he also thinks there's a body in the trunk. Which is partly accurate. But seriously. Santiago was waving for a cab. Where would he get a body?

Common sense here, people?

July 15th, 6:50am, The Inside of a Cab

Colton Navar

These kids sure are strange. They don't look like they're a couple. Both of them are sweaty. And the boy put *something* in the trunk. Something or some*one*. I have no idea.

There's a huge, bleeding cut over the girl's eyebrow. She keeps wiping the blood out of her eye. The boy keeps glancing over his shoulder, his blonde hair falling into his eyes. They don't talk to or look at each other. She's biting her nails.

"Okay stop," the boy whispers. "You're making weird little noises. I can't stand it."

"Oh shut up," she grumbles.

Why do they want to go to Exit 207 off the 287? It leads to an abandoned observatory, fifty miles down a gravel road. My grandpa used to take me there when I was a kid. Many years after he died, it closed down, supposedly bought for private research. It was around the time my wife left me. I don't know what kids like them want with it. We drive for a long while in silence. Through the Holland Tunnel, down the 78 to the 95, and finally onto the 287. Farthest I've been outside the city in a long time.

I look in the mirror in time to see the boy glance back again. He looks at the girl with wide eyes.

"What's the matter, kid?" I ask, uneasy.

"Um, we really need to get out of the city," he replies.

The girl just glares straight ahead. Okay then. I look back at the road. "We're close to the edge."

The boy nods, his jaw clenched. There are three black cars behind us.

"What's this?" I say, referring to the cars following us.

The boy runs his hand through his hair, looking down. The girl's fidgeting with the hem of her hoodie. The cut is—I do a double take. The car swerves. There's no cut on her head. It's gone.

"Hey." My voice wavers. "What happened to the cut on your face?"

Whoever these kids are, something is very wrong. Or I'm going crazy. We roar past suburban houses as they slowly become further and further apart. The boy is staring at the cars over his shoulder. The girl touches where the cut was. Her eyes are large. She bites her lip.

"I—I don't know what you're talking about. There wasn't a cut on my face."

My heart is beating way too fast to be healthy for me. I'm getting hallucinations? Panic is spreading through me when I see the blood on her sweater cuff. So she's lying.

"Why's there blood on your sweater then?" I raise my eyebrows.

Sirens start wailing. They share a frantic look.

"Hey, kids, what's this about?"

Anger and fear rise in my stomach. I pull over on the side of the highway.

"No. You can't stop," the girl pleads, abandoning her composure. "Please."

"You're gonna have to explain yourself," I say sternly.

I'm freaking out. This girl just made a huge cut disappear, they want to go to an abandoned observatory, and the police are chasing us. Well, them. Not me. Unless I'm an accomplice now. God*damn*.

The boy's skin is even paler than before. The sirens are very close now.

"Get outta my car," I nearly yell.

I think the girl is about to cry. They jump out, running into the forest beside the highway.

"Get back here!" I shout. I didn't expect for them to run. The boy stops, then he runs back. The girl yells at him from the edge of the trees. He's shaking his head.

"Can you unlock the doors?" His voice is muffled by the windows. "Oh, never mind!"

The door locks click open on their own. I gasp. The boy opens the trunk and another girl jumps out. What the hell?! She's got dark skin and a bun of springy curls on her head. Then she disappears. *Into thin air.* I choke on my yell as they vanish into the green.

Their pursuers pull over next to me. Instead of the officers I expected, they're a hazmat team with mirrored glass helmets. I try to calm my frayed nerves. My heart is pounding like it's intent on escaping from my rib cage. I'm dizzy. Sweating. My chest feels like it's collapsing. Can't I get enough air?

CHAPTER 9

chapter 9

July 15th, 5:33pm

Location: Somewhere in the Woods

Tiago

I don't know how long we've been blindly crashing through these woods, but I do know that I'm just about done. Rosemary has insisted that we keep running, even though *there is no one following us.* Tiny, burning cuts are scattered on my face from pine needles and twigs. It's really weird that the guards didn't chase after us. I'm slightly concerned that we're not being pursued, which is an odd thing to worry about, but still. If they really were guards from the home, what else could Madame Ester have up her sleeve that she could use to catch us with? Or maybe she doesn't care. That's possible? Maybe?

Rosemary is a few steps behind me. She's breathing heavily. *Thank goodness I have long legs*, I think, half delirious. That means she can't keep up. That means she's getting tired. That means we can stop this marathon of ridiculousness. Genevieve is... well, I have no idea where she is. I'm assuming she's with us, because she was a few minutes ago. She must be invisible now. Or maybe she was just using us as a way of getting out of the home. The invisibility is definitely going to take some getting used to. If she's even here.

"Tiago. Can we. Stop?" Rosemary gasps. "It's getting. Dark."

I stop and slowly turn around. She almost runs into me. "Be my guest, Miss Let's–keep–running–even–though–we're–not–being–chased–anymore."

The end of my sentence is lost in a burst of violent laughter from me. She looks awful. It's hilarious. She glares at me, not quite meeting my eyes, since she refuses to look up. Her bun is gone, replaced by a nest of sticks. I guess she fell a few times because the knees of her jeans are ripped and muddy. Her sweater has dark stains on the cuffs. Absolutely filthy. I snort.

"You look... ravishing," I tease.

"Well you don't look much better," she grumbles, still out of breath. Her face is blotchy, as she bends over and places her hands on her knees.

"You wanna bet on that?"

She looks up at me and rolls her eyes. I focus on being clean. The pieces of dirt *want* to be back on the ground. The particles hum and sing to me as I disperse them, feeling the tiny pieces poof into the air.

"That's just not fair. You close your eyes for like three seconds, and I see all the dirt literally disappear into thin air."

I wink at her. "Magic." I spin around, showing off. "Is there any evidence of a day–long run through the woods?"

She glowers.

"Oh cheer up, Miss Sunshine." I mock–pout (a handy expression I learned from Emeline). "You only got us kicked out of our ride. And made us get lost in this forest. But does that really matter?"

"This isn't *just* my fault."

"Really? I was the one who freaked out the driver by making a two–inch gash heal in twenty minutes?"

"Okay. Fine," she counters, "but to be fair, he would've pulled over anyways because of the guards *chasing* us."

"Yes and if you hadn't fallen down the stairs and slowed us down, we wouldn't have been chased at all!"

"You're going to blame this *all* on me?"

"Yes. Rosemary, it's your fault. I shouldn't have let you come."

"Are you kidding me right now?" Her voice is rising, like the red in her cheeks.

"No. I'm not. *I* shouldn't even be here! I should be eating dinner with Em. At least then I'd be happy!" I yell, though I don't know if that's even true. Rosemary looks hurt. More than hurt. Wounded. Betrayed, even.

"So you'd rather ignore the fact that he's gone," she says flatly.

She walks over to a tree. Resting her head on the trunk, her back to me, she whispers, "I don't understand why you're even here, Santiago. I thought it was because you cared about him a little bit. Regretted everything you fucked up. Maybe I was wrong. Did you just want a little adventure? Was this your way of getting a good adrenaline rush? Do you have a death wish?"

Her words flood over my head like a bucket of freezing water. Of course I care about him. (Not that I want anyone to know that I care, but Rosemary might storm off into the woods if I don't tell her.) Why else would I be here? Is it to get away from our prison? Am I really that selfish?

"I should've come alone," she finishes.

My heart squeezes painfully. I don't know why. "Rosemary. Rosemary, I—"

"I think you've said *enough*." She doesn't move from the tree.

Genevieve appears beside a tree on the far side of the clearing. "Are you guys finished with this yet? Because I am." She looks kind of pissed off. "You guys are stupid for running off together without knowing each other first." Then she sits down with her back to the tree, opens her bag, pulls out a small book, and starts to read.

Okay then. I stay silent. Genevieve is very perceptive. The ground is dry, since it's been decently sunny. The sun really isn't helping my current mood though. Sitting down, I wait for either of them to move or acknowledge me in some way. The sunset is pink, but that's all I can see because of the trees.

"Rosemary?"

She turns around but doesn't look me in the eyes. She slides roughly down the tree trunk, mirroring Genevieve.

"What." It's not a question.

"Um... are... you hungry?" I ask nervously, offering the bag of assorted sandwiches from yesterday's lunch. She takes it listlessly.

"I do. Care. About him. Just so you know," I say, looking at her. (It's really hard for me to say it out loud.) (But *why?*)

Her large dark eyes meet mine for the first time since the taxi. She looks skeptical. Genevieve raises her eyebrows, but doesn't look up. Rosemary purses her lips.

"You told him you hated him on countless occasions, electrocuted him at least twice by putting some magical electricity into those wires he was playing with and convincing him to put a fork into a goddamn electrical socket, and oh! Let's not forget the time you shoved him off the roof of a three–story building," she scoffs. "Do you really expect me to believe you care about him?"

I open my mouth to say something (something like *I didn't push him off the roof,* because wherever she believes, it's not true), but I just leave my jaw unlocked. The thing is, I did electrocute him *more* than two times. I accidentally set him on fire. Ezra would really benefit from being less gullible, but he didn't even need convincing to put the fork in the socket. I just said it would be funny if he did. He didn't even think twice before doing it. It wasn't funny at all. It was terrifying. That was when we were thirteen. It was the last time I had a hand in electrocuting Ezra. Also, the roof was in a category of its own. I *was* going to push him, but then he fell off (mostly) on his own.

I squint at her, unsure of what to say. I close my mouth and run my tongue over my teeth. I raise my eyebrows. "Can I have the sandwiches?"

She smirks. "Can you answer my question?"

My heart contracts again as I wonder if she picked that up from Ezra.

I feign shock. "Is that an Ezra–ism I hear?"

"How do you know his isms?" she asks, looking upset.

"Are you angry I know his isms?" I start laughing. The hurt melts from her face.

"Maybe I thought I was the only person who knows Ezra–isms."

"Well, in that case, you'd be mistaken."

She laughs softly, grabbing a sandwich. "'Kay," she says with her mouth full, "when does he do this?" She opens her eyes really wide, kind of pathetically.

"Oh that's an easy one. He does that when he wants you to answer his question when you've said no a million times." I smile.

"You're right, that's too easy," she says. She starts rocking from side to side slightly.

"When he's worried or scared."

A huge smile lights up her face.

"That's him the rest of the time." This feels like a game show that I've been studying for since I was three.

"You know the way he always needs eye contact?" she asks.

"Or the way he says my name all the time? He's always like, Tiago, Tiago. Tiago. Tiago? Tiago. Tiago? Tiago?"

She bursts out laughing. "And how he snorts when he laughs? How he can never lie? The fact that he has an empty notebook and an obsession with quotes and anything poetic, but has the messiest writing humanly possible? He's so afraid of heights, yet he followed you onto the roof? The way he looks like a lost puppy when he's upset? And how everyone loves him?"

"Well not everyone..." I mumble.

She raises her eyebrows. "And who are you referring to?"

"Me."

"Then why are you here?"

"She got you there, buddy," Genevieve mumbles under her breath, coming into our conversation for the first time.

Rosemary's trying to get me to say something I'll regret, and Genevieve is making a very valid point. I swallow.

"How he had the tendency to disappear?" I whisper, going back to our game-show, avoiding the question entirely.

"How he *has*, Santiago. He can't be..." She trails off like she did before. "He always... survives."

I have to believe her. If he isn't alive, what are we doing here? We need to find him. Which would be much easier if we weren't in a random forest.

Genevieve

Tiago and Rosemary's relationship is so weird. One moment, they're yelling at each other and the next, they're reminiscing about the one thing they have in common. Ezra. But Rosemary is Ezra's best friend, according to her mind. And Santiago? I can't really figure that out. During their whole conversation, his thoughts went something like this: *I hate Ezra. Why am I even here? Because I hate Ezra, right?* Over and over and over. Except when he was thinking about him. *Green eyes, crazy mess of curls, kinda short. I hate him.*

So why is he here? Apparently, *he* doesn't even know. I hate to admit, but I kind of forgot how complicated people are. For the last couple months, I've been observing and keeping to myself. As I watch them, I find myself wanting to hide. Shy. I'm feeling *shy* around them. Rosemary and Tiago have fallen silent, their minds humming a little. They brought sandwiches, which I knew. I, on the other hand, brought cookies, mango juice boxes, salad containers, lots of saltines (because they remind me of home for some odd reason), and the beaten copy of The Hobbit, because it wasn't being read back at the home. And it's full of messy annotations too, in several different hands. I like the little thoughts.

"Hey Genevieve?"

I look up at Santiago. My heart skips a bit. I'm not normally like this. Oh boy.

"What?" I close the book, because there are a few things he wants to ask.

Rosemary stares at me too. I avoid her gaze. It's piercing.

"How long were you at the home?" Then he smirks. "Or the prison, as I like to call it."

I have to bite my tongue to keep from saying, *Oh I know you like to call it that. You say it in your head A LOT.* But I don't say that. Instead, I do a kind of exhale-y laugh. "Nice, that's clever," I respond. "I'd been there awhile, I guess."

They look at each other, thinking, *How did we not notice her?*

"Honestly... I kind of retreated in on myself. I think it's a trauma response. So I stayed invisible and hung out in the library mostly," I say, answering the question in their heads as I wave the book around for emphasis.

As usual, they look a little freaked out. Because I answered what they were thinking. I forgot how hard socializing is. Goddammit.

"Some crazy shit went down at home and my parents had no choice but to send me there," I say. "I might have told the entire population of my high school that the popular girl was running away with a teacher and then disappeared into thin air."

Santiago's eyes go wide as he puffs up his cheeks and lets out a breathe.

"That's... ballsy," he says, his nod somewhere between discomfort and admiration.

I force a laugh. "Well. Yeah. That girl reminded me of Emeline, actually."

"A fake little liar?" Rosemary chimes in, glaring at Tiago. He just rolls his eyes, mostly lost in thought.

He wants to know what happened after, but he doesn't ask out loud. Rosemary still feels bad for not noticing me. I think she has a thing for outcasts. I'm pretty sure Ezra was an underdog too. But not because of his gift, like me. Because he didn't *have* a gift. But he has one now? I wonder if I'd get along with *the famous Ezra Colton.*

The companionable forest filled silence starts edging towards awkward as Rosemary and Tiago start thinking deeper inside their own heads.

"I'm going to sleep now," I say. The sky is a deep bruise–ish purple, with the beginnings of stars. "I assume we have to walk tomorrow?"

Santiago glances at me quickly. My voice dragged him out of another Ezra spiral, but he was also enjoying the sky.

"Oh, uh yeah, good idea." He pauses. "Goodnight, I guess."

Rosemary stays silent. *Her* Ezra spiral wasn't disrupted by me.

July 15th, 8:12pm, Ester Myrtle Kellwether's Home for Unusually Gifted Youth and Children

Ester

The incompetence of my guards is unbelievable. All of them are in their late twenties, early thirties, some in their forties—all at least four years older than Rosemary, Santiago, and Genevieve, yet they let them get into the forest. Now, I will have to track them down myself and somehow make sure they arrive at my lab. I can be there within an hour, if need be.

I pace my office. Nothing was deleted or changed on my laptop when it was found. The signal was traced to a fast food restaurant. The computer was in the garbage can. Those three are smarter than I gave them credit for. Those three, I suppose. I know that they either had my passwords, or hacked into my email. Of course, my lab workers sent the update on Ezra in the twenty hours my computer was not with me. Though I knew it was coming, I did forget to check my email before the computer was stolen.

Miss Mae–Anderson, Miss Legend, and Mr. Grey would be at the lab by now, if my guards had found them. They definitely are not. Currently, I am guessing those two rascals are either yelling at each other or sleeping in a forest somewhere. I have no idea what that Genevieve character would do. I could send some of my creatures to chase them in the right direction, but I do not think I will just yet. I will wait.

It is hard to believe that we moved Ezra just two nights ago. Everything is so unorganized at the moment. My mind simply will not slow down. That is the reason that I am having trouble sleeping, which is why I am in my office staring at the video of Ezra that was attached in the email. Watching it for the twelfth time, I feel a twinge of pity. I quickly drown the feeling. That is not something I want to start.

CHAPTER 10

chapter 10

*J*uly 15th, 5:15pm

Location: That same tiny room

Ezra

I stare at the words. Still afraid, even though it's been days. Or maybe it's been minutes. I've read the note over and over and over.

Ezra Colton, it says.

FlAmes IlLuminate yoUr fRozEn soul.

I wasn't supposed to see those words ever again. They seem normal enough, to a normal person. Maybe a little odd. But all I see is FAILURE. Words hidden inside of other words. I used to write poems like that because I liked having small secrets. People are unobservant, so they usually don't find the hidden meaning. But this place, these scientists, they turned the poetry into a cruel game. Because I see the secret messages, they use the poetry to remind me of what I am.

My vision swims. Fear takes over, seeping violently through me. I bash myself into the door, screaming. I need to get out. This place. It's full of begging for mercy, but getting none. It's full of agony. Terror.

My body goes hot. At first, I ignore it. (I have to *ignore it.*) I get hotter. My hands. They're on fire. (*Oh god.*) I drop to the ground, by instinct. Not real instinct. I can't be seen like this not again—

Memories flood my mind. Like they have. Over the past few blurry days. I'm not actually burning. The heat is comforting. It's soothing, understanding, almost like a homecoming. These flames, they're mine. My gift. They're supposed to be mine, but Ester tried to take them away. I remember now. For real. I—

almost don't want to remember.

(Is the pain worth it? Just to burn?)

The door bursts open. Hazmat people rush in. I back away. Breathing is a foreign memory. They soak me with powerful hoses. The flames are gone. I crouch, cowering, trying to disappear, as they advance on me. The fear is back, stronger than the memories of my gift. I scream when their gloved hands grab my arms. I kick and fight as hard as I can. I'm no match for them. I'm so cold. I can't keep this up, but I can't let them take me. Not this again. I can hardly breathe.

Something pricks my neck. I scream, but nothing comes out of my mouth. My limbs won't work. The burning cold starts in my feet, spreading like an unforgiving blizzard. I'm powerless. Just like I remember. Agony is something you never get used to. It gets worse every time.

I feel myself twitching. My breathing is shallow. I try to remember things that make me happy. Rosemary. She has blonde hair. No. That's wrong. She has curly hair. Her eyes are—another scream builds up inside me. There's nowhere for it to go.

Tiago.

July 15th, 9:15pm, The Woods

Rosemary

I can't shake Santiago's words from my mind. *He* had *the tendency to disappear.* What if Ezra *is* dead? I know it wasn't what he meant to say, but still. The dry ground is making it hard to get comfortable. Genevieve didn't eat and she's with her back to us, breathing evenly. I think she's asleep. Santiago keeps squinting up at the stars as they slowly appear, his face unreadable. I think I would pay to know what's on his mind.

The sun has now set completely, leaving us in an ominously moonlit forest. A while ago, Tiago suggested we should try to sleep. I'm pretty sure neither of us is actually doing that. Yeah, I do hate him, but he's the only one here with me right now who knew—knows!—Ezra well.

"Santiago?" I whisper.

He turns his head to face me, his eyes catching the moonlight. I'm still sitting with my back to the tree. He's lying down, looking up.

"I can't stop thinking about him."

A small, pained smile plays at his lips. "Don't worry. Me neither," he says, almost inaudibly.

He looks up again. I kind of feel bad for hurting him, but why does he suddenly care about Ezra?

"How long have you cared?" I ask.

"Rosemary," he replies bitterly, "I've always cared."

"Even when you shoved him off the roof when he was trying to apologize for something he didn't do?"

"You know he fell," he states flatly. "He *is* kind of clumsy."

"I don't believe you." I know Ezra wouldn't fall off a roof.

"I swear I didn't push him. I was going to jump after him, but he hit the ground before I could think."

"You know that jumping after him wouldn't help, right?"

"Yeah. I know. I'm not an idiot." He's getting upset again. Maybe I'll ask him tomorrow. "Sorry."

"What?" I'm confused. "Why?" Why is he saying sorry?

"I really need to stop getting so angry. We need to, well, get along for a bit, I guess. I'm really not helping," he mumbles. "But neither are you..."

Oh, God. Why is he pulling this stunt? I roll my eyes and turn away from him. There is *no* way I'm going to agree to get along with him.

"Goodnight then," he grumbles.

The feeling of regret I was suppressing fights its way up now. I can't push it down. Why did I decide to hate Tiago anyways? I turn around. He's lying on his side with his hair strewn across his face. I'm not sure anyone should be allowed to look that serene. *Why did I make it my job to despise him?* Couldn't someone else do that? Ezra didn't want me to. Not that it matters what Ezra said (because I am my own person). But I guess I should try to get along with him. For Ezra's sake, right?

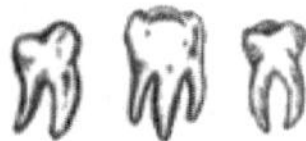

Sunlight streams through the dense pines. I open my eyes slowly, propping myself up on my elbows. Santiago's sitting with his back against a tree, eating a sandwich. Genevieve is laying on her back on the other side of the clearing, hands clasped over her stomach.

"How was your beauty sleep, darling?" Santiago asks, mocking me.

I have to work really hard not to glare. Instead, I force a smile.

"Um, great, thanks?" It wasn't meant to sound like a question. But it is. I don't even know what I'm doing.

He throws the bag with the sandwiches in it at me. Surprisingly, my finger hooks onto the opening in the Ziploc seal.

"Nice catch." He's just as surprised as I am.

I choose my favourite kind—peanut butter and jam. (I know. I'm boring.) The bread is getting a bit soggy. I throw the bag back, less successfully than my catch. He leans over, but ends up falling on his side. (Still snags it, though.)

"I'm sorry about last night."

I wasn't really planning on saying it so fast and frantic.

"The epic blurter strikes again," he chides.

My face goes hot. I have a habit of yelling things out at random times. The embarrassed blush makes my neck itch. I don't restrain my glare this time. He puts his hands up, trying to look innocent (and failing).

"Oh stop it," I growl. "That innocence is reserved for Ezra only."

He laughs. "You're right. I'm sorry."

"So, um should we try to, well…" I rub the back of my itchy neck. "Get along? For Ezra's sake?"

"I suppose that would make sense." He grins. "It wouldn't do anyone any good if we killed each other by arguing."

I sigh. It's really just an unfortunate situation.

"I suppose so."

He extends his hand. I'm confused. He clues into my perplexed expression.

"Shake on it," he says with his eyebrow raised. "To make it official."

Santiago–ism.

"Eew. You want me to shake your hand?" I ask with pretend disgust.

"It's not that gross." He suddenly looks concerned. "Is it?" He glances at his hand. "No. It's not even dirty. But you, my dear, are filthy."

"That one's your fault, bozo. You could use your magical powers to clean me up, you know." I pop the last bit of sandwich in my mouth. Then I plug my nose and extend my other hand. "I still think you're gross."

He sticks his tongue out at me.

"Okay, fine. I'll shake on it." I can hardly keep my face straight. My voice is all weird. He chuckles, then shakes my hand. He plugs his nose too. Then, the dirt is swirling off of me. I see it rising off of my sweater like mist as twigs unknot themselves from my hair before they disperse into the air. It's kind of a tickly sensation that passes in a few seconds. A smile tugs at my lips.

"Great. Lovely. Thank you for your compliance, Miss Germaphobe."

"What is this, some kind of initiation?" Genevieve is staring at us, eating a cookie. "Because if you want me to plug my nose and do some kind of dance, that's not happening. You guys are so... weird."

I shake my head, laughing. He stands up, stretching but also smiling. He offers me his hand again, to help me up. I don't take it. I refuse. (I still have standards.)

"Don't worry. You won't have to dance." A grin spreads across his face. "If you give me a cookie. Where'd you get that?"

Genevieve laughs. "There's literally a table with cookies and cake sometimes." She grimaces. "The cake is awful, though."

Santiago looks absolutely appalled. "How did I not know this?!" Genevieve hands him a cookie from her bag. His rant continues, and I can't help but smile. "There was dessert that I didn't know existed! I've lived there for almost my whole life! How did this happen?" He takes a bite. "Oh my God. Ginger cookies. Wow. I haven't had a cookie since I was three."

She holds out a cookie to me, but I shake my head.

"Which way are we going to go?" I ask.

"Well, Exit 207 is that way, I think." He points to the left, his mouth full. "Since we didn't turn when we were running. So if we go diagonally, we should find the road at some point." He seems confident.

"Okee dokee." God, that's dorky.

Genevieve is more skeptical. "We're just gonna walk in a diagonal line and hope we find the road?"

"Um." Santiago is a little thrown off, but he recovers quickly. "Yeah. We are."

She shrugs. "Okay. It's your funeral. See where mansplaining gets you."

Santiago frowns at her. "Mansplaining?

Genevieve huffs out a sigh, shaking her head. "You're all so woefully uninformed."

"No what does it mean?" he asks, concerned.

As she starts telling him what that is, (a man explaining things to someone who's generally a woman in a condescending or patronizing tone) I pick up my bag, still cringing at myself. Honestly, I don't even remember what's in there. He takes the sandwich bag and shoves it in his pack. I'm not sure why his bag is so much more full than mine. He had less time to grab things. Genevieve is packed and ready. She's been packed and ready this whole time. (How is everyone packed and ready???)

"Are you coming?" Santiago's voice is far ahead.

I was too busy judging his ugly bag again to notice they're already walking. (Which is incredibly stupid because the bag was moving and getting smaller as he trudged away.)

"Oops! Sorry. I was a bit distracted by the hypnotic effect of your hideous backpack." I say as I run to catch up.

He just looks at me. "Uhhh..." Clearly he has no idea how to respond. "Never mind."

Genevieve gives me a little laugh, so at least my joke didn't *completely* fail.

Today is sunny, like yesterday, but today I can actually feel the warmth. Ezra was right—Santiago's hair shines a lot in the sun. (Ezra said that a lot, now that I think about it.)

Last night, the silence was uncomfortable, but as the three of us beat back the undergrowth, it feels... less awkward. We've kinda got a purpose, I guess? Genevieve pulls ahead at some point, but she keeps checking back on us, flashing me a bright grin over her shoulder. I really like her. She's... cool.

"Why did you run away to find your mortal enemy again?" I ask after about an hour of trudging through bushes without saying anything. I've been thinking about the fact that Santiago gave Ezra his sweater. (Honestly, I'm really confused by the fact he did exactly that. He ran away with nothing but a backpack full of random stuff, to find his nemesis. It's just weird.)

"I guess I wasn't really being rational." He looks over his shoulder at me, smirking. "But what fun would life be if I didn't have my *mortal enemy*?"

"Are you sure he's your mortal enemy?" Genevieve yells, walking backwards so she's facing us.

He just shrugs. The sun is hot. Thank goodness for the trees. Dappled light patches pass over me as we walk. The forest is alive with gentle yellow and green. It screams LIFE in the most subtle way.

"One sec, I want to take off my sweater." Genevieve doesn't hear me so I yell, "Can you stop? I want to take off my sweater!" She turns around and walks back towards us, like she's taking a leisurely stroll through the park.

Santiago plugs his ears and turns around to look at me. "You're really loud."

I duck out of my boring, plain sweater and shove it in my bag, ignoring him.

"Do you actually think he's my mortal enemy?" Santiago asks.

I look up at him with my eyebrows raised. "Really?"

He runs both of his hands through his hair (Santiago–ism) with an unhappy expression on his face. Genevieve rubs her eyes with her palms, then gives me a look that says *This? Again?* I ignore that too.

"Santiago, the last thing you said before he disappeared was that you hated him," I point out, shouldering my bag.

His expression becomes mildly distressed. "But I'm here now. I'm trying to make it right. Doesn't that count for something?"

"Something pretty small. Remember the times you told him he should play with the live wires? Or when you decided it was a wonderful idea to push him off the—"

"Stop bringing up the roof thing, okay?" he cuts me off, frustration shadowing his face. "I. Did not. Push him."

I'm taken aback by the passion in his voice.

"I'm done hearing you lie about the roof!" I start to yell, but Genevieve shushes me.

"Can you just tell us what happened then?" she asks softly. "As someone who wasn't a part of it, I'd like to hear both sides of this story?"

He makes an exhausted huff, then glares at me. "Fine. As long as you don't bring it up again. That day was like hell. But fine."

Tiago

I can't see Rosemary's expression, because I'm walking in front of her. Genevieve is beside me at the moment, with this very odd look on her face. I'm tempted to ask her what's wrong, but then Rosemary would accuse me of diverting the conversation away from myself or something stupid like that.

"I just need a minute." To calm down. To get myself together.

"'Kay," Rosemary responds, suddenly smug.

"Would you mind walking beside or in front of me, Rosemary? It makes me nervous when you're back there. I can't tell how you're reacting to the stuff I'm saying." I know it's a weird request and I know she knows it is too.

"Weird request, man." Genevieve says with a little, tense laugh. Why is she so... it's like she knows what I'm thinking.

"Um, sure." Rosemary speeds up, bushwacking beside me now.

I breathe in deeply, inhaling the cool, forest air. There are so many incredible things here that I've never seen before. This forest is just bursting with poetry. Ezra would love it. I shake my head. What is that cheesy nonsense? Where are these thoughts *coming* from? Genevieve snorts. I squint at her, trying to figure out what's so funny. She gives exactly no clues.

"Hellooo. Earth to Santiago. Are you still alive in there?" Rosemary is waving her hand in front of my eyes.

"Stop." I shove her hand down. "Stop, you're gonna trip or something."

"Are you going to tell me?" She smiles expectantly (a bit manipulatively, if you ask me).

"Okay, okay..." I sigh. "I didn't push him off the goddamn roof."

Genevieve feigns surprise. "*Really.*"

I keep my eyes forward. Rosemary looks at me, disappointed and about to say something stupid.

"Shhh. Don't say it. I'll keep going."

"Thank you," she says sarcastically.

"Okay. So. I *wanted* to push him off the roof."

"That really doesn't help your case, Santiago."

"Shut up," I mutter. "You wanted to hear. So just be quiet for a single minute of your life."

She rolls her eyes.

"You don't *have* to tell us if you're this uncomfortable, Tiago," Genevieve offers.

Rosemary lets out a strangled cry. "*No* you have to tell us," she begs.

I give Genevieve a grateful look, then sarcastically pat Rosemary on the arm. "Be not afraid, small annoying bird. I shall tell the tale."

To this, Genevieve snorts and Rosemary literally growls. I yank my hand away, turning my haze back to the forest ahead.

I continue, a little nervous because no one (except for Ezra, that *weirdo*) believes that this version of the story is true.

"I *wanted* to push him off the roof." I pause to see if she'll interject. She clenches her jaw. "We were only thirteen, and I was a jerk."

"Was?" she mutters to herself. I ignore it, but my cheeks flush.

"I knew he loved the sunset and the roof had a good view. So, I walked past him at dinner with some friends. I said, 'I think I'm gonna sneak up on the roof to watch the SUNSET, ALONE, AFTER SUPPER.' He heard. I had gotten so mad at him for asking me a million questions the day before about some stupid things like my favourite authors, my favourite colours, my favourite animals, blah blah blah, so I knew he was looking for a time to apologize to me, and the fact that he loved sunsets was, well, the perfect way to get him up on the roof, so I could just shove him off and be done with it."

Genevieve laughs for some reason. Rosemary gasps quietly, horrified.

"This story isn't helping me like you any more than before," she says through clenched teeth.

"Anyways, he came up," I continue, tuning her out yet again. "And I laughed at him for being stupid. Then he saw the sunset and forgot I was there... which made me even more angry so, um, yeah."

She squints at me. "So you *did* push him."

I shake my head.

"No. I came up behind him and said, 'What are you sorry for?' And he slipped and fell because I scared him. *By accident.*" I articulate the last two words.

Rosemary darts in front of me.

"You're telling me"—she jabs her pointer finger into my chest—"that you scared him into slipping off the roof because he thought the sunset was pretty?" she yells. The anger in her eyes is so intense I find it hard to look at her.

"Remember, this was like, five years ago, right?" I match her volume.

Rosemary looks like she's going to hit me.

"Woah, woah, woah, guys. Chill out." Suddenly, Genevieve is in between us. She's holding Rosemary's wrist and has a hand up in my direction.

I breathe deeply again, trying to control my rising fury.

"Okay. Fine. Fine. I guess I should let it go. For now." Rosemary pauses, then shakes her head angrily. "You horrible little *fucker*," she says under her breath. "If we make it out of this... ohh boy. You're in for it," Rosemary says threateningly. We stare at each other for a long moment until she looks up at the sky.

"Thank you for being honest," Genevieve says quietly, giving me an understanding nod.

July 16th, 11:10am, Ester Myrtle Kellwether's Home for Unusually Gifted Youth and Children

Emeline

"We are very sorry to inform you all, but Rosemary Mae-Anderson, Genevieve Legend, Santiago Grey, and Ezra Colton are dead."

The room is, like, perfectly silent.

"Their bodies were found beside the highway last night. We do not know the cause of their untimely deaths." Madam Ester's voice goes silent as the intercom shuts off.

I don't believe it. Who even is Genevieve Legend? That girl from the library? How can they be dead? How can *Santiago* be dead? He's dead. Gone. I cover my mouth. Kenzie looks numb. The pain in my heart is growing. I never got to say goodbye. None of us did. Mason wraps her arms around my shoulders and cries into my sweater. Everybody either looks like Kenzie, who's shell shocked, or like Mason, who's sobbing uncontrollably into her hands. Our friends are all in various states of disbelief. There won't be one person here who takes Ezra's loss lightly. The only person who would is—no, *was* Tiago. My vision blurs with hot tears.

How can he be gone?

Ester

Unwelcome tears prick my eyes as I announce they are dead. I know they are alive, but just thinking of them dead upsets me. It should *not*. I watch the reactions of everyone in the dining hall on the security camera feed. Nobody moves. Then, people start crying into the shoulders of their friends. Some just stare blankly. I hope no one gets too devastated. They will move on... I think.

It is not that I am worried about them. I merely did what was necessary for my plan to proceed. If it works, all of these unfortunate youth will be free. They will not remember each other, nor will they know the pain they felt while grieving for their friends who are not really dead. With luck, none of these children will remember their time here.

I do have pity on the poor youngsters who have been abandoned at such an early age. Like Ezra was. And Santiago, I suppose. Those little ones are wandering around the halls right now, bawling just because everyone else is. They have no idea what is happening. I page some caregivers with my hearing aids to take the small children to the nursery.

I shut my computer, sighing. This idea of mine really is a gamble. I think it would be wise to start as soon as possible, to leave a margin for error.

July 16th, 5:33pm, The Woods

Rosemary

I don't trust myself to even look at him. If I do, I might punch him or let loose a furious stream of insults. We didn't stop walking after his story. We haven't stopped all day. My feet are really aching from my worn–out sneakers. I didn't think we'd be hiking. (Not that I have any better footwear.) Genevieve is walking beside me, slowing down her pace to match mine. She's actually quite a bit shorter than me. I didn't realize that before.

My anger cools to resentment, but I will *not* turn around and look at Santiago. Earlier, I tried to focus on the beauty of everything around me. I haven't really ever seen anything like this before. Pure, untouched nature. That strategy worked until I realized Santiago hadn't magically disappeared. Then, Genevieve started telling me about this book series, about these characters named like, Bilbo, and Sam, Frodo, and how they went on several great adventures. She was reading one of the books earlier. Her voice is calming. I wish she could read the stories to me out loud.

It takes me a while to realize that Santiago's footsteps have stopped. I clench my jaw and turn around. Genevieve sighs quietly and turns around too, glancing between us with a combination of trepidation and hope.

"What," I demand, "are you doing?"

He gives me an exasperated look. "Rosemary, you can't ignore me forever."

"I've only been ignoring you for what?" I snap. "Four hours?"

"Guys...?" Genevieve interjects. She's probably regretting coming with us. Because we're a fucking circus.

"Please," he says, angry, but at himself. "I'm sorry."

"You should be apologizing to Ezra. Not me," I glare at him harshly before turning back around.

"Ezra's not here," he mumbles. "Also, he wasn't mad."

Ezra's not here. Why did that hurt me? Santiago's right. He isn't here. But I haven't been anywhere without him in years. We're each other's support. And it kind of feels like I'm walking around with half a body.

"Rosemary, we won't ever find him if we're always at each other's throats."

"I'm not at your throat," I retort, looking at him again (and contemplating how satisfying it would be to actually punch him in the throat).

He throws his hands in the air. "You're impossible, Rosemary."

"Thank you."

He smiles.

"What's so funny?"

"Well, the first time we went looking for Ezra, we said almost exactly that."

"Oh yeah..."

We're laughing again. His eyes are so bright.

"But no, I really am sorry. I was young and dumb."

A sarcastic snort escapes my lips.

He sighs with fake frustration. "Well, maybe I am still young and dumb. But not *that* dumb. No going on roofs for the rest of my days. I swear."

I realize that he's standing a few feet away from me now. I punch his arm.

"Ow." He narrows his eyes at me.

"Oops. Too hard?" I wince. "You did deserve it."

Santiago frowns a bit. "Maybe you're right."

Genevieve raises one eyebrow. (OH MY GOD! She can do it too! Why can't I? This is completely unfair.) "I really didn't expect you to be the violent type, Rosemary."

I laugh awkwardly. "Um, yeah, me neither to be completely honest..."

She shakes her head, like her mind is blown. The sun is slowly sinking.

"Let's just stop here?" Santiago says to us. The three of us weirdly nod at each other.

A part of me wants to cry with relief. I don't think I've ever done this much activity in my life. I throw my bag on the ground. We sink to the dry forest floor. Santiago hands me the bag of sandwiches. They're not holding up so well. (At least there aren't any ham ones.) (The ham ones are gross when they're *fresh*. I can't imagine how awful they'd be days old.) If I weren't so hungry, there's no way I'd eat the soggy lettuce and cheese between the mush that used to be bread. Genevieve takes a sandwich too, but she just removes the cheese and eats it. Santiago takes her leftovers. My water bottle (which I didn't realize I had until a few hours ago) is almost empty. After my sandwich (I'm not sure you could even call it that anymore), I drain my water to try to get the disgusting, stale taste out of my mouth.

Then, I take the cookie Genevieve offers. It's a bit dry, but oooh so good. Crispy chocolate chip heaven. After we eat, she proceeds to hand out mango juice boxes. Santiago's thrilled.

"Thank for being smart," he says to her.

"Yeah, well." She frowns a bit. "I wasn't really planning on sharing, but out of the sheer goodness of my heart, you have juice and cookies."

He laughs and slings his arm around her shoulders. She tenses up, as do I. What? Why? There's a little twinge in my stomach and I frown, rubbing my arms. They're covered in goosebumps.

"Are you cold?" Santiago asks me.

"No, I'm going for the plucked chicken look." He just stares at me, totally confused. I reach for my pack. "I'm going to grab my sweater."

"Nah. It's fine. You can have mine."

He throws his sweatshirt at me. I don't catch it gracefully. I catch it *un*gracefully, and pull it over my head, only to discover that it's huge on me. Genevieve furrows her brow at me, so I smooth down my hair.

"Wow." He laughs. "I didn't realize you were that small."

"Yup, because five foot seven is tiny. I'm practically a gnome," I grumble. "She's way smaller than me." I nod towards Genevieve, who looks a little uncomfortable.

She shrugs. "Buying kids shoes is way cheaper," she says under her breath.

"C'mon, your mouldy sandwich made you grumpy?" Santiago teases in my direction. "I can't see why. Also, you can't go picking on people who are smaller than you, Rosemary."

"Really. Would *you* care to have another sandwich? And you can't tell me that, because Ezra is wayyy shorter than your tall ass, and you've had no problem picking on him all these years."

Genevieve smirks. "Touché."

"Um, no I don't want more sandwiches, and fine. Fine, fine, *fine*."

"Exactly," I say triumphantly.

There's a pause.

"I, um, I'll be right back, okay?" I say.

"Where are you going?" he asks, suddenly concerned.

"You know..." I gesture vaguely into the trees. Genevieve slips out from under his arm.

"Oh. Right. Yeah."

I run into the trees until I can't see him anymore. My bladder feels like it's going to burst.

CHAPTER 11

chapter 11

July 16th, 7:07pm
Location: The Woods

Genevieve

Rosemary runs into the trees. One of the pluses of being able to turn invisible is that I can go to the bathroom whenever I want. So that's good. Santiago's thinking about asking me something, but I don't listen too hard. I'm going to ask my own question.

I wait until I can't hear Rosemary anymore. We both start talking at the same time and immediately stop, telling the other person to go first. But after a brief argument over who should actually talk, I give in and ask:

"So what's the famous Ezra Colton like?" Yeah, I already know this from both of their minds, but I want to hear it out loud.

Santiago regards me for a thoughtful moment. "I don't know if I'm the best person to ask about that." He looks at the ground between his knees, his hands clasped. "He and I, well, we have a problematic relationship."

I stare at him, trying very hard to tune out his thoughts. To let him tell me the whole story, without me reading into it.

He continues, "Actually, he doesn't cause any problems. That's me. I, um, well, I am the problem."

That's the vibe I've been getting from him. Problem child 101. (He's just super lost and lonely, I think.) Nice confirmation, though.

"Okay, but what's he like?" I shove his shoulder, and he almost falls over. At least it makes him look up from the ground. "Tiago, I know you like to talk about yourself, but you're with me right now and he's not. Just tell me about him. We're rescuing someone I've never even talked to."

He rolls his eyes, but is compliant enough. "Ezra's... something. Almost inhuman. But he *is* a human! He's so curious. It normally drives me insane, to the point where I wanted to push him off a roof... but everyone else loves him." Santiago leans in closer and whispers, "But he isn't really friends with anyone except for Rosemary. Not *close* friends at least."

I lean back, nodding. "So, he *does* have a gift? At the fast food place, I kinda saw that video, but not really."

"He does. Apparently he can light on fire. But we didn't think he could. It's like his gift just appeared late and he happened to be in a really unfortunate place. Aka, Ester's home. There was this monster, on the day he got kidnapped, that he incinerated. I think that's when his gift started to come back. It makes more sense now. That day was. Messed up. But anyways, somehow, Ezra made a bunch of power hungry kids forget that he didn't have powers. He's so unbelievably kind to everyone. Even me. Which does *not* make sense. But that's him. He's such a weirdo, obsessed with dumb poetry that he never puts in a notebook..."

I don't catch the rest of what he says, because of the poetry. The poetry on his walls. That he never put in a notebook. Because it needed a bigger canvas than those tiny pages.

"Huh," I interrupt, catching myself by surprise. "So why'd you give him your jacket? Or your sweater?"

He turns his head slowly towards me, his face slightly pinched. Shoot floot flibbity bloot. He didn't tell me about the jacket.

I stare at him, a super fake little grin pursing my lips. Maybe... I'll just stop talking now.

Rosemary

I listen to Santiago talk about Ezra like he was *his* best friend for a few minutes from the trees. Until I can't stand it anymore. But just as I'm about to burst in, their voices turn hushed, then go silent altogether. Genevieve abruptly gets to her feet, stretches, gives Santiago a fast salute, then marches across the clearing to her bag, where she starts rummaging around. Santiago watches her for a moment, then looks up, but as I approach, I see a slight crease in between his eyes.

"What are you looking at?"

He isn't startled that I'm back. "The stars," he answers simply.

I sit beside him. "Aren't you cold? I can go get my own sweater."

He looks at me, smirking, all traces of his concern gone. Maybe I imagined it.

"Do you have a problem with sweater–lending, Rosie?"

"Please don't call me that," I whisper.

"Why?"

"My parents used to."

"Oh."

They used to, before they abandoned me. I sniff, because I'm cold. Not because I'm crying. Santiago doesn't get that. He puts his arm around me. I freeze. My heart does a fluttering dance. What's that supposed to mean? I'd like it to stop. I swallow, hard.

"Are you okay?"

"Yeah. I'm just cold," I say evenly.

"Oh. Well." He pulls me closer to him. "For warmth."

My heart pounds so loudly, I'm scared he'll hear it.

What is happening to me? Am I getting sick? His arm is so warm around my shoulders. I sniff again.

"Are you sure you're not crying?" he inquires, glancing at me suspiciously.

I wipe my nose. "Yeah," I say. "I'm sure."

I can't see anything anymore, except for the patch of stars above my head. Honestly, I don't think I've ever seen anything so sad, yet somehow, so beautiful. The stars are just tiny specks of light, millions, if not billions of miles away. They're all alone up there, sparkling coldly in hopes that someone will look at them for a fraction of a second. In the city, there are no stars, or even trees. There's really no nature at all.

"It's amazing, isn't it?" Santiago whispers.

I look at him, my brow playfully furrowed.

"Are you sure you can't read my mind?" Well, part of it …

"No I can't, but your expression gave you away."

He pulls the hood on the sweater down over my eyes.

"Hey!" I brush it off, laughing.

He smiles and he looks genuinely happy. It's not his usual smirk or the grin that doesn't reach his eyes. God, he's very. Attractive. I scrunch my face up. What on earth am I thinking? The only reason I'm with him is to find Ezra. My best and *only* friend. Santiago Grey is *not* my friend. Or anything else to me. He's just *Santiago*.

"I'm going to try to get some sleep, okay?" I say, pulling away from him and lying down by my bag.

"Good idea."

I hear him getting comfortable (or as comfortable as you can get on a forest floor of sticks, old leaves, and pine cones). Soon, his breathing becomes soft and even. My sweater is in my pack beside me. I grab it, then slip out of Santiago's hoodie. Careful not to make any noise that will wake him, I shove his sweatshirt back into his large, ugly backpack. (Even in the dark, its hideousness has been burnt into my retinas.)

Then, I lie on my back, gazing up.

July 16th, 9:45 pm, The Lab

Ezra

"Ezra, you're a failure. Ezra, you're pathetic. You can't do anything." The recording plays over and over as I writhe, trying to escape the pain that's made its home inside me. I can't breathe—

The pain starts to wear off. I'm trembling. The voice stops. Lights come on quickly, making my head throb. I'm in a small room with an observation window. The floor is cold. I try to relax. Not possible. The Hazmat team comes in. It's exactly like I remember. Resisting them isn't worth my energy. Nothing is worth the energy. Or the pain.

The next time I'm conscious, I'm lying on the floor in my room, staring up at the ceiling. My vision is blurry. My glasses. Even sitting up feels impossible right now, but I pat the floor next to me. I accidentally knock my glasses across the room. At least they're here. I'm so alone. And I always have been. I always will be, in this endless cycle of futility—

Rosemary. No. I'm *not* alone. Well. I am. But there are people who care about me. Maybe she'll find me. Probably not, though. I'll just be stuck in a loop of agony and exhaustion until I die. (Which might not take too long now that I think about it. By then, death will be a cool relief.) Hope feels so far away. If hope is even a thing anymore.

Darling, whispers the dark voice at the back of my mind, *wishes cannot save you now.*

I wish I had a marker. I'm still wearing my T-shirt. Where did the sweater go? If I've lost it and I see Tiago again (which probably won't happen), he'll kill me. My wrists ache as I struggle to my hands and knees. The shackle cuts hurt. The bed is low enough for me to see that the sweater is on it. My arms can't take the strain anymore. I collapse onto the cold floor, face first. I smile. It's okay.

It'll be okay.

July 17th, 6:55am, ???

Tiago

Ezra's burning. He's on fire. My heart is in my throat. How can he look so peaceful? My instinct says to find water, to put the fire out, but that seems wrong. I don't think I've ever seen him so... calm. Whenever I've been around him, he's either been smiling, miserable, or in intense pain. I cautiously walk towards him. The air gets hotter. He's sprawled out on the floor, eyes closed.

"Ezra?" I whisper, leaning down a little. The fire does nothing to me.

His eyes flutter open. They grow wide with fear.

"No," he says, panicked. "Y–you have to leave."

His face is pale, hollow.

"What do you mean?" I ask, kneeling down beside him, hands fluttering uselessly in the air.

"Tiago," he implores. "Please."

Why is he trembling? My fingers twitch, wishing they could help.

"Tiago, you have to leave." He struggles to sit up, then grabs my arms. Pity maims my insides as his grip tightens. He's somewhere beyond horror now, gaping at me like a dying fish. I have the urge to pull him close to me. I don't. I reach out, hands stopping inches from his chest.

"Oh, Ezra. What have they done to you?" I whisper.

"Don't you understand?" he yells, right in my face, fingers crushing my biceps. I jerk back a little, but have nowhere to go.

"You need to leave!" he practically screams.

My hand acts on its own accord. It brushes his dull hair off his forehead.

"Ezra," I whisper again.

He freezes, like an animal in headlights. The door behind me bursts open. A jet of frigid water hits my back.

July 17th, 6:59am, Tiago's Dream

Genevieve

That boy is burning. He's on fire. My heart is in my throat. How can he look so peaceful? My instinct says to find water, to put the fire out, but that seems wrong. I don't think I've ever seen anyone so... calm. I cautiously walk towards him. The air gets hotter. He's sprawled out on the floor, eyes closed.

"Ezra?" I whisper, leaning down a little. The fire does nothing to me.

It's not my voice I'm speaking with. I'm not in my own head.

His eyes flutter open. They grow wide with fear.

"No," he says, panicked. "You–you have to leave."

Our hands twitch. We want to help but we don't know how. Ezra's face is pale, hollow. It looks unhealthy. I wonder whose dream I'm in. This happens sometimes when I sleep around other people.

"What do you mean?" I/the dreamer ask, kneeling down beside him, hands fluttering uselessly in the air.

"Tiago," he implores. "Please."

So I'm in Santiago's dream. Great. Why is Ezra trembling? Tiago's fingers twitch, wishing they could help.

"Tiago, you have to leave." Ezra struggles to sit up in a frenzied kind of pain. He grabs our arms as pity maims our insides as his grip tightens. He's somewhere beyond horror now, gaping at us like a dying fish. We have the urge to pull him close to us. We don't. We reach out, hands stopping inches from his chest. (I'm not in control here.)

"Oh, Ezra. What have they done to you?" We whisper.

"Don't you understand?" Ezra yells, right in our face, fingers crushing our biceps. We jerk back a little, but have nowhere to go.

"You need to leave!" he practically screams.

Our hand brushes the dull hair off his forehead. Woah. (I am *not* in control here.)

"Ezra," we whisper again.

He freezes, like an animal in headlights. The door behind us bursts open. A jet of frigid water hits our back.

I bolt upright, my breathing ragged. I *hate* sleeping around other people. Rubbing my arms, I glance around to see the forest waking around me in sleepy little rustles and sounds of leaves. I'm myself again. Thank *fuck*.

July 17th, 7:12am, The Lab

Ezra

When I wake up, my glasses are on my face. There's a cup of broth beside me. I gulp it down hungrily. I don't care that it tastes like over–salted chicken. It's gone too soon, like the dream I had. I can't remember what it was, but my heart is racing and my forehead is burning like I have a fever.

Now that the broth's gone, I notice that a marker was left with the cup. (Well that's creepy... wasn't I just wishing for a marker?) With a somewhat steady hand, I take it. Writing saved me last time I was here. I take off the cap and start writing on the floor. (Writing on the wall would be more poetic, but since I can't get up, the floor will have to do.)

For nOthing i sLowly stoLe yOu a Wayit was as siMple as can bEAlthough it's over iLl remember your Light

I pause, feeling the flames rise under my skin.

Time will not Heal you anymorEdarling Wishes cAnnot save You now-Darling they will nOt remember you When you've falleNbut will—

I know I'm burning. I feel alive again. More alive than ever. Just as alive as when I wrote this poem in the first place. The last time I was here was when I was eight. That was the last time I ignited before the pain broke me. I lost my gift. I lost *so much*, convincing myself that I was making up the torture for attention, but Ester brought me here every week. I remember it all now… I won't break this time. I can't. There's too much for me to lose.

July 17th, 7:17am, The Woods

Tiago

I scramble upright, breathing ragged as I rake my hands through my hair. Ezra's not here. I'm back in the woods. I was always in the woods? Yeah. Sweat soaks my back. What the *fuck*? It's still dark, but the sky is lighter than when I fell asleep. A hundred questions bubble up as my thoughts race. The image of his lifeless eyes is burned in my mind even worse than the video of him on fire that we saw on Madame Ester's laptop. What was dream–me doing? How much longer will Ezra live? Was that real or did I make it all up? And how the *hell* did Genevieve know about the *sweater*? (I guess this is how Ezra ends up asking thousands of questions at a time.)

Rubbing my neck, I look around. Rosemary's sleeping shape is a few feet away. Genevieve is further from me, but she's also awake, breathing so evenly that it can't be normal. When she looks at me, confusion and anxiety flash across her face. Our eyes lock. For a second, I swear she knows about my dream. But that's ridiculous. My sweater is sticking out of my bag. I grab it, comforted by the familiarity. Rosemary rolls over to face me.

"Why are you up?" she grumbles sleepily.

The thought of talking about the dream makes me uncomfortable for some reason. Genevieve is slurping the dregs from an old juice box fully engrossed with something in her bag.

"I wanted to… see the sunrise?" I say, unconvincingly.

"Is that a question?"

"It is question*able*, since there are so many damn trees." I try to save my pathetic excuse.

"Yeah, that's true."

"Go back to sleep, Rosemary."

I need some more time to process. And maybe talk to Genevieve. I swear she knows. She obviously knows *something*. Which is unnerving. Extremely unnerving. (Or... maybe it's not.)

"I'm awake now." Rosemary rubs her eyes, sitting up. "And I wasn't sleeping well, anyways."

I hold back a sigh. I had hoped to have a bit more time alone. But Rosemary's stomach growls. I pull out the sandwich mush. Genevieve pretends to gag. I laugh under my breath, holding up the bag.

"I think I can fix it," I suggest, shrugging.

"You'd better." Rosemary wrinkles her nose. "There's no way I'm eating that."

"And this," Genevieve mutters, "is why you bring cookies."

"You're so right," Rosemary agrees, staring at the bag in mild fear.

I close my eyes, feeling the particles that make up the bread and the mold, trying to convince the mold to separate from the bread, and for the components of the sandwiches to restore themselves. My hands tingle a little as the mold feeling pieces disperse through the plastic bag.

"Oh thank God," Rosemary sighs, relieved. "You resurrected them."

When I open my eyes, I see that she's right. Our mush has become whole, thriving sandwiches. I mentally start making a sarcastic monologue. *Do you need a guy who can resurrect five day old sandwiches!? Do you need a guy who can make mold disappear? Well, I'm the man for the job!* I stop myself, passing her one. She looks happy that it's peanut butter. (How boring, and also unfortunate, since that's my favourite too.)

"Do you want one?" I offer the bag to Genevieve.

She shakes her head. "No, thanks. But could you resurrect this too?" She smiles and pulls out a plastic clamshell of wilted salad.

"Yes I can, but I don't like the idea of being the resident food resurrection expert."

They both laugh. The sky is grey, so the sun must actually be rising now. After I fix the salad, we eat in silence, listening to the sounds of the forest. A tiny little bird lands on the ground close to us. Rosemary smiles, breaking off a chunk of the bread. She throws it to the bird. It hops closer curiously and pecks at the crumb. All three of us watch the sparrow flit around for a little until it takes to the sky again, sweet melodies filling the morning air.

"Rosemary, you're just so confusing." Genevieve shakes her head. "First you punch people, scream at Tiago, then you feed some innocent bird."

Rosemary laughs contentedly. I grab my water bottle. It's almost empty. That might prove to be a problem.

"Guys." My voice shatters the calm mood. "Do you have any water?"

"Uh, no."

"Not a drop."

"I think we should start walking," I say. "Maybe I can use my gift to find a stream."

Rosemary throws her bag over her shoulder and stands up. Genevieve and I do the same. I close my eyes again, imagining water molecules. Or just water in general. Maybe a lake or a stream or *something*? (I know nothing about atoms or particles or molecules...) (I'm just making all of this up.)

Suddenly, I see Rosemary, Genevieve, and myself from above, seeking the water. I'm apparently out of my body...? My vision speeds forwards, disorienting me for a second, as I my mind flies along, exactly on our path, stopping over a wide creek. *Yes.* We might be able to get there today. I found water. Now to get back... to my body. I have to strain to get my eyes open, feeling the strong urge to pry at them with my fingers. But when they unstick, I'm back where I was standing. On the ground. Rosemary and Genevieve are staring at me, frowning slightly. I glance in the direction of the water. It's singing to me. Almost. It's kind of calling to me, I guess. I'm really dizzy. When I turn back to them, Rosemary looks expectant. Genevieve looks bored. Maybe even amused. The bird that Rosemary fed looks hungry. (It's back, hopping around, looking for more bread.)

"There's a stream a ways ahead on our path," I say, pressing a hand to my eyes. (I honestly didn't know I could... throw my mind towards specific molecules? That. Was. Strange.)

"Oh, good. We won't die of thirst before we find..." Rosemary trails off, gaze focused on something in the distance.

Genevieve raises a discrete eyebrow, as she shuffles her feet in the dirt.

I understand why Rosemary didn't finish the sentence about Ezra and his possible... death, but why didn't she say his *name*? I give her an inquisitive look. She ignores it. And then we walk. Trudge through the forest, our feet softly crunching against the pine needles and leaves.

After I feel more... stable in my body, a question comes to mind.

"Hey Rosemary, why do you hate nicknames? Or... being called Rosie?"

"You hate nicknames?" Genevieve asks her.

Rosemary swallows, her face troubled. "Yeah, I do but I don't really know why. Partially because my parents loved nicknames and also, why would you name somebody something, then call them something else? It just doesn't make sense to me."

"But what if that person really hates the name given to them?" I ask, scratching the back of my neck. It's sticky with sweat. And then I cringe, not meaning to make the conversation about me. She's quick to catch on. They both are, because Genevieve is doing that tiny little laugh that she thinks people won't notice.

"Would you prefer that I call you Tiago?" Rosemary says, frowning.

"Um, yeah," I cough awkwardly. "Maybe."

I'm clearly not as subtle as I thought. She makes the same disgusted face as when we shook hands.

"What, are you preparing to shake hands again?" Genevieve asks.

I stare hard at Genevieve for a moment, and when she doesn't acknowledge me, I look at Rosemary.

"What's so gross about that? What's so bad about taking away the 'San'?" I ask her playfully.

Rosemary grimaces. "It sounds wrong in my mouth."

"It's quite incredible what a 'San' can do to a person," I say sagely. Rosemary shoves me. She's actually really strong (for a gnome).

"What did the 'San' ever do to you?" Rosemary asks.

"Well, *it* didn't do anything to me," I sigh.

She grows somber. Parents. I have a feeling she's thinking about the people who named us and gave us up. She nods. "I get it."

I'm glad she doesn't push it any further. Green envelops us again as we break through the foliage. A few small rodents dart from under bushes and up trees. Some of them are squirrels, which I've seen before. The others are smaller, with lighter colouring and a thick stripe along their backs. Rosemary says they're chipmunks. She read about rodents in the library several years ago. Genevieve asks if she's read anything since. Rosemary scoffs. I tell them about my astrology book and Genevieve says she had a telescope at home.

I can't stop myself from blurting out, "No way!" And then, "Aw *man*, I'm so jealous."

Rosemary laughs, shocked, and Genevieve grins. "When we find Ezra, we can go back to my place. Sort shit out. And use the telescope."

I whoop, excited and also because the way my voice bounces off the trees is satisfying.

Today isn't as warm as yesterday, but it's still sunny. The shade is pleasantly cool. But all joking (and the prospect of making it out of here, alive and well enough to look through a telescope)aside, my dream hangs heavily over my head. I want to tell Rosemary about it, but I can't get over how she wouldn't say his name. I decide to bring him up, to see how she reacts. She's in a good enough mood right now, talking to Genevieve about how bad they are at origami.

"Why did you help Ezra when he was young? What made you hang out with him?" I butt in. Genevieve scowls at me as Rosemary's face falls.

What? I mouth at Genevieve. She just keeps glaring. Rosemary doesn't answer for a long time, so I'm stuck beneath Genevieve's scrutiny and disappointment.

"I... I guess ..." Rosemary struggles for a moment. "He was so helpless, and I wanted to be the one to... give him hope."

"Oh?" That's not quite what I expected. Genevieve clenches her jaw. I guess i ruined a good moment between them. (Go me, all I ever do is ruin things.)

"I was hoping..." She goes quiet. "Never mind."

"You were hoping what?" And I can't *shut up.* "You really can't start to say something then stop like that. Also, you owe me." I'm just saying whatever bullshit words appear in my mouth at this point because I'm used to it.

"What? No, I don't."

"I told you about the roof thing." Oh man. It was Genevieve who asked for that story. Fuck me.

She glowers at me. I put my hands up defensively. Genevieve swallows, putting her face in her hands, watching through her fingers. We've regressed back to animosity.

"It's not like I have anyone to tell your secrets to," I say brazenly. Apparently fighting with Rosemary is more comfortable than being happy with her. But I really want to know what she was going to say.

For a second, I think she isn't going to say anything as she walks on in silence. "Fine," she mutters. "I was hoping the caregivers would treat me special because they all liked him. They said he was special because he didn't have a gift. And *I* wanted to protect him from everyone who didn't understand that and everyone who picked on him." She pauses, looking up at the branches overhead. We stop walking. She keeps talking. "Then he grew up. People forgot how they hated him for being *'special.'*" She uses air quotes when she says it. "He got good looking and friendly. No one cared that he didn't have a gift. And I didn't get acknowledged by anyone, but him, and since everyone suddenly loved Ezra, he changed to be the happy–go–lucky idiot he is today."

I stare at her, dumbfounded. She gazes at me without seeing, then covers her mouth like she's trying to stuff her words back in.

"*See*?" Rosemary asks bitterly, looking between Genevieve and I, almost desperately. "That's why I didn't want to say it," she whispers. "I knew I'd say something wrong. I just—"

"Oh," is all I can think to say, accidentally cutting her off. It just comes out of my mouth. I didn't mean to say anything.

She's upset, watching something just over my shoulder with tired, watery eyes. Pity. I feel so *bad* for her. I wrap my arms around her. She goes stiff, inhaling sharply. It takes a long moment for her to relax and hug me back.

"Santiago, can we just not talk about him?"

I don't say anything. But I do stop breathing.

She steps away, looking up at me with tears in danger of flooding out of her eyes. I raise my eyebrow.

"We're going to save him from—" My heart convulses painfully. (What the *hell*?) "From possible death and we're not allowed to talk about him?" I have to fight to keep my voice even.

"Please?" The tears slip down her freckled face.

"Why, Rosemary?" I ask, sort of confused.

She swipes the tears away viciously, but says nothing.

CHAPTER 12

chapter 12

July 17th, 11:10am
Location: The Woods

Rosemary

Santiago obviously cares about Ezra. Maybe more than me. And I hate that. It's not true. It's not true. It can't be true. My mind is *lying* to me. There's this dark sinking feeling in my stomach. I don't know how to get it to stop. Ezra is my everything. I love him. He's my best friend in the world. But what if I was using him? What if I was bad for him? Ezra is so pure and innocent. (Or is he?) What if he thought I was like that too? What if I was manipulating him? That's not the girl I want to be. If I did that, I'd be just like Emeline, using whoever was around her for her benefit. But this would be worse. With Emeline, she uses you, then moves on. Ezra and I have been friends for ten or eleven years. And what if Ezra is really dead? (He *can't* be. Santiago is just freaking out for no reason.)

But... if he is in trouble... I can't help him. I can't heal him like I always do. What if I'm not the person I thought I was? The things that just came out of my mouth were awful. So awful. Maybe not awful, if they were in a funny joking way. But they *weren't*. I *meant* it. I'm the worst friend ever. And if he is dead, then I'll never get to tell him the truth about me. But maybe it isn't true. He *is* my best friend. My reasons for becoming his friend shouldn't matter. But what if they're the reasons I stayed his friend? No. No, that can't be it.

Tears are pooling in my eyes, gathering like my thoughts. How do I know what's true? *Oh, Ezra.* I wish he was here. I wish he was okay. I wish he would live and live and live long enough for me to figure all this out. And we could figure it out together. I could apologize. I could laugh with him. So we could just be Rosemary and Ezra again. Not Rosemary-in-the-woods-having-a-crisis and Ezra-suffering-in-some-mysterious-lab.

Tiago's staring at me, bewildered. He watched all those emotions written on my face, waiting for an answer to his question. I close my eyes, and the tears jump down my cheeks, finally free to fall.

"It makes me too upset. What if he really *is* dead?" I whisper. The ground crunches as I start walking again. Tiago doesn't follow me, but Genevieve does. She grabs my arm and pulls me out of his sight. Then she hugs me. I bury my face in her shoulder, starting to sob.

"It'll be alright. Shhh, shhh, shh."

This is weird. The last woman I hugged was my mother. Suddenly, for no real reason, I feel like Genevieve understands me.

"This is just so, so difficult." I manage to choke out.

"Yeah, well, you guys didn't really think this through," she says softly. "It's gonna be okay."

"I–I just don't know how to deal with this."

Genevieve

I want to say, 'Yeah, Rosemary, neither do I. I've no clue how to deal with trekking through the great wilderness, no idea how to deal with this crazy confusing drama you've got going on, no idea how to deal with the fact that you're crying into my shoulder. It's all so hard. And that's just a stupid part of being human.

Maybe in a normal situation, I'd have been the mediator. But this is not a normal situation at all. I know about Santiago's dreams and Ezra spirals. I know about your feelings and how you're trying to figure things out. I think you're lying to yourself. I don't know what this all means yet, but you're starting to think of Ezra as dead. A dead pet project. I think you know this deep down, but aren't willing to face those demons yet. Or maybe I'm misreading it. I think normal people would be appalled by this. Or maybe confused. I'm not. Appalled or confused. It just gives me this crazy strong urge to protect you.

Ezra and Tiago didn't know their parents, but we did. You still think about yours, like I think about mine. I know your parents said you were special. Mine did the same. Until we were too special. Too different. Some-times, kids lash out. Your way of lashing out was sort of manipulative. To take in some little underdog and train him. Or maybe you just wanted a friend. But why choose him? (No offence to you, Ezra, just trying to make a point. I'm sure you've been a great friend.) I don't think you even knew you were doing it, Rosemary, until now. To be completely honest, Rosemary, I wish I could say I'm sorry for all the people who hurt you. I'm sorry the caregivers didn't pay attention to you until you were a side–kick. Until you were someone to rely on.

You tried to be two things at once. The help you thought that poor kid needed, and a friend. I know you're lonely, love, and I'm sorry. So, so sorry.'

But "I understand. I really do" is all I say to her.

Tiago

She finished a sentence about Ezra being dead. Not that it should mean anything, but discomfort stirs in my stomach anyways. I can hear her crying, and Genevieve muttering things too low for me to distinguish. I busy myself with ripping a thread off my sweater cuff. It's filthy. Then I tie the string in as many knots as I can. Eventually, after a long, silent, awkward period of time, they walk back onto our path, towards me. The shoulder of Genevieve's blue T–shirt is wet and Rosemary's eyes are puffy. She wipes her nose with the back of her dirty sleeve.

"Don't worry," I say as Genevieve looks at me like *dude, just stop.* I continue anyways. "He always survives." I shove Rosemary lightheartedly as we continue onward. Those words have become my mantra when we aren't joking or talking. *Don't worry. He always survives. It's okay. He always survives*, and so on and so forth.

"But Tiago, I was always with him to help with the survival part," she says gravely.

She's right. He's alone. Ezra hates being alone. But he isn't powerless anymore.

"He's not completely helpless," I remind her.

She nods, dejected and small.

Rosemary

I stop talking altogether. I guess it's unfair of me to ask him to stop talking about Ezra, but I don't want to deal with those feelings again. Not yet, at least. Not now, please not now. I can feel him walking close behind me. Genevieve stays beside me. All of a sudden I get super self–conscious, because somehow, I managed to get gross again and I'm *not* asking Tiago to make me clean. Once was enough. And it would be awkward. My hair is wild, I smell horrible, and I'm a mess. He doesn't seem to notice. Not that

I should care what he notices. A high, whirring buzz invades my ear. I slap my neck. Nothing happens. Without fail, an itchy welt appears on the side of my neck.

"My Dad and I used to hike a lot," Genevieve says, pulling her backpack around to the front of her body and digging in the front pocket. "This cream should help with the mosquito bites."

She hands the small tube to me.

"Thanks."

I'm so thirsty. I'm tired and miserable and I can't *deal* with these feelings right now, so I suppress them. As we go further, more bugs start to swarm me. Santiago walks in silence, either ignoring the pests or using his gift to keep them away. Honestly, I'm bitter about his gift. He puts his mind to nearly anything and it happens. I don't know what he can't do.

"I feel like mind–reading would be nice," I say, trying to distract myself from the annoying bug noises and the internal turmoil. "It would be a useful gift, I think."

"Which is *not* something I can do," Santiago says, giving me a point-ed look, then glances at Genevieve, who's suddenly coughing. "Are you okay?"

She nods, almost frantically. "All good. Swallowed a bug."

"Ew," I reply.

"Yeah it tastes like blood," she grimaces.

Whatever I was about to say next is erased from my mind as we come out of the dense trees into a wide, grassy meadow. Sunlight warms my face. I smile. There are small flowers sprinkled throughout the grass. I look over to see Santiago, but he's running. (Why can't I ever tell when he's suddenly not where I expect him to be?)

"Where are you going?" I yell.

He looks over his shoulder, a huge smile spreading across his face. It's almost impossible to watch him in the bright light. His hair is shining, his eyes are so alive, and when he smiles, I think the sun gets embarrassed. Genevieve looks embarrassed, that's for sure.

"C'mon!" he hollers back.

I grin in spite of myself and start to run after him. Full on light, no trees obstructing it. Joy. He throws his bag down about halfway across the meadow. Catching up, I realize it's a stream, wide and clear. I drop to my knees on the bank, plunging my hands into the icy water and drinking. My throat seizes up at the temperature, but I don't care. It feels so good. I'm about to get up when my head gets dunked in the water. Shocked and gasping, I turn around, my hair dripping in my face. Santiago's whistling in the least subtle way as he skips along the rocky bank behind me. I raise my eyebrows. A suppressed snort of laughter escapes his lips. Genevieve is just now catching up to us, strolling at a leisurely pace, breathing deeply.

"You've just started something," I say gravely to Tiago, "that you're going to regret."

Standing up quickly, I shove him towards the water. He lands upright with a splash, his legs submerged up to his calves. I snicker. He scoops some water in his hands and throws it at me, giggling almost maniacally. I shriek. Some of the water hits Genevieve as well. She inhales sharply. I make eye contact with her and it's clear we're on the same team. His hand on my wrist takes me by surprise. He yanks me into the stream. I splash him, running up against the current. I gasp as the cold soaks through my jeans. Santiago stands downstream, plotting his next move, swaying back and forth, fingers wiggling in the air. Genevieve is invisible. I stifle a smile.

"Are you running away?" he asks innocently, as a stream of water gushes over his head.

I hear Genevieve snickering as Tiago whips around. She splashes him from the other side. "Okay, that's just not fair!" he yelps, shielding his head.

I run towards them, kicking as much water as I possibly can. Santiago closes his eyes for a second and suddenly there are very large waves in the stream.

"*Not fair* says the guy who can control water?" Genevieve reappears, dripping wet and scowling. "That's BS, man. I call bull*shit.*"

Santiago and I laugh. Her sarcastic facade cracks, showing a genuine grin.

I'm about to respond when suddenly he's right beside me. He throws me over his shoulder and drops me fully in the water before I can even comprehend what's happening. Absolutely drenched, I emerge from the stream, staring incredulously at him as he laughs. I push as much water as I can at him. He jumps, making an offended scoff. Genevieve cackles, soaking him from behind again. I shake my hair, throwing droplets everywhere.

"I know you were trying to help there, Rosemary," Genevieve says, "but I feel like that got us both wetter."

"Yeahhh, sorry I'm not the best team player," I reply sheepishly.

"There were two of you, and I still think I won," Tiago announces. "Fair and square."

Genevieve purses her lips, crossing her arms. "It's men like you who perpetrate the patriarchy and the continual oppression of women," she sighs, shaking her head as she walks towards the bank.

"Fine!" he retorts, throwing his hands in the air. "Don't really know what a patriarchy is, but it sounds bad, so fine. You win."

"Much better. Thank you." Genevieve grins as she ties her hair back into a thick ponytail. "Also. Y'know there's water in the air, right? You could've probably just... pulled it into our bottles."

Santiago's eyes bug out. "Are you *kidding* me right now? Why didn't you say something earlier? You're smart. You're so, so smart! I'm *stupid*," he laughs, smacking his forehead with his palm.

Genevieve just smiles. "Wanted to see how this would turn out," she says with a shrug.

Tiago huffs and offers me his hand. This time, I take it. Standing up makes me realize I'm actually really cold. He drops my hand, the ghost of a smile on his face. We wade out of the stream together.

July 17th, 8:23pm, The Lab

Ezra

This time, it's stabbing.
　Constantly.
　When I light
　on fire,
　they punish me.
　It gets worse each time.
　I don't remember.
　(stab)
　Her name.
　(stab.)
　Her face.
　(stab.)
　Her voice.
　(stab).

She is just.
(stab)
Another.
(stab.)
Person I
(stab.)
can't
(stab.)
remember.   (stab.)
How can
(stab.)
they take
(stab.)
my memories   (stab.)
away like this?(stab).
I don't
remember
(stab).
Happiness.
(stab.)
All I know   (stab.)
is pain
(stab.)
is flames   (stab.)
is cold
(stab.)
Is
Tiago   (stab).
(stab). And that

(stab). I am

(stab).

A Failure.

July 17th, 8:45pm, The Woods

Tiago

Rosemary looks like a drowned cat. Her hair is tangled and her clothes are sopping.

Genevieve is at her bag, pulling out clothes. She disappears, along with the clothes in her hand. That is one handy skill for changing. Or, literally anything. I can't be invisible. If I tried, which I have, I just start to violently shake and feel really sick.

"Do you want me to go somewhere?" I ask Rosemary, gesturing vaguely to the field. "So you can change?"

She pushes her hair out of her face, still smiling. I feel weird about offering to use my gift to dry her off. It seems oddly intimate for some reason. I dry *myself* off thinking of the water rising off my body and clothes. I should change but I only brought one extra shirt. I'm not sure how I managed to have four sweaters. (And I don't want to try making a shirt out of a sweater. I'm emotionally attached to them all.)

"Oh!" she exclaims. "I have other clothes!"

Her teeth are chattering. That reminds me so much of *Ezra*. Always cold. Except when he was feverish. The joy drains out of me. How could we possibly have had so much fun, while he's out there somewhere, maybe dying or suffering or... dead?

"Yeah. I'm going to change," Rosemary decides with a happy nod.

"Okay." I walk away from the creek.

"Thanks, Tiago!" she hollers cheerfully.

I'm glad she didn't realize that I'm not in a good mood anymore. The grass shines in the twilight, the whole meadow bathed in a golden glow. Little bugs and pollen float lazily through the warm dusk. I try to bring any positive thought into my mind, but I can't. Ezra's stuck there, in pain and shrouded with mystery.

I press the heels of my hands into my eyes. When I close them, he's right in front of me. When I open them, there he is, haunting my thoughts like a ghost. It reminds me of how ashen he looked in my dream. He was warm, though. At least he was warm. That's a small victory. But his eyes. I've never seen him look so broken. He didn't ask me a single question. He didn't answer mine either. (How rude.) *It was just a dream.* Then again, I don't think I've ever dreamed so vividly. It felt so *real.*

I pick up a stone and throw it into the water. It's so clear. The rock sinks to the bottom. Ripples spread, but quickly get lost in the gentle current. Why can't I get him out of my mind?

Footsteps crunch up behind me. "Hey, Tiago?"

Genevieve

I walk up behind Santiago, invisible. That way Rosemary won't know I'm talking to him. I'm about to do something that could go very wrong. But I think he already knows. He turns around.

"Hey, Genevieve. That's you, right?"

I nod, but then remember he can't see me. "No, actually it's Florence O'Tooleo. Your new invisible best friend."

He snorts humorlessly.

"Yup," I say after a second. "It's me. Obviously."

Neither of us says anything for a moment.

"Will you tell me more about him?" I ask.

He smiles a little, staring at the crystal water. "Yeah. I guess so."

His thoughts: *Oh, thank god. Rosemary won't let me talk about him. Why is he on my mind so much?*

"He's got these really..." *Intense, beautiful, innocent.* "Green eyes."

It's kinda funny to think everyone else would just hear "He's got these really green eyes."

"Oh yeah?" My heart pounds because of what I'm about to do.

"And he wears these ridiculous T–shirts with weird quotes..." *That he somehow manages to pull off.* "He feels everything so deeply..." *In a way I wish I could understand.* "And his—"

"Clear framed glasses he wears on top of his head more than on his eyes... and he's got brown curly hair that's always a bit of a mess, but it was dull in the dream, and you're worried, because he's never looked so broken, and you've seen him in really extreme pain, so he must be hurting," I blurt out.

Santiago freezes, looking forward with wide eyes.

"Can..." He struggles for a second. "Can you... read my mind?"

I clear my throat nervously. "Uh, yeah."

He swallows.

"Please, don't tell Rosemary." I stop and glance back at her. She's busy with something in a backpack that I don't think is hers. "Just so you know, I'm not telling her about what you're thinking and vice versa. I'm not messing with you privacy like that."

Santiago runs his hands over his face, nervous, shocked, and confused. But not angry.

"So you saw the dream?" he asks after a moment, cast adrift like a dandelion seed in the wind.

"You're not angry?" My turn to be confused now.

"Nope." He finally turns towards my voice. "I guess I trust you." He massages the back of his neck, the bags under his eyes suddenly visible. "I trust you a lot, Genevieve."

"Okay." Well, that went better than expected. "Yeah, I saw the dream. Sometimes when I'm sleeping around other people, I get into their dreams. It's weird."

"Oh. Right." He looks at me again. Is he about to cry?

I put my hand on his shoulder. "Are you okay?"

He shakes his head a little, but otherwise doesn't answer. So, no. He's not okay. I don't pry. He rubs his eyes with his palms again.

"I really don't," he whispers, "think he's okay."

"Tiago, we can't know if that dream is true. But what about you? Are you okay?"

Tiago

"You can come back now!" Rosemary calls over the meadow.

Genevieve's hand slides off my shoulder. "It's gonna be alright," she whispers before her quiet footsteps recede into the field.

Well this is... surprising. I really don't know how to deal with that... so I think I'll just try to *not* think about it.

I breathe deeply, pasting a fake smile on my face. "Coming."

I'm not sure she heard me, because she doesn't look up from my bag. My bag. Why is she going through my bag? She pulls out our sandwiches, which are slowly dwindling. Then, she takes out a small box. She doesn't look nearly as disheveled as before.

"Tiago, did you know you have a fire starting kit?" she says, holding it up.

"Oh yeah! I have no idea where that came from. I think it was in the bag when they gave it to me." I pause. "Why are you going through my stuff?"

"Um..." She's uncomfortable.

"Whatever," I reassure her. "I have nothing to hide." (It's still a weird thing to do...? But we're in a weird circumstance?)

She smiles, handing the kit to me. I pop the small metal tin open. It's brand new, with a little instruction book, matches, and some fire starter (I think that's what the grey wool thing is). Thank goodness there are those instructions, though. I've never lit a fire before.

"Could you start a fire with your gift?" she asks, leaning forwards on her hands.

"I'll try?" I've tried before. I can't.

But I focus on... making the grass on the ground into fire. Even if I *could* start one, I think I'm too preoccupied to do *anything* of use.

"Nope." Her voice breaks my concentration after a while. (I don't think I was concentrating on fire...)

"Sucks to suck, I guess." I sound so fake, but she buys it, laughing.

"Too bad he—" She breaks off mid-sentence.

She was going to mention Ezra. She was going to mention him. But she *stopped.* I don't get it. Apparently Ezra's taboo now.

"I'll just have to follow these instructions," I say, waving the handy booklet in the air.

"Good idea," she says, gazing into space.

CHAPTER 13

chapter 13

July 17th, 11:17pm
Location: The Woods

Rosemary

I almost broke my own rule. Nearly said something about Ezra. My throat is closing up with bottled emotions. I tell them to go away inside my head. *No no no no. You don't get to be here, feelings. Go die in a fucking hole.* Santiago's footsteps crunch across the ground, off towards the trees with his fire starting booklet. Right now, I should be urging us forwards. I should want to find Ezra more than anything else. And I do want to find him. But, I also don't want this to be over. Tiago is such a good guy... and I might have feelings for him. A crush. Ugh. I've never really had feelings for anyone before.

A little voice inside my head reminds me of the note and the sweater and the innocent eyes thing, but that little voice somehow gets squashed by an imaginary steamroller. Because maybe that was made up. Or maybe it was a slip of the tongue. People say dumb things when they're angry, right? The sky is darkening, from gold, to grey, to deep blue. Soon, the stars will be out. Tiago loves the stars. I always notice him looking up at night in quiet awe. And he's so obsessed with that space book. Maybe I'll ask him why he thinks they're so incredible. To me, they're pretty, but they don't hold magnitude like they do for him.

I hear soft footsteps behind me. I turn around. My stomach sinks a little when it's Genevieve instead of Tiago. She's wearing a grey turtleneck and loose jeans. So that's where she was. Changing. The rocks shift as she sits beside me and looks up.

"They're pretty, right?" she says.

I nod, my heart a little lonely.

I think she's done, but she continues. "But they're kinda boring."

It's unexpected. I laugh. She smiles.

"Yeah. Like, what's the big deal about tiny dots in the sky?"

Genevieve looks deeply thoughtful. "I think people are fascinated by the untouchable."

"The untouchable?"

"Yeah. People like to fixate on things they can't have."

I haven't really seen this side of her. She looks at me. It's cooling off as the darkness sets in, but those untouchable, cold, pinpricks of light reflect in her eyes. I've never seen her eyes this close up. One is the colour of the sea in a rainstorm. A deep grey with a hint of blue. The other looks like honey. And on her face, is a map of the sky.

Her freckles are only a few shades darker than her skin. I didn't notice those either. I reach out and run my finger down her face.

"*I* can touch the stars," I whisper.

She laughs quietly, pulling away from me. "What are you talking about?"

"You have the sky on your face."

Smiling, she focuses on the ground. "And I could say the same about you."

I blush. Thank god it's sort of dark.

Suddenly, her mood changes. She clears her throat uncomfortably. "Do you, y'know... have feelings for Tiago?"

Her question catches me off guard. It's so out of pocket. My cheeks flush again. (Why am I so prone to blushing? This is a problem.) "Uh..."

"It's fine if you do, I think you should just not..." She sounds nervous. "Get too attached to him."

I'm about to object and say that I don't have feelings for him, but something stops me. Because I do have feelings for him. And while that's terrifying, it's also... I dunno. Exciting. New. It's mine, at the very least.

"Okay. Your concern is noted," I say, kind of coldly. Then I feel a little bad about it.

She bites her lip. "I just... I think he might be—"

"You think I might be what?" Tiago asks jokingly, crashing into our conversation like a dumb dog photo-bombing an otherwise decent photograph. "Am I interrupting something?"

We both whip around. My stomach sinks as my heart speeds up. From nerves, guilt, or um, other things. I don't know.

"Oh, not at all," Genevieve says casually. "I was just saying I think you might be three times my height."

I'm almost certain that wasn't what she was going to say, but damn. She is *smooth*.

"Huh. I can't tell if that's a compliment or not."

Genevieve smirks. "You're welcome."

Tiago's holding a pile of twigs and sticks. My heart is still thundering. (Actually, I feel a bit sick.) Smiling, I watch him dump the wood on the ground. He returns my smile, but it falls short of his eyes yet again. Grr.

"What's on your mind?" I interrupt the near silence of the field. He doesn't respond.

Genevieve cringes. The tall grass rustles. He starts to set the wood in a stacked shape on the rocky bank of the creek.

He keeps his focus on the brochure in his hand. "I'm not allowed to tell you because the thing on my mind has been forbidden."

My face flushes red (OH. MY. GOD.) at the sarcastic frustration in his voice. I busy myself picking at the short grass I'm sitting on. He fumbles around for a while.

"There we go." He sounds satisfied.

I look up to see fire licking the bottom of the stacked logs. I do feel kinda bad for going through Tiago's stuff, but I was hungry. I didn't find anything other than sandwiches, which I didn't want to eat. I *did* find the fire kit, though.

"Handy little kit, huh?" Genevieve says with a grin.

"Don't tell me you knew how to start a fire this whole time," Tiago whines.

His anger is better hidden now, but it's still there. I push down my embarrassment, standing up to join him by the growing fire. Genevieve shrugs mischievously, wrapping hear arms around her waist.

Santiago stares at the flames, no doubt thinking about Ezra. I sigh. He looks directly into my eyes. "We're going to find him, okay?"

I know he's trying to comfort me. I still don't know what's wrong with me. There's those ravenous feelings again, trying to claw their way up my throat. I miss Ezra. But I also don't miss him. I'm confused. I'm confus*ing*. I sit down on the stones. Tiago settles down beside me a moment later. Genevieve yawns, stretching wide.

"Man, I am *tired*," she says, rubbing her eyes.

Tiago nods in agreement, not really paying attention as she walks across the bank, making herself comfortable away from the fire. She doesn't disappear, only turns her back to us. I could try to pretend we're alone, but I know she's there. And it feels weird to ignore her.

"Genevieve?" I call.

She sits up again, raising her eyebrow at me.

"Do you wanna sit with us?" I ask.

Genevieve shakes her head, frowning and smiling at the same time. "I'm going to try and sleep. A little bit, at least, because rocks are *not* an optimal place to rest."

"Okay," I say, a little disappointed. And a bit scared. I'm gonna be sort of alone with Tiago. "Goodnight. Hope you get a bit of sleep at least."

She salutes to me with a falsely serious face. "You as well." The rocks crunch as she tries to find a decently okay spot to rest.

After she stops moving around, Santiago doesn't say anything for a long time. I start fidgeting. Clothes, hair, fingers. Oh lord. I wish Genevieve was awake and sitting with us.

"Do you hate *me* too?" I blurt. That was the only thing I could think of to break the awkward silence. (Pure brilliance on my part.) (The intellectual world is quaking in its fancy boots.)

He scrutinizes me. "Rosemary," he says, his voice even. Dead serious.

A spark of hope ignites in my heart. Could it be possible?

"Over these past... days, you guys have become some of my best friends. Even if *you're* slightly annoying and difficult at times. And I'm sure you'd say the same about me."

The hope dies a horrible death. (Like the kind of horrible death where it got hit by eighty arrows, run over by multiple trains, and dropped off a cliff into a river full of stakes. And piranhas. And sharks with spears.) I fight to keep from crying. The evil feelings with flaming pitchforks use the momentary distraction to storm out of the castle I locked them in.

"I don't know if I would've made it this far alone." He nudges my arm with his elbow. I rub my eyes to hold back the tears. Like last night, he pulls me closer. A sob wracks my shoulders. Here comes the army of demon feelings that I can't control.

"It's going to be okay, okay?" He comforts me in the wrong way again. God, I'm so selfish. I rest my head on his shoulder, staring into the fire, trying not to picture Ezra's face in the center. Something happened to Santiago. He hated Ezra, and all of a sudden *his* life depends on saving him. I really didn't think this through. I never think things through.

Being with Tiago is so different than being with Ezra for these reasons: a) I never had feelings for Ezra, b) Tiago is actually a really easy going guy; not so energetic and optimistic, and c) I can suddenly be the person who isn't always strong. Not that Ezra cares about that. It's just something I feel obligated to do around him for some reason. Part of me wants things to go back to normal, but a bigger part of me wants things to stay how they are right here, right now. And there is my answer. I'm a terrible, manipulative person. I *have* to save Ezra now. I have to say I'm sorry. I'm sure that once I see him, all of this will be fine.

July 18th, 12:02am, The Lab

Ezra

The only wounds I have are inside my head, although I feel like I've been torn apart and crudely sewn back together. Failure. Failure. Tiago? Tiago. Weak. Tiago.

The sweater. It smells like him. Artificial mint and cedar. Cheap deodorant. As long as I remember him, I'll be okay. It'll be okay. I hug the sweater to my chest. I shiver. I won't let them break me this time. I find the heat, deep down inside. *Failure*, my mind whispers. I bite the inside of my cheek. And I ignite. I know they'll be here any moment to put me out. But now I know this warmth. Whatever they do won't take it away from me. But they will take me. They'll fill my head with lies. They'll take my voice, so I can't beg or scream. They'll push me to the edge.

The only thing out there is Tiago. He keeps me from falling. I'm completely, absolutely stupid. I'm nothing to him. He's made it his personal responsibility to hate me. I'll bet he threw a party when I disappeared. He probably told everyone that it was my own fault. I'll just be a joke. Again.

How is it possible that the person I love more than anything hates me?

July 18th, 12:17am, Ester Myrtle Kellwether's Home for Unusually Gifted Youth and Children

Ester

Ezra is not getting any better. When he was younger, he would stop igniting for weeks after one treatment. I suppose he has feelings, people, and memories to keep fighting for now. He had nobody before. The lab workers have been sending me daily updates. I have decided to tell them to start my experimental process. Things aren't improving, and it is possible for this kind of pain to make him grow stronger.

The system I have been creating is a mixture of pain and fear. Ezra is afraid of many things. This intelligent machine will pick his worst fears and create pain—based experiences with them. It is rather fortunate that Rosemary, Santiago, and Genevieve have decided to save him. I will use it on them too, after Ezra completes the program. With luck, he will be able to walk past them in a hallway and not remember anything about them. He will be able to start fresh, and live a better life than one doomed with a gift. If—no, *when*—it works, I will be able to fix all the unfortunately cursed children and youth. Hopefully, once I am finished, "gifts" will no longer be a problem that plagues the world.

July 18th, 12:19am, The Woods

Genevieve

I pretty much have the best gift for eavesdropping, but I'm not even invisible right now.

I can't be angry. Yes, I can. But, I can't. Can I? I have no idea.

They're both asleep, I think, or close to it, at least. Rosemary was crying, because Santiago thinks of her as a friend. I tried to tell her! I really did. But Tiago has excellent timing. To ruin things. He even ran into her mind when we were having a moment without him. I was the one who brought him up, but only because Rosemary was fixating on him.

People are obsessed with things they can't have. I stand by that. Things they're not sure about. I've always known this, but never *really* experienced it. I'm not stupid. I know who wants who here. People are gonna get hurt. And now, I'm in the process of digging my own grave. Going deeper and deeper into something I know know very little about. Feelings, drama, sleep deprivation, people, and *Ezra* for God's sake. But honestly... it's not the worst thing ever. Santiago and Rosemary are fun to be around, when they're not fighting. Santiago's a good story teller. I find Rosemary watching me curiously a lot. I can't make my heart shut up about it.

It's almost as uncomfortable as lying on these rocks. Weirdly enough, before Rosemary told me she liked Tiago, she ran her finger down my face in the most gay coded way and I just about lost it. But I have to remember that she hasn't been friends with a girl for a long time. Ever. (Telling myself that does *not* help anything...)

It's all okay. It's so fine. I'm not rushing into anything again. I've sat in the principal's office at my old school, while my parents tried to explain how I disappeared after telling the entire school Lucy was going to run away with Mr. Reynolds. It was a long uncomfortable hour that stretched on, slowly filling with regret and the question, *'why didn't I slow down and think about this?'* Rosemary wants to tell Santiago about her feelings and they've only really known each other for two (?) days. (I have no clue how long it's been... time's all messed up in the woods.) I'm attached to them, that's for sure. Because they're funny, dishonest, innocent weirdos. So incredibly unlike all the people I've hung out with before, but also oddly similar, in the ways that matter.

I don't know how Rosemary is asleep— there is just no way to get comfortable. And it's gonna be such a long day tomorrow.

I just wish I could have told her...

She probably wouldn't have believed me anyways, but at least I tried.

July 18th, 12:20am, The Lab

Ezra

I'm getting used to being soaked, but I'm still afraid. I wish I could disappear. Fighting won't do me any good.

I go limp as they drag me out of the room. Opening my eyes slowly, I see that somebody finished the poem that I wrote on the floor. Sort of. My glasses are on the floor again. But I can see that the ending lines of the poem are written in the same black marker, but in much neater handwriting. Great. Maybe that means the sociopath I meant it for saw it. And got someone to finish writing it, of all things. How thoughtful.

I think someone's cutting my hair. Or maybe they're just... moving my hair around.

Before I can really contemplate that, somebody else sedates me. A prick of a needle, then there's no more pain. Only cool darkness.

Is this death?

July 18th, 12:23am, The Woods

Tiago

I think Rosemary's asleep. My eyes are starting to droop every few minutes. Her breathing is almost silent. The sun sank below the horizon hours ago, while I sat by the fire holding her as she cried. I'm not sure why she was crying. She wouldn't tell me, but I'm guessing it's about Ezra. Maybe. probably not.

Gently, I lie back. She nestles into my side. I'm glad I'm not alone, though I never expected to be in the middle of some forest with Rosemary Mae–Anderson and enjoying her company (for the most part). And Genevieve. I wish she would come over here. It's better when she's around.

She's quiet, but she's ridiculously smart and kind and sarcastic and goofy. I like talking to her about the Lord of the Rings. I have to read it one day. She's such a good listener. I'm a bit mad we had to run away to become friends. Mad at myself. I'm so mad at myself.

The embers glow dimly in the darkness. It's mesmerizing, the way the heat dances from coal to coal. This is the closest to peaceful I've felt in a very long time. Except for Ezra, lurking in the back of my mind. Something stirs inside me. I push it down. Maybe I should ignore him for just one night. There's no way for me to help him this second. I force the thoughts of Ezra to the very deepest part of my mind. They struggle for a moment, but eventually settle down. I sigh. Then, I let my eyes close and the gentle waves of sleep wash over me.

I don't know how much time has passed when I wake. It's still dark. Rosemary isn't here. I frown, pushing myself up to look for her. I'm a bit dizzy. Grass crunches behind me.

"Rosemary?"

No answer.

I turn around. No one's there, but the footsteps get closer. Maybe it's Genevieve?

"Hey, Genevieve?"

Still nothing.

Out of nowhere, fear suddenly courses through my veins. I take a tentative step back. The footsteps speed up. Nobody's there. *Nobody's there.* I turn around and run. The creek water sends jolting shivers down my spine as I stumble through it. The footsteps slosh across after me, following me. I keep looking over my shoulder. Adrenaline is taking over. I've reached the forest on the other side of the meadow. My pursuer is closer now, crashing into the ominous undergrowth. My heart is pounding so hard. I'm drenched. What's happening? Dodging trees, I barrel forwards, vaulting over a fallen log.

There's a door in front of me. What? Stopping, I yank the handle. The footsteps come to an abrupt halt. I whip around, my sweaty hair sticking to my face. I listen hard. Nothing. My hand grips the doorknob. The door creaks open. A sharp inhale starts my heart pounding again. Below me is a cavernous hole. There's no bottom that I can see. I'm about to slam the door shut when somebody falls past the opening. I tense in surprise, frozen for a small moment. Holding my breath, I cautiously peer down, my stomach churning. No. It can't be.

But it is.

I grit my teeth and jump. I have no choice.

The feeling is insane. My gut wants to stay at the top. My heart feels like it's going to come out of my mouth. And the air rushing past my ears sounds like a waterfall.

As we fall, his eyes open. A smile spreads across his gaunt face. It's all wrong. Wrong because his cheeks are hollow; his skin is more grey than brown; his eyes are rimmed with watery red. Sallow. Breaking at the seams. How long has it been since he smiled?

"Tiago," he whispers.

I reach out. He's too far away. He lifts one arm. Our fingers brush. He speeds up, plummeting down. How is he falling so fast?

"Ezra!" My scream is lost in the choking blackness.

July 18th, 7:25am, Tiago's Dream

Genevieve

Whoop! I jolt awake. Look who's screaming! Tiago. He's making weird high pitched noises. Is that screaming? I don't know.

I sit up. My back pops in multiple places as I rub sleep out of my eyes. The rocks have bruised me all over. It's still dark. Santiago is definitely dreaming (and whimpering) again. I close my eyes and then I'm in his head.

I wasn't expecting for our stomach to be yanked backwards. We're falling. There's a boy below us, also falling. We get closer to him, but I still have no idea who he is. His eyes open, and a smile spreads across his face. His skin is kind of grey. He looks so *sick*. Our eyes are watering from the speed of the fall; his are rimmed red. His eyes though... they're green. So green. These are the eyes I've heard so much about. This is Ezra.

The smile literally cracks his chapped lips. What's wrong with him? A surge of Santiago's violent pity surges through me. It's painful.

"Tiago." Ezra's voice is so quiet.

We reach out for him. He reaches for us. Our fingers touch. We're suddenly very warm. Ezra falls from our reach. Faster and faster until we can't see him anymore.

"Ezra!" we scream.

July 18th, 7:45am, The Woods

Rosemary

The screams jolt me awake. The sun is bright. It hurts my eyes. I squint over at Santiago. He's rolling over, his forehead glistening with sweat that shines in the light. He just yelled Ezra's name. Genevieve is curled into a ball, her hands clenched into tight fists. She *also* just yelled Ezra's name. At the exact same time as Tiago. What in the *hell*. I should wake them up. This is fucking weird if you ask me. What are the chances of them *both* yelling his name at the *exact same time?* Tiago looks like he's having a nightmare. Except for the fact that it's day now. (That would make it a daymare.) I lie there on the uncomfortable stones for another minute, soaking up the sun. Then I get up. I shake Tiago a little too roughly. His eyes fly open, panicked. He grabs my arms and I jerk back, surprised.

"What...?" he mutters, really seeing me. He closes his eyes again, his chest heaving.

"You were screaming about... yeah..." I say, avoiding Ezra. Ezra Ezra Ezra...

Tiago sits up slowly, pressing his hands into his eyes. When he takes them away, he looks at Genevieve, who's still asleep. (What is *happening* between them?)

"Oh," he mumbles. "Oh god."

"It's okay."

I'm awful at comforting people. Genevieve isn't. She'd know what to say.

"I was being chased. Then I fell—no, wait, we—I jumped down into a pit after—after Ezra."

We?

I'm about to probe him but then he glares at me before getting up and going to the stream. Why is he mad? I didn't say anything! I hear him gasp quietly as he splashes his face. Worry knots my insides. He's getting frustrated about the Ezra thing. I chew my thumbnail, forehead creased. I won't ask him about Genevieve. Then it hits me. *Oh my god. Is this why she didn't want me to get attached to him? Because they're a* thing?

She bolts upright the moment I think of that, looking at me with huge eyes. I jerk my head away. I will not talk to her or acknowledge her. She's so selfish. And such a good liar too, if that's true. *Fuck.*

"Are you hungry?" I ask Santiago weakly.

He's crouched down by his still-ugly bag, changing his shirt. I quickly look away because a blush is creeping up my neck. And then I look back at him just as fast because Genevieve is on the other side. I end up staring straight at the sky.

"No," he says curtly. "I'm fine."

He didn't eat last night either. None of us ate. Genevieve is drinking another juice box. Not that I care. I take my water bottle out to fill it in the stream. He really should eat. *It isn't my job to take care of him*, I remind myself as I dunk my bottle. He's suddenly beside me, filling his. (How is he so stealthy?) I let my hair fall in a curtain between us. I don't want him to look at me. I'm so embarrassed. But this silence is worse.

"Um, why did you jump in the pit? Was he okay?" I ask shakily. I sense his head turn. I don't know what to say next and he's clearly expecting me to say more. I stand up, screwing the lid on my cheap, plastic bottle. It's scratched and filthy. Ezra got it for me a while ago. I'm pretty sure it used to have some quote on it.

"No. I don't think... " He trails off.

Tiago's looking up at me. A shadow of something passes over his sunlit face. Momentarily, I panic inside. Has he somehow guessed that I'm having an internal war? Or about my feelings? He scrunches his eyebrows together in understanding pity. I relax a little.

"Rosemary, it's going to be okay. They're just dreams. He's going to be fine. We're getting closer. We have to be." He stands up, but doesn't move to hug me. "This whole thing will be over soon."

Frustration bubbles inside me. *I don't* want *this to be over.* Guilt follows in suit, playing a polo game with my heart. He walks over to the remnants of our fire, kicking the ashes everywhere, and says, "It's later than usual. Let's go."

I guess I don't get to eat now either. *Wonderful.* Resentfully, I grab my bag.

"Stop," he demands. "Take off your shoes."

"What? *Why*?" I wrinkle my nose at him.

"You'll get blisters if you walk with wet shoes. I'm not drying them off for you," he says, pointing at the stream.

"Dude, shut up," Genevieve interjects. "That tone is so unnecessary."

"I'm capable of taking care of myself," I snap at both of them. "We were wearing shoes yesterday when we were in the water."

"Yeah, but we weren't walking," Tiago grumbles, aggressively umping into the stream.

I take off my shoes and socks as Genevieve follows Tiago into the stream, quietly asking why he couldn't just part the water for us. I roll up my jeans as high as they go. They'll still get wet, but whatever. The two of them get out of the water.

"Are you coming?" Tiago asks impatiently as he sits to put his shoes back on.

"Can you just give me a moment?" I bite out.

Technically, I could heal the blisters. I'm such an idiot sometimes, but I don't care. Whatever makes him happy. On the opposite bank, he's struggling to put his wet feet into his socks. I jump into the freezing water, my feet numbing instantly. Like I predicted, my jeans get soaked up to my knees.

Genevieve's just standing there, watching me, concerned. I ignore her, even though I... already feel bad for assuming things. I should just ask her.

By the time I get to the other side, Tiago's already standing with his shoes back on. He looks anxious to move, his feet shuffling on top of the grass. The bitter part of me wants me to go as slow as I possibly can. I sit down again. My feet are so incredibly sore. Sliding the sock over my foot hurts so bad. And there's Genevieve, standing next to me.

"Rosemary, what size are your feet?" she asks softly.

Not making eye contact, I grit my teeth and answer. "Eight."

Genevieve places a pair of thick, dry, clean socks on the ground beside me. "Okay." She puts her fancy looking mountain shoes next to them. "You can have my hikers."

She proceeds to put on her own socks and *my* sneakers. I look at her for the first time today, in disbelief. What is she doing? And now she's just walking away. She doesn't look back. Santiago looks at me, also looking kind of confused. He follows Genevieve, leaving me to put on her shoes. I growl quietly as I lace the 'hikers.'

The meadow is less pretty now that I'm not happy. Bright flowers look dull. Vivid green grass is muted. Even the blue sky looks bleak. I don't even try to catch up to them. They're not walking together, which makes me a bit happier. (And guiltier. How could they be a thing. I've literally been with them almost every second of this stupid fucking walk.) (Now I'm embarrassed *and* in a shit mood.)

Tiago's power marching, so far ahead I can barely see him while Genevieve hovers between us, looking back and forth.

I need a bit of a break from them both. So I just keep trudging along as slow as I can.

I'm glad when I finally reach the cool darkness of the forest. It matches how bad I feel.

CHAPTER 14

chapter 14

July 18th, 10:23am
Location: The Woods

Tiago

I know I shouldn't be angry with Rosemary. It makes sense. She has solid reasoning behind not wanting to talk about Ezra. It just really bothers me that we're ignoring the person we're supposedly going to save. I want to get to him so badly. I'm getting more and more convinced that he's in pain and it's hurting me.

For some reason.

Even though I'm constantly moving, I can't seem to outrun the ache. Actually, it's like a void. Like the hole in my dream. I think I absorbed that pit. I didn't know it was there until now. It's growing every day I don't see him.

Rosemary is lagging so far behind that I actually can't see her when I turn around. Genevieve keeps stopping to wait for her. I hate how slow we're going. I wish Genevieve would just come up here with me. I need to talk to her.

But as the day continues, I'm stuck in an uncomfortable quiet. I'm used to being able to talk while we're walking. This feels wrong and the annoying thing is that I don't know if it's my fault. The forest does a decent job of filling in the silence, but it's kind of eerie. Twigs snap under my feet. Wind rustles the evergreens. Birds twitter. I walk through patches of sunlight. The ground has less undergrowth on it now. It's covered in a carpet of fallen pine needles, so when sticks do pop under my feet, it's surprising.

Eventually, I get so far ahead that I can't see or hear either of the girls, so I just. Stop under a big tree and wait for them. Genevieve catches up first, but she doesn't notice me right away.

"Hey wait," I have to call out.

She gives me a confused look, about to say something as Rosemary appears, clearly in a sour mood. She huffs, frustrated. Yesterday, I would've asked if she was okay. But something's changed in her. Whatever it is, it happened quickly. It makes me uneasy.

"Guys, we've been walking for hours. Can we please eat something?" she whines. I forgot about eating. The thought of food makes me realize how hungry I am. "Well, we didn't start until late today. Let's eat while we walk."

I really want to keep moving. We've already wasted so much time. The void will grow. Also, I don't want to stop until we absolutely have to because Rosemary's making me uncomfortable, hovering a few feet away, her arms crossed, avoiding both of our eyes. Genevieve presses her fingertips to her temples, apprehension written clearly across her face. I wonder what Rosemary's thinking that's making Genevieve nervous. I'm nervous just being around her, let alone hearing what's in her mind.

"Fine," Rosemary snaps.

What is making her so *upset*? I grab the sandwiches and throw my backpack on again. I wasn't planning on being with somebody in the woods (frankly, I wasn't planning on being in the woods at all), so there are only five left. Well, three after we eat this meal. (Genevieve doesn't eat very much of our food. That's good. She brought her own stuff, unlike Rosemary.)

"I guess we get one today," Rosemary complains quietly.

I nod, not quite sure what to say. I gave her the last peanut butter one. My sandwich is gross. It's cucumber, hummus, tomato, and mashed peas. (Why in the world would someone think it was a good idea to put mashed peas in a sandwich?) I never take this kind at the home. We keep walking in silence. All together now at least, but maybe it's not the best choice, because the tension is so thick. Genevieve pulls away from us a bit, looking up at the trees.

"Did you know looking at the tops of trees is actually really healthy?" she offers. "It's helped patients with depression, apparently."

Rosemary doesn't even acknowledge the comment.

"Did I do something to make you angry?" I ask, concerned. She shakes her head at the ground and stops. Genevieve walks slowly back to us.

"Then," I continue, "what's wrong?"

Why am I even asking? She's just going to say she's upset about Ezra. But for some reason, I feel like she might be lying. Her expressions are different when she talks about him now, like there's an internal struggle happening within her eyes. She looks at me, pained.

"I need to be honest with you. I don't—" She stops abruptly, neck tensing.

I throw my hands in the air. "You don't *what*?"

In the corner of my vision, I see Genevieve covering her face with her hands. Is she crying? Or just so fed up with us? Because I would be too—I'm about to turn to her when Rosemary's eyes go wide. She brings her finger to her lips.

"*What*?" I demand.

"Shhh!"

"Okay. *Seriously*. Stop—" Then I hear it too.

Buzzing.

July 18th, 1:34pm, Ester Myrtle Kellwether's Home for Unusually Gifted Youth and Children

Ester

I have decided it is a good idea to speed up their progress. I am eager, perhaps impatient, for their arrival. This latest strategy should cause a minor panic, and corral them in the correct direction. They will have to thank me later. If they remember me, that is.

July 18th, 1:45pm, The Woods

Genevieve

I'm so over-stimulated from the aggression of their thoughts. I would try to step in, but their minds are so *loud*. I've been listening to Tiago angsting all morning, and Rosemary feeling like shit about Tiago and about thinking that I was with Tiago... oh man. And when they fight, especially right now? When they've had all day to stew in their own feelings? This is the potential disaster right here, where people get hurt, and I cannot stop it, because Rosemary's made up her mind. She's gonna tell him about her feelings. She's nervous and it's gonna go wrong and we'll never make it out of here alive. Santiago's angry. So angry. There's this conversation going on in their heads, that the other can't hear, but I can.

Santiago: *This needs to stop. Why is she doing this? I can't fucking believe her.*

Rosemary: *I need to tell him. I need to tell him. I need to tell him. Oh god what was Genevieve trying to tell me about him—SHUT UP oh my god...*

Santiago: *She's lying about Ezra. I need to get moving; this is ridiculous. Why is she stopping us? Oh my god. What the hell. I'm so confused what's even happening how was everyting so fine yesterday and just awful now—*

Rosemary: *Why am I so oblivious? I need to tell him. I'll throw up if I don't. Or maybe I'll explode. Here goes nothing—wait...*

Santiago: *Genevieve.... oh fuck what—what? What's she gonna say?*

Rosemary: *Wait, what's that noise?*

Then I suddenly stop focusing on their minds, trying to hear the noise. I lift my face out of my hands.

A weird, high pitched buzz.

July 18th, 1:47pm, The Lab?

Ezra

I can't ignite. Lights flick on. What is this? Is it real? I look down at the floor, then notice I'm wearing minty green hospital scrubs. Where did they come from? *Where* are my real clothes? Where are my *glasses?* Why can I see without them? And where's the sweater...? (Yeah, I'm totally dead. Tiago must've killed me for losing his hoodie.)

The single bulb on the ceiling buzzes. There's no one. Anywhere. My heart's already in my throat. Then I notice the walls. They start to close in on me. I spin around. A door. Except, it's upside down. I have to crawl. The walls come closer so fast. Breathing raggedly, I grab the door handle. It's locked. *Big surprise there*, the small, rational part of my mind snorts. The rest of me is not rational. The walls brush my shoulders. Panic roars through me. Alone, in a shrinking space, with a locked door. Aching spreads as the walls fight against my body, trying to crush me. My eyes blur with tears. The door falls off its hinges. I can't make it. My arms burn as I pull myself towards the opening.

Grunting with effort, I reach the door-frame. Suddenly, I wish I'd stayed in the room. Below me is a drop. I can't see the bottom. If there was anything in my stomach, it'd be gone now. The floor supporting my legs disappears. I inhale sharply. My arms give out. I fall, screaming. Light streams out of the door-frame. Someone looks out. Tiago. He jumps down after me. He's so close. I smile.

"Tiago."

He looks at me with a tenderness I've never seen on his face.

I reach up with one arm. It's all I have the strength for. He reaches for me too. Our fingers brush. I plummet away, into darkness. The image is gone, but the feeling of falling stays in the pit of my stomach.

The feeling of Tiago's brief touch.

July 18th, 1:48pm, The Woods

Rosemary

The buzzing is like a dentist drill. Invasive and unrelenting. So in other words, awful. Tiago looks back to where it's coming from. Tiny specks start to emerge from the trees.

"What are they?" I whisper.

He shrugs, confused. Out of instinct, I step back. Genevieve rushes forward. She tries to catch his arm, as if to hold him in place, but she misses. He walks closer. (Oh lord. His survival instincts are terrible.) The number of things multiplies by the second. Genevieve and I share a worried look, all problems suddenly pushed aside.

"Ow," he mumbles, slapping his neck. "They sting."

Then, without warning, thousands of them swarm him. I can't see him anymore. He's surrounded by the stinging things. He cries out.

"Santiago!" I yell, afraid to get any closer, but horrified for him.

His figure stumbles forwards, covered in little black dots. I scream, terrified. My legs start running in the opposite direction. I need to go back and help him, but I don't have the willpower to turn around. Fear pools in my throat, my stomach, my limbs, sloshing around like an over–filled cup. Something crashes into a tree behind me. I wince behind the panic. It's him. He can't see where he's going. More of the insects appear, chasing us through the trees. I can't bear to look back again. My rational side knows I can't outrun things with wings. My moral compass is still yelling at me. My legs start to burn. I feel sick every time I hear him charge into something or fall. A prick stings my neck. I bring my hand to the pain. It's wet. Bleeding. Alarmed dread swamps me. Where's Genevieve?

"Santiago! You need to use your gift!"

I don't recognize the hoarse scream that escapes my lips. Suddenly, my mouth goes dry. A sting rips into my calf. I feel blood soaking the leg of my jeans. Burning spreads at each point where I've been punctured. I fight to keep running, but my feet are so clumsy. Rocks move under my slurred steps. Why are there rocks? Blue sky floods my blurred vision. Where are the trees? I'm about to stop when my feet slip.

Rocks dig into my palms as I tumble down the sharp slope. It's so steep. Feet first, I slide down. At least four suns kaleidoscope feverishly with puffy, white clouds and little black bugs. For a second, I think I see the shape of a person flying through the air. I hear a rock tear something. My backpack. The shapes in my vision go blurry, then dark. Pain shoots through my body as I jolt to a stop. I think I was rolling. (I don't remember the last time I rolled down a hill.) As I lose consciousness, I think I hear Santiago crash over the edge.

So he wasn't the one flying.

Tiago

I can't feel my body.

I think I fall. I think I get up. I think I see someone flying through the air. I *think* I'm hallucinating. Nothing exists but my mind. Someone told me to use my gift. I try. Except, I don't know why I need to use it. Or what to focus on.

I'm pretty sure I'm falling. I know for a fact I'm bleeding. A lot. There's this awful buzzing noise. I focus on it being gone. Maybe that's what the person wanted me to do. Ouch. My eyes burn. The buzzing stops. I slide off of something, soar through space and time, then land with a crunch. Sparks appear. Feverish heat expands, overtaking my body. Things I can't identify slide across my vision. My eyes shut against my will.

What's happening?

July 18th, 6:19pm, Ester Myrtle Kellwether's Home for Unusually Gifted Youth and Children

Ester

Around six o'clock, a call comes in. I accept it when I see it is from the lab. They do not call me unless something is wrong.

"What is the problem?" I ask as soon as I pick up.

The man on the other side of the phone clears his throat. A lab assistant.

"Well?" I demand.

"The boy, Ezra, got out of a simulation. He was twitching and…"

"And what?" My heart pounds.

"He opened his eyes. Only for a moment. We can't be sure it even happened," he finishes.

I stifle a gasp of shock.

"We sedated him as soon as it happened. I really don't think he was conscious. He—"

"Was obviously conscious to get out of a simulation," I finish the sentence icily. "What was the simulation about?"

Silence.

"What was the simulation about?" I repeat impatiently.

"Well, you see, it didn't involve physical pain. He talked back to the person who was yelling at him. I didn't know he had the power to do that."

The course of action is very clear.

"Please change the settings. Have every simulation be based on his fears that cause physical pain. He will not have the power to resist that," I say, devoid of emotion.

"Alright."

The line goes dead. I listen to the dial tone buzz. It makes me wonder if the troublesome trio got my insects. Worry stirs inside of me. How was it possible for him to be conscious in a simulation? It just does not make sense. I should not worry. Adding in regular pain will help this come to an end.

The phone rings again.

July 19th, 2:06am, The Lab...? and *The endless darkness in between*

Ezra

Everything stopped feeling so real for a time. Now, I'm not sure *why* I felt like that. I think I'm dead. Or, I should be dead. I don't know where I am. Maybe some sort of in between. Is hell real? Is *heaven* real? Because this isn't it.

Sometimes, I float aimlessly through darkness. Times like now, I'm in a place I've never seen before. The only thing I can count on is pain. Sometimes I have to fight shadowy figures to the death with my bare hands. I get torn apart and somehow end up back together. Other times, I'm tormented and tortured by Santiago. Tiago. I...

Right this second, I walk on coals. It doesn't hurt, even though it should. Why doesn't it hurt?

Because of the warmth. There's warmth living inside of me somewhere. These coals are warm. Wait, no coals anymore. Only ice. I can't move my feet. Now I feel burning. It isn't the warm kind. Snow stings my bare face. Or, I think it's snow. I've never actually seen snow. It's kind of like needles. Just less awful. And more cold.

"Help," my voice cracks painfully.

I think I taste blood in my mouth. The burning spreads. A body falls from the blank, desolate sky. It hits the ice with a dreadful crack. I can't see the face until the wind turns the limp head towards me. His eyes stare blankly. The gale force wind stirs his blonde hair.

My mouth falls open in a silent '*No...*'

I reach for his hand, expecting some kind of cool darkness that doesn't come. *My* hand is shaking uncontrollably. *His* hand is freezing. It gets pulled away from mine. He's not dead. He's laughing at me. My heart twists. (It was a lie. A trick. Why do I keep *falling* for this?)

"Jesus, Ezra. What are you thinking? Are you *that* stupid?"

I can't move again. He sits up. A strange look comes over his face. I'm kneeling in front of him, my shins embedded in cold. He leans toward me. My heart goes ballistic, beating wildly. I hate it for that. I *hate it.*

"I'll never love you back," he hisses. A beautiful, horrible smile spreads over his face. "I'm real, Ezra."

"I don't believe you." But I do, don't I? And it hurts. It hurts so bad.

Everything is colliding. Is he real? Is this real? He stands up, smirking. Towering over me, he ruffles my hair, then grabs it, yanking my head back painfully. I try to avert my eyes but I can't.

"Just... stop," I beg feebly. "Please..."

He crouches down in front of me, still gripping my hair. I struggle a little. Tears fight to escape. I let them fall. Shivering, I hold his gaze of ice and hate. With his free hand, he gently wipes a tear off my cheek. I close my eyes and try to pull away. He's mocking me. (He's *mocking me.*)

"Shh. Shh. It's okay." The menace in his voice is hidden well. If I didn't know better, I'd think he cared.

"Please."

"Please what?"

"I need you—"

He snorts, cutting me off. "You need me?"

"I need you *to stop.*"

I feel his forehead against mine. "Oh, Ezra. You were always good for a laugh. Too bad you fucked it all up. Like you always do."

I don't open my eyes. This hurts too much. My body convulses. There's a knife in my hand. Small. Sharp. I scream, and it tears my throat bloody, raw, as I drive the blade between his ribs because what else can I do? He's laughing and we're throwing brutal punches and my skull rings and my body *hates this I'm gonna be sick and I'm kicking his knees out from under him and he's laughing, bleeding into the snow and just as I'm about to*—the ice beneath us cracks.

I plunge down; down into water. I gasp. My lungs fill with it. The water is scalding me. Inside and out. There's no point in fighting. I'll finally be done with this. It takes so much effort to hold my breath. My lungs scream for air, but I know there's none here. There's only pain.

Is there Tiago? Yes. My Tiago. But this Tiago isn't real. I made him up. I hoped the real Tiago would realize that he didn't hate me. He definitely hasn't. It's okay. All the Tiagos might be made up. Didn't I have a sweater? What came before this pain? Was it Tiago? If so, which one? Did I hurt him? My lungs scream for air. I'm imploding, folding in on myself as the water pulls me down–down, down. I'm wrapped in a blanket of pure, scalding cold that worms its way inside me and tries. To tear. Me apart.

And this time...

I let it.

July 19th, 2:09am, The Woods

Rosemary

My head is pounding. I open my eyes the tiniest bit, expecting sun. There isn't any. I see double for a moment. Double clouds. Grey. My whole body aches. What happened?

Slowly, I push myself to sitting. A clearing meets my eyes. It's large, with rocks scattered around the grass. I smell like dirt and blood. I gag. My jeans have dark stains every few inches. Noticing that I'm still wearing my backpack, I pull it off. The front is lodged with sharp stones that would have been in my back if it weren't for the bag. Behind me is the steepest, rockiest hill I've ever seen.

Oh my god. The bugs.

Where's Santiago? Where's Genevieve? *Did we fall down that?* I jump to my feet. All the blood rushes from my head. I'm so dizzy for a second that I consider lying back down, but it passes. None of the blood stains have an injury beneath them. I healed myself, like usual. (Quite handy.) How long have we been here? A few hours? A day? More? Santiago can't heal himself. Genevieve can't heal herself. Only I can do that. He was covered in those bugs, not to mention the fact that he ran into several trees and probably fell down the cliff. Frantically, I glance around, heart pounding.

I spot him. His arm is sticking out from under a huge rock. No. Oh no. I sprint over, neglecting my sore, screaming legs. When I reach him, I run around the boulder. His eyes are closed. I can't tell if he's breathing. His entire face is swollen and covered in gashes, dried blood, pine needles. I fight to keep from freaking out, but panic is quickly taking over. My breathing speeds up. One of his arms is definitely broken. I try not to think of his ribs underneath the rock.

"Santiago? I can't get this rock off you. I'm sorry. I need you to use your gift. Just focus on getting the weight off you," I plead, throwing my weight against the boulder.

Going into hysterics isn't an option right now. I stand up, breathing slowly to calm myself down. The rock is stubborn. I throw my shoulder into it, pushing with all my remaining strength. Santiago grunts softly. The rock rolls off him. And literally turns into thin air, because. His gift. I fly forwards, having to leap over him to keep my balance.

Dropping to my knees on his other side, I put my hands on his ribs. His pain wants to submerge me. I grit my teeth, thinking about what he looked like before all these injuries. I feel the separated bones coming back together. He gasps. I jump back. His face is still extremely puffy. The cuts have disappeared though. Clouds are covering the sunset tonight. I shiver.

I tentatively push his shoulder. "Santiago?"

He doesn't open his eyes. I gently turn him onto his side, which is hard to do considering his size versus my size. His backpack is mangled, like mine. The cursed sandwiches are shoved in the main pocket, surprisingly almost whole. I scarf one down without tasting it. I don't even notice what kind it is.

There are no stars tonight. No Tiago. And no Genevieve. Where is she?

"Genevieve?" I whisper into the dusk.

My voice is swallowed whole. There's no answer.

"Genevieve!" I say, a little louder, looking around the hill. She's not there. Or over there. Or over there. My throat closes up with panic again. I sink to the ground, too overwhelmed to do anything about anything.

When it's completely dark, I try to drag Tiago into the trees. He's way too heavy. I manage to move him about two feet, but then give up and sit down beside his head.

My bag isn't far, but I'm scared to go get it. The dark seems oppressive now that I don't have anyone to talk to. I wish there were stars. I think they'd be nice companions. Just my luck that Tiago almost dies and Genevieve goes missing on the day when the night is cloudy.

Shit. When did I get so selfish? I look down at him, even though I can't see at all.

"Please wake up," I whisper before lying down with my head next to where I think he is. The sounds of the forest aren't friendly at night when you're alone. Every now and then, a pebble tumbles down the slope. Trees creak. Little feet scuttle around in the blackness.

"Rosemary," someone whispers behind me.

I bolt up. The voice is female, but not Genevieve's.

"Hello?" I squeak.

"Rosemary," she says again, this time to my far left. I recognize the voice from somewhere.

My heart slams into my rib-cage as I slowly get to my feet. "Who are you?" I sound the opposite of confident. Because I'm terrified.

"Rosemary." She's angry this time, close to my face.

I step back, tripping over Santiago. (Aha! I found him!) Scrambling up, I run towards the trees. My hands are out in front of me, just in case I fall. It's a slow run, because I keep having to turn away from the trees my hands brush. Nobody's crashing after me. I stop. The moon suddenly appears, leering down at me from behind the trees, flooding the tall, dark forest in silver light. There isn't a soul in sight. I whip around, trying to find her.

Her voice is everywhere. "Rosemary."

"What do you want?" I scream, trembling.

"Silly Rosemary," she coos.

Pine needles begin to rise. My feet leave the ground. Hysteria clogs my throat.

"Put me down!"

She doesn't respond. I kick at the air. It does nothing. The higher I go, the more frantic I become. Pine needles spin around me in a frenzied tornado of chaos. I squeeze my eyes shut, hoping someone will shake me awake. Instead, something small and hard hits me in the arm.

A tooth.

CHAPTER 15

chapter 15

July 19th, 2:20am

Location: Ester Myrtle Kellwether's Home for Unusually Gifted Youth and Children

Ester

Most of the image feeds from the cameras that were inserted into the bugs fizzled out a while ago. They are dead. I am fairly certain that Santiago killed most of them with his gift. Unfortunately, with my cameras dead, I cannot immediately see their location. The ones who survived made it back to the lab. I close out of the screen full of black squares that used to be live video feeds. Pulling up the tracking map, I see the spot where much of my surveillance died. Assuming that Rosemary and Santiago have not moved since the bugs met their untimely demise, which would be likely, they are very close to the observatory.

The insects were courtesy of a girl who lives at the lab. Her gift was too dangerous to be kept with the other children. She turns things into something worse when she's afraid. We gave her a container of normal wasps and a fear inducing simulation, and we got venomous security wasps whose stings make people bleed and hallucinate. We added cameras into their heads for a situation exactly like the one we faced today. Even though I am excited, I am aware that I am getting older.

My feet are throbbing dully. The lack of sleep is also affecting my state of being. I am drowsy during the day with nearly no energy at all. But now? It is either the satisfaction of a success or the anticipation of what will come to pass making me feel quite nearly giddy. I dress quickly. A guard stands by my door. I ask him to ready my car. It is still dark when I leave. The mist is very thick. Sunrises are not my favourite thing. Today, it seems that things will go my way, because when the sun does rise, I cannot even tell it is there.

I will depart for the lab today, and await Miss Mae–Anderson and Mister Grey there. I have new matters to attend to now.

And, I can keep an eye on Ezra.

July 19th, 2:25am, The Woods

Tiago

My mind is filled with flashes of Ezra screaming, little insects, and a crushing weight. I don't feel the pain until the weight gets pushed. Shifted. I want it gone. It disappears. I feel like my bones are getting slowly soldered back together. Burning agony. Then, it's over. I slip away from consciousness. I fall into the void. How the hell did it get so deep? Being weightless is the oddest sensation. It's so calm in here. Nothing and everything. Just tranquil darkness.

And I float.

There are memories. But they're different from what actually happened. It's a day where Ezra was sitting alone. In real life, I laughed at him with my friends. In this memory, I go sit with him. We're laughing together. What's it like to laugh *with* someone who gets laughed at? I'd guess it's the same as laughing with people who do the laughing, but I don't know. Somehow, it seems more pure to laugh with a sweet underdog. The memory fades into the day I scared him off the roof. We're older in this one. And we're sitting on the edge, watching the sunset. Together.

Seriously. Was there ever a time when we were together where I didn't try to hurt him in some way?

I didn't realize I felt so guilty about everything I did to him. It changes again, to the day where I said I hated him. The day he disappeared. (I despise that day.) (It's the worst day of my life.) He's sitting in the hallway exactly like I remember. In this version, I feel a smile spread across my face when I see him. One side of his mouth lifts in an adorable crooked grin. I ruffle his reckless tumble of curls and slide down the wall beside him. When I look over, he's gone. He's gone.

Why didn't things happen like *this*? My stomach dives out of a plane, the plummeting feeling coated in grease and guilt. It's my fault. The reason things didn't happen like that was *me*. I was the one who told him I hated him. That's probably the last thing I'll ever get to say to him. If my dreams have any connection to reality, he's most likely...

No. I will *not* let myself think that. That's too horrible to be true. Ezra, so full of life, bursting at the seams with bad jokes and cheesy poetry, so curious that he makes you wish question marks didn't exist. Ezra, who could have a conversation with anyone, who was loved by everybody. He made a room full of people who based status on gift strength forget that he was powerless. Except for me.

Why did I take it upon myself to be the one to remind him of his childhood? Someone else could have made sure he fell off the roof and played with those live wires. It didn't have to be me. Fuck. Those things didn't even need to happen. He almost died enough times on his own accord. He really didn't need me trying to kill him as well. What if he is... dead? What if I never get to say I'm sorry? Not that an *"I'm sorry"* would cut it. What would I say to him if I knew he was going to die?

It hits me like a bus going 200 miles per hour. (And then the bus runs me over, reverses to run me over again, and speeds forwards, running me over one more time.)

Oh.

Rosemary

I'm literally in the fucking the air, rising, flying, but without any kind of control??? When the tooth hits me?? What's a *tooth* doing here? There are more every instant, swirling around me with the pine needles. Teeth. Hundreds. Thousands. What is *happening* to me? Breath—I can't—In a tornado of... teeth.

Oh god?

The day Tiago and I found Ezra, I didn't think much of the teeth, except that they were disgusting and out of place. Come to think of it, the voice was there too. (That's why it sounded familiar.) (The voice and the teeth. Were there that day.) (Fuck fuck fuck *fuck*—)

"What are you doing to me?!" I scream, the words catching in my throat, tears streaming down my face. I'm so high in the air that the treetops look fake. Struggling against the air? It's holding me up and I don't want to be held, not like this—

Having nothing under my feet is the worst feeling in the world. There's just. *Nothing and I've never been up this high before because how would I do this I can't fly—*

I don't even understand what's happening until all the air is violently ripped out of my lungs. A silent scream tears my mouth open as I'm swarmed teeth, ripping through the air in every direction. Some go up to where I was. Some fly sideways, avoiding my body. Others fall with me. Down. The ground is getting closer. The skin on my face is pulled back by speed. I hear teeth landing. My eyes are watering and the tears fly up, up, up. It's all happening so fast—

Thud.

The sound of my body hitting the ground, but. I don't feel it. My eyes are closed against my will. I peel them open, smelling pine. I lay on my stomach, face down on the forest floor. Teeth strike the earth around me. Sticking into the ground. Can't breathe. Need to get Santiago out of the open. The sky is getting lighter. Dimly behind the panic, I'm grateful this night is almost over. *Dimly behind the panic,* is more panic. Where is *Genevieve?*

Jumping to my feet, I have no pain. I *should.* I just fell from the fucking sky. (Did I? Is this real??) I sprint through the trees. The teeth hit me, leaving no marks. Why am I healing so fast? I'm healing so fast...

There's the clearing; ground's already covered in teeth. Tiago's bleeding again. I see my pack and throw it on as fast as I can. Fight or flight. Adrenaline in my body, so rampant I can't hesitate. (What is *happening?*) Clenching my jaw, I grab his arms and pull. He moves inch by inch. I grunt with the effort, trembling. The teeth fall more heavily, pounding us relentlessly like little fists. (This is my fault.) Looking behind me I see we're almost at the trees. Relief pumps through my exhausted arms. I take the final steps and collapse a few feet away from him.

Burying my head in my knees, I start to cry again. What is *happening to me?* I wish things would go back to normal. I'd trade anything to be back in the home, even if it was like a prison. I'd even trade real prison for this. Madam Ester was right. The real world is full of things we're not prepared for.

July 19th, 2:45am, The Woods **and** *Sterile Hallways*

Genevieve

One minute, I was flying. Then I saw sterile hallways. Then I saw nothing.

And now, a scream builds up in the back of my throat. But my lips won't open to let it out. I feel like I'm being torn apart.

July 19th, 2:49am, The Woods

Rosemary

Teeth bounce off my back and land in my hair. I'm so dirty. There are so many things I want right now. I want a hair elastic. I want a shower. I want to forget that I'm sitting in a forest, getting hit by falling teeth, hoping all my friends aren't dead. Why did I even come here? I wipe my eyes and look at the needle–padded forest floor. I wish Genevieve would turn up. I don't have the energy to search for her, but there's this weird ache inside me. I miss her now, which is surprising, because I didn't even know her two weeks ago. But I guess the same thing could be said about Tiago. Maybe it's just weird to miss a girl. I... don't know.

The sun is rising. A small comfort. At least another day is coming. I don't want another day of this wild goose chase (turned Gong Show). Is it really comforting that if I die out here, the sun will still rise? I've never experienced someone I love dying. Honestly, I don't know who I love. I haven't even *had* my first love. What if I die before my first kiss? So selfish, but it disturbs me. I've never thought about love in that way. It was always friendship–love. Not romantic love. Ezra was my chosen family. I never thought there could be more to life. Things used to be so... simple. Until Tiago and Genevieve showed me there could be more. I don't think they meant to introduce me to normal friendship. I'm pretty sure I never looked at Santiago's crowded table and thought, *I want that*. I was. More like Genevieve. Okay with being mostly alone.

It was always the two of us, Ezra and me. We would make fun of research studies from the library. We would try to play catch, but since we were both awful at it, we'd end up lying on the grass, naming shapes in the clouds. The things he saw were always unexpected. Where I saw a marshmallow, he would point out the way it looked like a smiling face. The number of cloud angels we found was too high to count. I glance at Santiago. The other day, while we were walking, he told me about his family of friends: Hunter, Emeline, Mason, Kenzie, Owen, Nathan, Declan, and James. Genevieve was there too, but she just laughed when Tiago said they were all real friends. She thought it was impossible to have a group that big without drama, without internal issues. I actually agreed with her. How can you possibly hold enough love for them in your heart?

Tiago said they were always there for each other. I never even considered having a pack like that. His time at Madam Ester Kellweather's home was the opposite of mine. His group was rowdy, their laughter always filling the dining hall. I'd glare or just ignore them as I ate with Ezra. Now, there's a big part of me (not the rational part) that's wishing I didn't go to Ezra that day when I first arrived. What would've happened if I'd joined Santiago's table instead?

Everybody idolized them, except for Ezra, of course. He saw them as people, not gods. To him, they weren't on a pedestal. He treated everyone so well, no matter what they did to him in the past. When Ezra was little, every last one of them made fun of him. Apart from that, I don't know anything else about his childhood. It used to bother me that I didn't know. Now, I'm not really sure. I don't think I need to fix all of his problems, like I used to. I don't think I *could,* even if I tried.

That thought makes me upset, but I have no tears left. My eyes are puffy from crying. The sun is almost halfway across the sky when I get up. Everything aches. I didn't notice that the teeth stopped falling. I'm glad they did. But I want them to go away. Bending down, I pick up one that looks like a molar. I throw it as hard as I can, a growl of frustration escaping my lips. I hate it here. *I hate it here.*

Turning around, I see that Santiago's still unconscious. His face isn't swollen anymore. Just smeared with dried blood. My bag is on my back. I pull it off and look for clean clothes. My stomach growls. I think about taking another sandwich, but he'll probably be hungry when he wakes up. Settling for water, I pull out my bottle. I'm careful to only drink a few sips. The coolness trickles down my raw throat, soothing the burning. Now that the water bottle is out, I see that there's a pair of folded leggings and a T–shirt in the bottom of the bag. I slip out of my destroyed jeans, and change quickly (glancing over a few times to make sure he stays uncon-scious.) (What a warped experience. Me hoping Santiago stays comatose so he doesn't see me changing.)

After I swap my shirt, I dump out the contents of my bag. There's my other clothes, damp from the stream, a useless toothbrush, and a small package of mysterious trail mix. (How long has that been in there?) My bloody sweater will have to do. I slip it back on. Shoving everything back in proves to be quite easy because I leave out all the clothing.

There's no point in carrying around disgusting fabric. I sit down again, ripping open the trail mix. The almonds are stale. I don't care. I have to fight to eat it slowly. Santiago groans. My attention snaps over to him. I put the package down and rush over. I need to heal the oozing cuts left from the teeth. Placing my hands on his face, I'm suddenly reminded of the last time I healed Ezra.

I gently place my hands on the cuts. "Let me fix your face," I whisper.

As I heal Santiago, I think of Ezra. His face got messed up so many times that it just became routine. Sometimes he'd call me ma'am or Mom as a joke. Like the day when I told him it was important to dress nicer than jeans and a T-shirt. (There was some event on. Or maybe it was Christmas?) He'd laughed his contagious laugh then said "Yes, Mom." I'd raised my eyebrows at him and he playfully shoulder checked me. I'd burst out laughing. A few minutes later, he'd come downstairs wearing a button up shirt with *jeans*. I guess that was as fancy as he could handle. Or there was the day when I fixed his face for the first time. I don't exactly remember how he broke his face, but I was eight. I *freaked* out.

"Geez," he'd mumbled. "It's okay. You're not my mom, mom."

The memory is so vivid. I'd been crying because of the huge burn that covered half his face and the tiny puncture wounds on his neck and arms. I was so scared. Maybe I thought he was dying, I don't know. What I *do* know, was that when he called me Mom, I laughed through the tears. He survived. Big surprise there. Santiago twitches. I pull my hands away jerkily. I forgot I was healing him. The cuts are definitely gone. His eyes dart back and forth beneath his eyelids. I feel the need to go look for Genevieve, but what if Tiago wakes up while I'm gone?

"Sorry, Tiago," I say, flicking a strand of hair off his face.

I stand up and go back to the chocolate I saved from the trail mix, even though my stomach is flipping over and over. Ezra always said it was important to enjoy your favorite part of something all the way through. I'm pretty sure he wasn't just referring to your favorite food that you saved for last. He said that if you can't find small joys throughout, you'll lose motivation to get to the end. Your anticipation for your favorite thing would eventually fade. Actually, I'm absolutely positive he wasn't talking about food at all, because it's a terrible example. Ezra always came up with awful analogies.

I see now that he was talking about life. He was right. My motivation to live any longer in this state of emotional turmoil is petering out. I don't know how much longer I can do this. It feels wrong to think that. Right now all I want is for Tiago to wake up. I want Genevieve to come back. I want to scream and cry and laugh. I want the teeth to leave me alone. I don't know what I'm feeling. Everything is trapped in a glass cage inside me, and the cage is cracking.

CHAPTER 16

chapter 16

July 19th, 4:08am

Location: The Woods

Tiago

Heat pulls me out of the emptiness.

Oh.

I struggle to stay. Yeah, that's not going to happen. There's no staying in the void. I have to go back. But I don't want to face life. I'm a coward. That's what got me into this whole situation.

Breath is a foreign sensation for a moment. I'm still alive. The bugs. I remember falling. Crashing into trees. Was there a flying person? No, I don't think so. Buzzing, falling again, but down a long way. I remember crunching, inside of me. Then darkness. My void.

Oh. Oh dear.

My eyes are stuck shut. I keep trying until whatever was holding them closed gives up. They fly open. I have no idea what I was expecting to see, but what I do see is not it. Above me are pine trees. Beyond them are the stars. My body is super stiff but nothing really hurts. How is that possible? Oh. Right. Rosemary. I rub my eyes slowly before rolling over onto my stomach.

Something pokes me. The ground is specked with white. What? I run my hand over the dirt. Teeth. My head pounds. I push my hair out of my face. The world wobbles and blurs momentarily.

"Rosemary?" I whisper into the darkness.

She doesn't answer. She's probably asleep. I'm glad. I turn onto my back again. Why is it so uncomfortable? I roll to my side. I'm wearing my backpack. That would be the source of my trouble. Sleeping doesn't feel possible right now. I shove the bag off my shoulders and shift onto my back again. My mind is happy to be conscious. I'm not so sure about the rest of me. I think I'd rather stay in the void. At least there, it doesn't matter that I screwed up. At least in there, the world is guaranteed to have him in it. That isn't the case here. He could already be gone.

Could I live in a world he isn't in?

Could I live with myself knowing I couldn't save him?

July 19th, 4:25am, The Lab

Ezra

I

Can't

Think

Straight

Nothing is

Right.Is

This

What

Itfeels

Liketo

Be

Ripped

Apart?

What's

Hisname.

No.

He is like the sun. His hair is wavy. blonde.

And

He

Hatesmy

Eyes.

Hehates

My

Laugh.

No.

He *is* taller than me. You can spot him the second you walk into a room because he's so bright. Like the stars. Like the sun.

Andhe

Hatesme

because

Iamme.

Nothing

matters

Anymore.

I

Givein. over and over.

Breaking

Doesn't

Sound

That

Bad

Right

Now...

The pain stops. It always does. I'm stuck in darkness waiting for it to start again. I'll have to kill someone. I always throw up. I always sit there sobbing, covered in blood and I don't... understand that its some kind of not real until the person I just killed gets up again, mangled and alive again, to kill me. And sometimes... he's there. His name. It just keeps disappearing. Where is it? If I lose it, how will I remember myself? I can't lose it. I just can't. Santiago. Tiago. I still have it. The only thing that's still mine. It's being taken from me too. Why? Why are they doing this to me? The heat. They don't like the heat. Where is the heat? It's getting smaller. The smaller it gets, the colder I become. Cold lives under my skin, inhabiting every inch of my body. Except for the heat. In the pit of my stomach. There it *is* warm. I think they're trying to help the cold take over. Why do they want to make me cold? Is there a problem with heat? They think there is. Otherwise, they wouldn't try to take it away.

Is there something wrong with Tiago then? Because they're trying to take him away too.

July 19th, 5:58am, The Lab

Ester

I am sick and tired of waiting. Ezra is useless. Annoyingly persistent. He will not let go. All of his simulations are about a boy. That is what my assistant from the lab told me earlier today. I do not know who this boy is, but clearly it is someone from Ezra's life. Now that I think about it, I might know who it could be.

I was also told that his temperature is dropping quickly. The heat in his core is disappearing. In speculation, I have assumed that the warmth will go away entirely when he forgets this boy. However, no matter what pain I have asked them to inject him with, he still clings to the memory. As I wait for an image of the simulation boy, my suspicions grow.

The sharp rap on my door pulls me out of my head. "Ah, yes." I call, "Come in."

A lab assistant walks briskly through the door. He swallows, obviously tense. I suppose I do have quite the reputation around here.

"Here are the pictures from the simulations..." he says, but trails off when I give him a stern look. "Madam. Sorry."

"Let me have a look, will you? Or would you just like to stand by the door for a few hours? Whichever suits you best is fine."

He walks to me, and shoves the paper into my hands.

"You may go," I say, without looking at the photograph.

"Thank you," he says nervously. "Madam."

And he is gone.

My heart thunders in my chest as I look down at the single sheet in my grasp. The sweet satisfaction of being correct floods through my body. The mysterious boy is actually our dear friend, Santiago Grey. A new plan starts formulating in my mind. To break Ezra, he will need to see Santiago get broken. But first, I need that troublesome pair to actually *be* at the lab. It is rather unfortunate to have to use the new batch of creatures so quickly.

Oh well. I will do what needs to be done.

July 19th, 8:17am, The Woods

Tiago

I wait until the sun rises to get up. As I lay here during the night, clouds drifted in. They covered the entire sky. The only reason I know the sun is rising is that the grey gets lighter every passing moment.

I push myself up to sitting. My vision goes spotty for a second. I clamp my eyes shut. After a minute, I open them, digging through my bag. I take out my water. After I chug half the bottle, I realize I might need it again. Hesitantly, I put it back in. Next, I grab the last sandwiches. They're completely flattened, and made of bologna with bright yellow mustard. Gross. I eat one in four bites. I leave the second one for Rosemary. Behind me, she turns over in her sleep. Genevieve must be invisible somewhere. I wish I could disappear from sight right now. I feel... exposed. The air is damp. I stand up and walk over to her, deciding that for the sake of my own sanity, I'll ignore the teeth. (I have no idea how they got here and I don't think I want to know.) I'm a little unsteady on my feet. How long was I lying on the ground? Actually, I don't think I want to know. But it was enough time to realize—

"Tiago?" Rosemary asks sleepily. "Are you awake?"

"Yeah," I say, standing over her.

She opens her eyes. "Jesus Christ!" she yells, jolting up to sitting. "I thought you were over there!"

"Oh." I didn't mean to scare her. "Sorry."

She puts her palm over her heart, exhaling carefully and laying back down. "You scared me so bad." She shakes her head, throwing an arm over her eyes.

"Not on purpose."

I'm really not in the mood to talk.

"Ah. No, I mean, I thought you weren't gonna wake up."

I laugh humorlessly. "Oh yeah. That."

She removes her arm from her face to glare up at me. "Yeah. *That.*"

Rosemary gets to her feet.

"Have you seen Genevieve?" I ask.

Concern creeps onto her face. "No. I haven't." She starts chewing on her thumbnail.

"What if...?" I don't know what I'm saying, but I'm suddenly full of uncertainty. Where *is* she?

Rosemary shakes her head, closing her eyes. "No. Just no. Just stop. Don't even think that. I only saw you fall over the hill. I'm sure she's fine."

She doesn't *sound* sure.

"Should we look for her?" I say.

"Uh..." Then, her eyes fly open. Completely afraid. She covers her mouth with both her hands.

"Are you okay?" I'm confused.

"No—"

"Are you going to tell me what's wrong?"

She starts hyperventilating, squeaking as she inhales.

"Woah, Rosemary!" I grab her shoulders, shaking her a little. "Calm down!"

"T—the bugs!" She covers her whole face now, muffling her voice. "They *took* her."

"Rosemary, that doesn't make sense." I have zero idea how to deal with this. She's panicking so I'm panicking and things seem to be going down-hill.

Her eyes are watery, rimmed with red as she looks at me through her fingers. "I know. I—I didn't think it made sense either, but when I fell, I saw this person. Flying."

"Excuse me?" My pulse hitches at the familiarity.

"Yes. I did." Her breathing is slowing slightly. "I thought I was halluci-nating."

"Oh no."

July 19th, 8:35am, The Lab

Genevieve

I don't remember losing consciousness, but when I come to, it feels like someone's drilling through my eye sockets. The feeling only gets worse as I force my eyes to open. I'm not in the forest anymore. I can tell because there were only two mind voices there. Wherever I am now, there are way more. It's that hum I'm used to. Except, under that hum is this disjointed stream of words that don't make sense. It's like someone is screaming every fifth word of a story. But quietly screaming. Screaming so no one else can hear. Just me.

My hands are shaking. And my gums ache. Now *that* is something that's never happened to me before. Where am I? Faint footsteps stop near me. I disappear. Become invisible. A door creaks open. Someone walks into the room I'm in. All I can see is white. A ceiling. Whoever is here mutters a stream of quiet curse words. They walk over to where I'm lying. Maybe on a bed? It feels kinda soft.

Now I can see him. He's a tall, brown haired man who's maybe in his late forties. His hair is going grey behind his ears. And he's wearing a lab coat.

His mind: *Madam Ester will kill me if she knows I've lost the invisible girl. Oh dear. What did I do to deserve this?*

My mind (not that he can hear me): *Haha sucker. I'm right here. But you'll never know. I win!*

But Madam Ester? The one who ran the home? The guy takes one last look around, his mind firing off a *very* long round of profanities before leaving the room. I almost burst out laughing, but my ribs hurt too bad. He even mentioned the fact that I was invisible. And didn't even bother to check the bed. Sometimes, when people are stressed, they make ridiculous choices.

Under the hum, the voice screams. *you can't. heat. will–refuse. will–not–break. need. there was a. sweater. stop. will–not–break. failure. sorry. sorry. helpme. i'm sorry.*

And then it stops. I shiver, wondering how that person's mind got so broken. My body is hurting less. If any other assistants come looking for me, they'll check the bed first. But where am I? I sit up slowly. It's almost agony. It feels like I've spent a long long long time running with a suit of armour on. Said suit of armour would have to have spikes on the inside, because I've run with armour before (my dad and I were really into medieval fairs when I was fifteen) and I didn't hurt this bad afterwards.

The room I'm in is tiny. Everything is a stark white. Even the floor. It smells like bleach. Clenching my jaw, I stand. And sway for a moment. Surprisingly, my legs work for the few steps it takes me to reach the closest corner of the room. Exhausted, I slide down the wall and crunch my limbs into a ball.

Why was I even in a bed, when I was in the forest with Santiago and Rosemary... Santiago and Rosemary! Are they here too? Is that fragmented voice one of theirs? Panic surges through me, but if that voice was one of theirs, then I'd know. I've spent so much time with them alone. I'd know their minds anywhere.

I take a deep breath and search for them. The endless chatter calms to a buzz. No voices pop out, which calms me down a bit. They're not here. But someone else is. Madam Ester. The bitter woman who runs the home. Who also, apparently runs a lab.

A lab... I think we were looking for a lab...

what's. hisname.

I can hear the voice again. It has this quality like microphone feedback. I wince, wishing I could block it out.

no.

Pity twists my insides. This poor broken person is literally screaming out and no one can hear him.

he is–like the–sun.

I wonder who the voice is talking about.

his–hair. is wavy. blond. and–he–hates. my eyes.

He hates my eyes? That's weird. Oddly specific.

hehatesmylaugh. no.

heis. taller than–me. you can–spot–him. the secondyou–walk. into a–room because. he's so bright. Likethestars. Like the sun.

He's taller? He hates my laugh? He hates my eyes? Wavy blonde hair...? We were looking for a lab. We were looking for a boy in a lab, who looked so broken in Tiago's dreams. His mind; it matches the image.

The broken mind... is Ezra Colton?

CHAPTER 17

chapter 17

July 19th, 9:07am

Location: The Woods

Tiago

I grab the last sandwich and hand it to Rosemary without saying anything. She answers my silence with more silence. I inhaled my sandwich, so I have zero patience for the slug's pace she's eating at.

"Can you speed up, please? This isn't your last meal before execution," I growl, after what feels like an hour (in slug time). We need to move. Genevieve is missing. She's just gone. Rosemary thinks the bugs things took her. I think she's right. Whatever happened, I don't want to be left out here alone. Maybe Genevieve is at the lab. Maybe we can find them both. Maybe, with luck (a *lot* of luck), they'll both be okay.

"It's my last meal for a while, since we have now," she shoves the last piece in her mouth, "run out of food."

I sigh. She's right.

"I'm sorry." I mean it.

She can tell. A small smile plays at her lips. But her eyes are still stormy as she replies with, "It's okay."

Is it okay?

"Let's go find them," I say wearily.

She just gets up and starts walking.

I'm pretty sure it isn't okay. We've been saying *It's going to be okay, it's okay, don't worry,* so much. But what if it's never been? My life was so normal. As normal as a life of a kid like me can get. I had a group of friends I was happy with. At least I think I was happy. Well... no. I wasn't happy. I was comfortable. I was a comfortable asshole. How many times did I laugh at the so–called weakling? (A very *specific* so–called weakling.) How many times was I a horrible person? Too many to count. My god, without even trying, Ezra taught me that it's important to be a decent human. Now, I'm risking my life for him. The person I considered my number one hate. My life has changed so quickly.

Rosemary walks ahead of me. In the mist, towering trees loom above us, and for the first time in my life, I feel small.

Rosemary

Fog, like the nighttime, makes the forest into a place that's out to get you. I can't tell what things are until I'm right in front of them. No birds are singing today. Our footsteps crunch, echoing eerily through the empty space. (We left the teeth behind. I'm not going to talk about them unless Tiago brings them up. Even thinking about them—)

"Tiago?" I ask, my voice sounding too loud.

"Yeah," he responds flatly.

I say the first thing that comes to mind. "What's your favourite colour?"

"Green green green."

What a weirdo. Then he doesn't even ask me *my* favourite colour. So I take it he doesn't want to talk. And all I know is his (oddly repetitive) favourite colour. Yay. What a major accomplishment.

Meek sunlight starts to stream through the mist, and I feel slightly less sarcastic. (Slightly.) I don't care if Tiago doesn't want to talk to me. He's just my friend and friends can keep silent company. I don't need his constant attention.

But… for some reason, I feel like I *do* need it. The fog has lifted now, and I'm trying to convince myself that I can be happy with the sunshine and my cheerful daydreams. Except for the fact that I'm not one to do that. I'm fairly sure that I've never felt this way about anyone. I've never *had* someone to daydream about. I've never daydreamed, period. (This is completely hopeless.) I can't help but wonder what's on his mind. He's just so unreadable.

I glance back at him; his expression is blank, but his eyes… there's something in them. I look forward again.

He breaks the silence. "Is there something you'd like to say?"

I bite my lip, trying to decide whether to say it or not. I give in.

"I was wondering… um… what's on your mind."

I hear him make a weird shivering noise and look back again, concerned. He's grinning. Sort of.

He grimaces. "I just can't get the feeling of those bugs off my skin." Now I feel bad that I didn't help him.

"Oh," I say sheepishly. "Sorry about that."

"Nah. It's okay."

I nod awkwardly and keep walking.

July 19th, 10:08am, The Lab

Genevieve

I need to talk to them. To let them know I found Ezra. But I don't know how. Maybe I can... I've never tried this before...

I close my eyes and search farther than I've ever searched. A throbbing starts behind my eyes, spreading to my head and down my neck. I ignore it.

I need to find her.

July 19th, 10:10am, The Woods

Tiago

There's the 'it's okay' again. I guess it's become a habit, built into my arsenal of instant responses. I think Rosemary can sense I'm in a weird head-space. It worries me, even though she's changed too. I didn't realize that people could change so fast. (Maybe they don't usually.) (This might be a special circumstance.)

Shove three people who hate each other or don't know each other into a forest trying to find someone who they think is dying or dead. Not to mention that one of the people searching is the dying person's best friend and the other person is the dying person's self-proclaimed number one hater, while the third person doesn't know the dying person, but might now be dying herself. Nothing makes sense anymore. The lines between friend and not-friend have definitely blurred.

"I'm done walking." Rosemary flops to the ground. "This clearing is nice."

I stop, glancing around the little gap in the trees. There's a bit of grass, shaded by branches.

If anyone should have the power to make us stop, it should be me, since I was unconscious for the past… however long. I'm about to say exactly that but. Rosemary makes a weird noise.

Suddenly, she starts convulsing on the ground. I drop my bag and rush to her side. My heart feels like it's going to come out of my mouth. She sounds like she's choking. I have no idea what to do. Her eyes roll back, so only the whites are showing. I… stop breathing. Everything feels nauseous.

"Rosemary!" I shake her, because what else am I supposed to do? She croaks, coughing violently. "Rosemary, come on!"

I grab under her arms, trying to get her upright. She goes limp. What is *happening?*

"No. Nonononono. You can't… you can't…" Now I'm borderline hysterical. She's not breathing. I'm *still* not breathing. I think I'm shaking her, begging her not to be dead, when she starts talking. But it's not her voice.

"Santiago? Is this working? I am *so* sorry about this…" It's Genevieve's voice.

"G–genevieve?" My throat is raw.

Rosemary coughs. "Yes! It's me!"

"You," I choke out, *"can speak through people?!"*

"Oh my god! That isn't what I meant to do!"

I breathe in and out. "Yeah, well that's what you've done. Rosemary had some kind of attack…" I look at Rosemary, who's sitting bolt upright, talking through Genevieve's voice. This is very concerning. But… handy.

"Oh my god, oh my god I feel so bad. Please please please tell her I'm sorry." Rosemary is starting to tremble. I bite my lip. "But I needed to talk to you," Genevieve continues. "I'm at the lab. Ezra's here too. He's alive, but he's… not okay. I haven't seen him but… he's not… doing well."

My lip trembles with the sheer volume of the relief that floods through me. He's alive. Alive. A ragged breath escapes my lips, and I blink hard to stop tears from falling. Alive. Rosemary slumps over. I catch her, holding under her arms. Her head lolls to the side. He's alive.

"Genevieve..." I struggle for words. "Are you—are you okay?"

"I'm fine—" She cuts herself off with a scream. Or Rosemary screams. Or they're both screaming. There's so much screaming, I want to cover my ears, but I'm still holding her up. Then her weight goes limp. She falls on top of me, knocking both of us over. I roll her off of me and grab her shoulders.

"Rosemary."

She coughs, but it sounds like a bark. Her eyes flutter open. She looks dazed, confused, but alive. (He's alive.) (Ezra's alive.)

"Oh thank god." I pull her into a tight hug. Rosemary weakly wraps her arms around me, shuddering.

"What—what just happened to me?"

I don't know what to say to her.

"You're shaking, Tiago." She pulls away from me. "I'm sorry, but *what just happened to me?* That's never happened before."

I'm pretty sure I'm crying now. Putting my face in my hands, I try to explain to her. "He's alive. He–he's alive. I–I think that Genevieve sort of... spoke through you? She's at the... the lab and Ezra's there too."

Rosemary flops down on her back and for a moment, I think she's going to have another attack, but she starts laughing. Laughing so hard she's crying. I might be delirious, and slightly traumatized, but it's contagious.

What the hell has my life become?

I start laughing too. We're both just laughing and laughing and laughing in the face of the weirdest situation ever.

July 19th, 10:28am, The Lab

Genevieve

Oh my *god*. I didn't know there was a security camera in my room. I didn't know I could speak through people. I didn't know that I became visible when I did so. I don't know if I hurt Rosemary. I don't know if I could live with myself if I did. And I don't know if I've ever slept this well. But this room smells like antiseptic. I'm waking up from this cool darkness, a semiconscious sleeplike state. I told Santiago what I needed to tell him. They know. But when I try to open my eyes, they don't. They're gelled shut. And not in a natural way. My wrists don't move. I'm strapped to a... gurney? A table? I have no idea. Someone walks in.

She is still unconscious. Good. This means the serum works for more than just Ezra. Though, the simulation tank will take time to prepare. We will have to keep injecting her.

I heard her mind a few times at the home. Madame Ester. She's going to put me in a simulation tank. Ezra's in a simulation tank. (Sounds like a sick nursery rhyme. *If you're going in a simulation tank, clap your hands. If your friend is in a simulation tank, clap your hands. If you're super terrified and don't know what a simulation tank is... feel the fear and stop trying to make a stupid rhyme to the tune of 'If You're Happy and You Know it' because that's not a good coping mechanism.*)

I struggle to keep my breathing even. My heart batters the inside of my rib cage. Did the simulation tank break him? She comes closer to me. I know she's standing beside my head. A cold finger trails down my cheek, like Rosemary did before. She was gentle. I bite my tongue as Madam Ester digs her nail into my jaw.

"Wake up," she whispers into my ear. "I know you are not unconscious."

I twitch involuntarily, but keep my eyes closed.

Such a pretty face, Genevieve Legend. So unsure of yourself, but such honest beauty. It is a pity you were cursed. And you are cursed worse than I thought.

It's weird, the way she's thinking. Almost like—

You can hear me, can you not?

I can't help it. I inhale sharply. Ester grabs my chin with her hand.

Just as I thought.

July 19th, 3:19pm, The Woods

Tiago

I breathe in the fresh air. Green is all around us, below and above. Rosemary looks dejected as she returns from the forest, collapsing into the grass. It's been a few hours since Genevieve... talked through Rosemary, who said she was going to the bathroom after we stopped deliriously cackling, but then she took at least forty–five minutes. I was worried about her, but if I've learned anything about Rosemary, it's that she can handle herself. Most of the time. She picks at the grass by her knees. I have to stop myself from saying *It's going to be okay*. Instead, I get up and sit next to her. I put my arm around her shoulders.

"Don't worry," I whisper.

I totally want to smack myself in the face. There's another one of those stupid instant responses. I *am* worried. What worries me even more is when she pulls away.

"What's wrong?" I ask.

"Nothing."

"I don't believe you, Rosemary."

"Trust me. I'm fine."

"Yeah right."

"Just shut up, Santiago," she mutters.

"I thought we were past these arguments."

"I said shut up, okay?" She's getting angrier.

"Did I do something?" I don't know what I *did*.

"No. It's not your fault."

"Will you please tell me?"

She ignores me. I think I understand now why Ezra gets so frustrated when people don't answer his questions. If I were him, I would be the death of me. I never answered more than a question a week. He asked at least three hundred. I was cruel to him. Horribly. Fuck.

Sighing, I look at her. She stares into space. Now, I *do* wish I could read her mind.

"Seriously," I say when the silence gets too awkward. "What are you thinking?"

She groans. "You're getting to be just as bad as..."

"Ezra. I'm getting to be just as bad as Ezra," I whisper. "What's your problem with him anyway?"

Genevieve isn't here to help us now. I think I was relying on her to save me from Rosemary's insensitivity and anger.

"Look, I don't have a problem with him. I just can't stand how you're so obsessed with him! That's my problem, Santiago. I've been trying not to think too much about him and you keep bringing him up!"

That stings. "Oh," I respond coldly.

She still won't say his name.

CHAPTER 18

chapter 18

*J*uly 19th, 10:43pm
Location: The Lab

Ester

After nightfall, I receive a message from the lab assistants. It reads: *They have been released and are tracking the pair.* A smile spreads across my face. At last, the time is close.

July 20th, 3:06am, The Woods

Tiago

A spasm rips through his frail body. I can't even get to him. There's a window in between us. I don't think he can hear me. I don't think he even knows I'm here.

So this is what it's like. This is what it's like to be completely powerless. There's nothing I can do. No matter what I try, he won't wake up. He's alive. But barely. My gift can't help him. *I* can't help him.

Putting my palms on the glass, I want nothing more than for it to shatter. And remarkably, it does. I'm hurling myself through the empty window frame when someone shakes my shoulders.

"Tiago? Tiago. Tiago!" Rosemary's the one who's shaking me.

"Stop. Stop, I'm awake," I whisper, not quite believing that I am.

She lies back down. The grass is shining with dew.

"You were screaming," she says quietly, and somewhat bitterly, though I don't see why. "Again."

I don't know how much longer I can live with dreams like this. I just can't help feeling that it's real, even if it's not. The stars are real. More real than dreams. I didn't know that many could possibly exist.

"I know they're hurting him, Rosemary," I say quietly.

She turns onto her side to face me.

"It's only been seven or eight days. What could they possibly do in seven days?" she says, trying to reassure herself, I think. Though, I could be wrong. I meet her eyes. I don't find any panic or worry there. Just the reflection of the moon and a hint of uncertainty.

"Aren't you afraid you could lose him?"

"Yes." But she says it so softly that I could've imagined it.

She rolls away from me. I should have known better than to ask that question. Genevieve would have at least give me a sympathetic look.

Soon, Rosemary's steady breath tells me she's asleep. I don't know if I want to sleep even though I haven't slept much this week. I watch the stars, thinking about the everything and the nothing that was inside me. Suddenly, I remember the notebook I took from Ezra's room. It's the only thing in the laptop pocket of my backpack now. I sit up and dig through my bag. The small journal is smooth in my hands. Opening it feels wrong, like an invasion of privacy. I decide to read just one page. The page I open to is blank. So is the one before it. And the one after. I'm about to close it when I see that a page in the middle is folded down. I flip to it. My god, why is his handwriting so messy? Does he know that erasers exist?

I fall.

This nigHtmare IsN't what i thinK.

I'm dreaMing. listen.

nothIng will make a souNd.

listen. The siLence is so full Of promises to be made and things neVer said bEfore.

The poem doesn't make *any* sense. It looks strange. I read it again, looking at it more closely. I'm lucky the moon is so bright. I recognize the strangeness. My eyes widen. It looks like the computer passwords. Does that... mean the random capital letters might not have been random? I need a pen.

I reach over and shake Rosemary's shoulder. "I think I figured something out."

She stirs.

"Do you have something I can write with?" I ask.

She sits up. "What did you figure out?" she answers groggily.

I ignore her question. "Get me a pen first. I'm not sure if it's anything."

She digs through her bag but doesn't find anything. Then she unzips the front pocket, reaches in, and produces a grimy, blue mechanical pencil. "Will this work?"

I nod and take it. She sits beside me, squinting at the poem.

Scowling, she grumbles, "Why is his handwriting so messy?"

"Exactly what I thought." I laugh.

She giggles begrudgingly before sobering up. "It looks like the passwords."

(It's nice to laugh with her. She has a laugh so unlike her personality, reckless almost, when in real life, she's normally pretty... rule abiding.) And also. *How* did she figure that out so fast?

"That's exactly what I thought too." I glance at her. "What if the capitals spell something?"

Rosemary's jaw drops.

"Do you remember the passwords?" I ask skeptically.

She acts like she doesn't hear me.

"Let's try it out on this one to see if it works."

"Okay." On the opposite page, I write the letters.

ITHINKIM

"Go faster!" she almost growls. I look up at her, eyes wide. She doesn't acknowledge me. "What does he think he is?"

"It's hard to tell which ones are capitalized, okay?" I grumble.

I continue.

ITHINKIMIMNLSOVSE

"Huh? He thinks he's IMNLSOVSE? That's not any word. Or words. Tiago, I think that's wrong."

I rake my hand through my hair, frowning at my not words. "Yeah."

"Let me try," Rosemary says, reaching for the journal.

I pass it to her.

She crosses out my attempt. (Ouch. I thought it was *decent,* at the very least.) Tapping the pencil on her chin, she reads it twice before writing.

I THINK IM IN

"See? That M has a little tail on it." She doesn't look up. "That's not a capital."

"Okay, *okay.*" I shake my head.

Rosemary inhales sharply.

"What?" I look at what she's written.

I THINK IM IN LOVE

With who? I take the book, turning the pages. There's nothing else. Our eyes meet. I close the journal. Rosemary laughs in a dejected, pitiful kind of way.

"Only Ezra," she says, bitter and fond and a little lost. "Only Ezra would write a single poem in the middle of a journal, telling the world he's in love, but not telling us who he's in love *with*."

Rosemary

I'm too riled up to go back to sleep now. Tiago and I sit beside each other, under the open, inky sky.

"Who do you think he was in love with?" I ask after a while.

"Who *is* he in love with, Rosemary. He's not dead," he says, mindlessly flipping the book's pages, scrutinizing them like there might be some other secret hidden within the empty expanse of white.

I shake my head, a little too forcefully. "Right. He always survives?" It comes out like a question. I don't mean to sound so pessimistic. I want to find him. I really do. But what if that means losing Tiago and Genevieve? And now, the idea that I was manipulating him is stuck in my head. It's all my fault. All of this is my—Tiago's voice brings me back to reality.

"Rosemary, do you remember the password—" He stops, eyes darting around the clearing. He leans forward. Listening.

"What's that?" he whispers, eyes glinting in the darkness.

I strain to pick up whatever noise he hears, squinting into the trees. Twigs snap somewhere behind us. Tiago jumps up. So do I. We stumble for a moment, my heart racing as we back up slowly, into the trees. The noise grows closer, faster, louder. It's harder to see in the dense forest. Tiago's eyes are wide, glinting in the night. My breath is fast in my throat. A tree creaks. Startled, I jump, letting out a startled gasp. He brings his finger to his lips. The noise stops. Like it's listening to us listening to it.

Then, Tiago takes off sprinting. I follow. So does the noise-maker. Something squawks and it echoes. Terrified, I look over my shoulder, trying to see our pursuer. I can't make it out in the shadows. All I know now is that there's more than one. An army of inhuman footsteps.

"Tiago!" I scream. "Do something!"

Nothing happens. He doesn't reply. The footsteps and horrendous bird-like trills crash after us. I almost run into a tree. Then I stumble over a fallen log, almost bailing face first onto the forest floor. I yelp as my palms hit the ground. Tiago's so far ahead. He slows down and looks over his shoulder, his expression a mixture of confusion and fear.

"Keep going!" I shriek, pushing myself up.

I don't need to tell him twice. The things, whatever they are, are close. I feel breath on my neck. I swerve to the right, into a patch of dense trees.

"Rosemary?"

His voice is muffled. I veer towards it. He's running, beside me, except there's a thicket between us. I jump into the brambles. The branches keep snagging my clothes, but I fight through them, the thorns leaving stinging cuts along my skin. When I trip out, I'm a bit behind Tiago. The trees open up. He stops abruptly. I nearly crash into him. He almost clotheslines me with his arm.

"Oh shit," he mutters under his breath.

July 20th, 3:18am, The Lab

Genevieve

Now, there's just a ringing. The complete absence of sound. It's like my mind is trying to make up for the silence with the buzz. My breath hitches in my throat. Ester knows about me. About the mind reading. She knows I talked to Tiago. She knows that they're coming here. What have I done? Wait, Ester *already* knew we were coming here. I just wish... that I wasn't tied up.

Someone sneezes. It's such a faint sound, but it's a sound. It's a person. So I'm not alone. Completely. My eyes open this time, but my eyelids are clammy.

All of me is clammy. There's a deep, unsettling pulse in my jaw. And a burning pinprick. More pain filled needles? Or anesthetic. Possibly both. I hate not being able to remember things.

I almost feel like I could float away. Just cease to exist. That's pretty much what I did in school (before the Lucy thing) and at The Home. I want to be invisible. I reach out, looking for anyone's mind. There aren't any thoughts. It must be this room. Somehow, Ester's managed to block the mind voices from entering. I feel like I've seen too many white ceilings in the past... fragment of time. Too many hours have been spent in pain or asleep to know how long I've been here. But I can guess.

Somehow, it's reassuring to think that it's been merely minutes. Maybe it's a dream. Maybe this is *someone else's* dream. The restraints bite into my wrists and ankles. It's not actually that reassuring. I hope this is almost over.

Actually. No. I'm done with this. I hate waiting around.

"Okay, people!" I yell into the silence. "I'm done!"

Nothing happens for a long moment. Just my voice, echoing through the vastness. I jerk my wrists around. They slam into metal, twinging with pain. The noise bounces around the room. I hiss through my teeth.

I have to get out of here. To warn Rosemary and Tiago.

July 20th, 3:18am, The Woods

Rosemary

I peer down, over Tiago's arm. We've ended up on a rocky overhang. Pebbles skitter over the edge from our abrupt stop. Holding my breath, and trying to slow my raging heart, I back up carefully, and turn around. Tiago follows in suit, and closes his eyes. He's trying to use his gift to stop them. Whatever was chasing us. A couple of the pebbles on the ground rise and tremble midair. Like they're struggling. I, on the other hand, am completely powerless. Our pursuers start to catch up. I can see what they are now. Horrible. They're so... horrible. The creatures form a semicircle around us, hissing through thick beaks. Their bodies are like ostriches, but their legs are scaly and muscular. Fangs protrude out of their mouths, glistening in the sun. My mind is blank. I'm going to throw up. This can't be real. If it is... we're going to die. We're going to fucking die.

Tiago wheezes and my head jerks over to see him fall on his hands and knees, like he just got punched in the stomach. My heart dives off the overhang behind us. His gift isn't working. Why isn't it working? We're going to die. Fucking hell.

"I can't. They're... they must be—" He shakes his head, his face contorted in pain, and whispers, "You have to figure out what to do."

I collapse down beside him, trying to haul him up. Those awful *things* slowly get closer to us.

"Come on!" I yell, crying all of a sudden, his arm in my grasp. "I can't either!"

I feel his pain. I try to heal it. The creatures are so close now. Tiago's pain won't go away. Seven. Seven monsters.

What created them? There's no way they're real. This can't be real. There's no *real animals that look like this.* One of them snaps its demented, fanged beak at me. I can feel the pain all around me; a subtle throbbing in their bodies. The monster things are radiating it, and it invades my body, hurting like electric shocks. For some reason, I find myself focusing on the pulsing ache expanding instead of shrinking. Growing the pain instead of making it smaller. It's a radiating heat that burns the air around me without touching me. (What am I doing?) (I'm... really scared.) The creature closest to me starts to twitch. A few collapse. One flails off the cliff. The others shriek and run, crazed, back into the trees.

The ones that are still here start to bubble. Their feathered skin looks like boiling water on the surface of a pot. I don't know how to react. I'm frozen as they transform. Because that's what they're doing. They're changing into something else.

People. They're turning into people. And now, the bodies of four humans lay in front of me. I can't tell who they are. But I killed them. A supernova explodes in my chest. The inside of me is collapsing, being eaten by some massive force. I'm rooted to the ground. These people in front of me were people I knew. People that were in group twelve. Eevie, Julia, Maddox, Carson... they were people I knew. This can't be real. This can't be real and I'm dreaming some sick kind of fucking messed up nightmare.

I start to shake. I cover my mouth, crying again. I killed them. They were people I knew. I fall to my knees, sobbing and dry heaving and coming undone. Who did this to them? How? Julia was ten. Eevie was twelve. They were children. Carson and Maddox were brothers. Twins. Fifteen years old. And I killed them. Their eyes are glossy, blank, staring at nothing. But I feel like they're staring at me. They're staring and staring and staring. That's all they'll ever do. They'll never blink again. I retch. Can't look away. They're dead. Dead, dead, dead—

Tiago crawls over to each body. I barely notice him as he gently closes their eyes. I can't move. I still feel them staring at me. I killed them.

"What happened to them?" he whispers, horrified as he pauses over one of the... bodies.

"I–I killed them."

I can't control my emotions. Acid is crawling up my throat, scalding me from the inside. Tiago sits beside me, pulling me into him. His touch is cold.

"No. You didn't kill them. I think they were already dead," he says into my hair.

I laugh bitterly. Tears stream down my face. They're dead.

"It's okay," he chants. "It's going to be okay. It's okay."

"I'm supposed to help," I whisper. I *heal* people. "Not make the pain worse."

"You didn't have much of a choice." He looks over the forest below us.

I feel his jaw drop. I follow his gaze. There it is. (I killed them.)

"Rosemary! We found it!" he says, suddenly elated. (And obviously forgetting about me and them. Them. They're dead.)

Up, on a hilltop across from us, is the "abandoned" observatory. Anxiety swamps me, mixing with the pain behind my eyes. I'm still shaking. I killed people. Children. I want to find Ezra. I want to tell him everything. But I also want Tiago. I'm supposed to be happy. We're about to find my best friend. And my new friend, Genevieve. But seeing Santiago so excited just fills me with intense jealousy. I'm stuck in a torrential downpour of hate and pain and love and fear and oh–it–hurts–it–hurts–it–hurts, like a branding iron. It's destroying my insides. Why, why, why did this have to get so messy? So confusing? So *broken*? Tiago stands up, grinning like a fool. I take his hand and he helps me up. I should be happy, like Tiago is. But finding Ezra won't make me any happier. My legs almost give out at the realization. I killed people. I'm unravelling.

I step in front of Santiago. He looks down at me, bewildered. "Tiago. We don't have to find him. We could run away. Never come back. Leave all this behind. Please. I–I ..." I sound frantic. I sound like I've lost my mind. And I can't make myself stop.

He looks confused. I take his other hand.

"Please."

I'm pathetic. He's about to say something. I don't want to hear it. So, I do the only thing I can think of, the thing I've wanted to do for so long. I wrap my arms around his neck and kiss him. It's an infinite moment. Everything is still, except my heart, beating through my lips.

Until he pulls away. I've screwed up. I know I have. I knew before I did anything. I killed people. I haven't slept in days. I'm so. Lost.

There's regret in his eyes. He feels bad. I try to kiss him again. (Because why stop at rock bottom? I brought a shovel so I can go even fucking lower.)

"Rosemary," he says gently. "Rosemary I... can't."

"Is something wrong?" I ask, distressed. (Everything is wrong.)

"No. No... it's just ..." He takes a deep breath. "I think I love him."

Tiago

The words spill from my mouth like a breaking dam. I wasn't planning on saying that... but it's true.

It's taken me way too long to realize, to finally accept it. A lifetime of pretending. I can't do that anymore, that's not for me. I love him. I love him more than anything.

I understand now. I get it. Rosemary's face goes from confusion, to sadness, to hard anger in a matter of seconds. She tears her arms from my shoulders.

Rosemary

This hurts even worse than if he just didn't like me. I *knew* he didn't like me. But this... oh god. A tiny, malicious, voice yells *I told you so! I knew he was gay from the start! The sweater, the sweater, the sweaterrrrr*—then, I stomp on the voice.

"Oh god, Tiago," I snarl coldly. "*Not* you *too*."

After everything we've been through together, he fell for Ezra. Ezra isn't even here. I don't understand. I turn my back to him and walk towards the woods. I don't know where I'm going. Only that I'm leaving. I've screwed up time and time again. I've broken myself. I'm done. I'm finished. I just... have to go.

"Rosemary."

I won't look at him, because I might be tempted to forgive him. Genevieve had said *I just... I think he might be...* Well, I know the end of the sentence now. So they weren't a couple. And Santiago is in love with Ezra. Great. Just great. If he was in love with anyone but *Ezra*, I'd be so happy for him. Ezra?

"Rosemary, please."

Why is he pleading? I stop. Like I thought, when I see the struggle in his eyes, I feel awful. I felt awful this whole time. The awfulness swamps me, and leaves me floundering. I'm drowning.

"Rosemary, please. I need you. I need your help."

His eyebrows are scrunched together. He looks miserable. Hearing the words *I need you* crumbles my resolve. Even if he does love my dying friend, I'll help him. I have to. Where else would I go?

"Okay," I say as softly as I can. "I'll help you. I'm sorry."

A wave of relief crashes over his face. He smiles. I can see his pity behind his gaze, but I ignore it. I don't need his pity. I can be a strong, independent woman. I try to smile. It ends up looking like what's probably more of an ugly grimace. I can't help thinking how Ezra was stupidly somehow slightly attractive with a grimace. I probably look like some demented, dumb–ass gargoyle.

"I need a couple minutes," I say, sitting down without looking at him. I hear him walk back to the point. Anger burns inside of me. And self–loathing. And fear. And that horrible, horrible feeling, left over from breaking. It's like hand sanitizer in my throat and broken glass in my lungs. I have to help him. Clouds are covering the sunrise. Mist descends. Like yesterday. The dew makes my dirty sweater damp. Everything is damp now. I breathe in, inhaling the cool (damp) air. (The glass clatters around inside me. It hurts.)

Exhaling, I make a deal with myself. I'm going to forget my anger. And all my feelings for Santiago.

God, that's going to be hard.

July 20th, 3:19am, The Lab

Genevieve

A door opens behind me as I'm struggling. But I stop immediately. They might make a mistake if they think I'm sedated. I clench my eyes shut. A flood of mind voices crashes into my ears before being cut off again as the door closes. The person in the room isn't Ester. Another lab assistant. This one is nervous.

Is she sedated?

For her sake, I'll pretend to be. I focus on evening out my breath, to make it seem like I'm asleep. When the woman sees this, she relaxes.

Good. I hate to be the one to do this.

Do *what*? I can't handle it. Tears leak out of my closed eyes. I'm full of pent up anxiety. Fear and anger and fight are trapped in my veins and my teeth chatter as she injects something into my arm. It pinches and then burns through my body like wildfire. This isn't fucking fair. Just as I get friends who actually care about me, who wouldn't throw me under the bus if they messed up, these people are trying to take it from me. Like they did with my parents.

My parents. I lost them. They're alone, grieving their only daughter because we lost each other. We could have run away. (No we couldn't. There wasn't time.) It was the darkest part of my life, and I did it alone. Yes, I want to fight for myself, but I also want people to fight for me. I want someone to care for me so I don't have to fend for myself. *I don't want to be alone like this.* And now this lady, pushing some kind of medication or tracker or *something* into my blood. She's taking away my freedoms, my choices, and throwing them carelessly to the floor while pretending to *feel sorry* for me.

How dare she? I grind my teeth together and dig my nails into my palms. It's cold and I'm alone again. *I'm alone again.* At some point, she finished doing her job and walked out of the room, leaving me with the ghosts of my past. My parents had to let those guards take me away. They'd come after me, if I had asked. My parents didn't leave me. This doesn't have to be the end. It's just a gross part in a life full of adventures and stories and poetry and happiness. Of course I was lonely. I just let myself disappear. I won't do that again.

I struggle against the restraints as whatever the fuck that woman injected into me scalds my insides. I'm worth something. More than something. I *am* worth fighting for. I scream in effort. I am worth fighting for. *I. Am. Worth. Fighting for.* My back arches and my hands curl into fists. Blood trickles down my wrists, the smell of iron wafting around me. They won't break me again. I have people to care about. I have a future to look forward to. I have *hope.*

And then, the restraints are no longer holding me.

July 20th, 4:00am, The Lab

Tiago

I thought we were friends. Good friends, but just friends. I thought *they* were friends. Rosemary and Ezra. But she wanted to leave him. To forget about him. How could she want to give up when we're so close? And she wanted to leave Genevieve too? It seemed like they were close. I just...don't understand.

Rosemary's been silent the whole time we've been walking. The observatory is on the crest of the next hill. It's so foggy. And yet there it is. The road we could've followed if we hadn't been kicked out of that cab. We could've been here days ago. It could've been so easy.

"Rosemary," I say as she starts along the crunchy gravel of the road.

She's exhausted, her shoulder sloping, her feet dragging. We're both filthy and hungry.

"What?" she asks wearily.

I don't know what I was going to say.

"It's going to be okay."

I actually can't stop saying that. What the fuck? It might *not* be okay. I know she isn't okay. I don't think I'm okay. Genevieve might not be okay. Ezra's almost definitely not okay. I don't think anything is okay. So why does it keep coming out of my mouth? She just shakes her head and walks down the road. Everything's so quiet here. Rosemary looks back.

"Come on, Santiago."

I jog to catch up. Our bags are gone. It's easier to run without a backpack anyway.

July 20th, 3:50pm, The Lab

Ester

Birdie Lee is the most dangerous twelve year old I have ever known. She made our ordinary wasps into powerful weapons. She turned seven humans into monsters. We have used her to create abominations and beasts. All she needs is to be afraid. Our theory is that once she is afraid, any living things or objects in the room will take on the shape of the worst thing it can be at that time. When we injected the serum last time, the worst thing the annoying brats of group twelve could be were ostriches with teeth and huge reptilian legs. She is always unconscious when she has the serum in her system.

We had previously tried it with a rooster, a rat, and a goat. She somehow combined all of the creatures and they multiplied. We do not understand her gift very well, and it is for the best that we keep her locked away. Her most recent creations were the ones I sent after Rosemary and Santiago.

Of course, we add cameras afterwards to the creatures she creates. I have just received an alert from our security system, that the meddlesome pair have come into the one mile radius of the lab. Finally.

Genevieve

I don't know what just happened. Sitting up, I run my hands through my hair. The injection is still prickling, but no longer ravaging through my body.

I was holding onto the past. It's time to let go. I don't need to hide from the future. I don't need to stay invisible. I don't need to pretend. There *will* be people to love me, and to find them, I need to live fully. I need to care about myself. When I breathe in, I feel lighter. It's nice. A burden lifted. A shaky smile spreads across my face. I look at my wrists, my ankles. They're weak, feeling like bird bones instead of human ones. And they've got nasty cuts on them. I don't know how I got out of the shackles. I'm wearing a mint coloured hospital gown. My bare feet touch the hard floor. I push myself off the table. It looks like an iron door with shackles attached. Shackles that couldn't hold me. I'm worth fighting for.

Blinking, I look around this room. It's like the last one, just bigger. The size of my school's gym. With a single door. And a single table in the middle. And the remnants of my other life. My new one starts here. Reborn with purpose. Maybe even confidence.

"Hey!" someone shouts as the mind voices surge into my head.

I turn to see about five people in hazmat suits at the open door. The one at the front has a tranquilizer gun. Actually, they each have one. And they're pointing them at me. I blink. They're all afraid...

"Come here," the man at the front beckons with his empty hand, "and we can do this peacefully. We're just gonna sedate you. You must be confused. You're not supposed to be awake."

I'm not confused. I know *exactly* what's going on. (If they knew me, they'd know I'm actually pretty smart. But they don't know me. Which is okay.) I don't respond, but start walking towards them.

"Stop right there!" he orders, panic creeping into his voice.

"I don't want to be sedated. Just let me go," I answer quietly. "I swear I won't hurt anyone. I don't want to."

His mind: *Oh I really wish I didn't have to do this...*

My mind: *Then why are you* here?

All these people, wishing they didn't have to do what they're about to do really makes me question the morals of this place. I sigh. If I hadn't been watching closely, I wouldn't have noticed the slight flick of the leader's head. Not that it would really matter. No one could have reacted that fast. The barrage of five, ten, fifteen darts fly towards me. All I can do is close my eyes and wait for them to hit me. Twenty flaming pinpricks of sedation drugs. I suck in a breath. And the pain doesn't come.

I dare to peek at the room. In front of me are five stunned guards.

Behind me, are twenty darts sticking into the wall.

CHAPTER 19

chapter 19

July 20th, 4:03pm
Location: The Lab

Rosemary

The observatory is polished, but it has an abandoned air to it. Like it's haunted. I shiver. What's inside? I have no idea. Santiago stands behind me. There's a black van parked beside a bay door. Someone must be here. The whole world is grey, the mist tingling against my face and hands. Miserable.

"How do we get in?" I whisper.

If we open the bay door, that'll pretty much alert everyone who's inside as to where we are. (Not that there's a way to open it from the outside.)

"I could attempt to erase the door..." Santiago replies.

He's not really present. I'm sure he's worrying. About everything.

"Um..." I'm skeptical. "Are you sure?"

"No," he says simply.

Okay, he's thinking about something else. That something probably being Ezra. I wonder how much he thinks about Ezra. That isn't important, though. But it kind of is. Is it? Yes. I must cause myself more pain.

"How often do you think about him?"

He looks at me, a nearly invisible smile dancing across his mouth. "You think this is important right now?"

I roll my eyes. "Not really, I guess."

"Yeah, well, a lot."

"A lot what?"

"I think about him a lot."

"Oh."

There's the answer to my question. (*Why* was that so important?) I force myself not to think about anything regarding Santiago. Moving on to more pressing matters... we have to get inside without getting caught and also get Ezra out and also we don't know what kind of state he's in and then we also have to get away from here quickly. Not to mention Genevieve. We have no plan (aside from possibly making part of the bay door disappear). We're exhausted, hungry, dirty, tired, thirsty... exhausted. Yeah, we should've thought this through, at least a little bit.

I turn to face him. "Santiago."

He doesn't even blink.

"Santiago." I wave in front of his eyes. "Hello?"

What is he *doing*? Any more frustration will make me explode. I'm about to yank on his arm or say something else when he grabs my wrist, walking briskly towards the bay doors. Oh my fucking god. I don't want him holding my hand. He's dragging me after him like a tiny child. This is so embarrassing. I yank myself free. He doesn't even notice.

I stop and cross my arms. With this pout, I probably look about three years old. I don't care. He puts his palms on the huge metal door. At first, nothing happens. I'm about to tell him that we should find another way in, when the metal around his hands starts to turn... fuzzy looking. It chatters like TV static, making my eyes focus weirdly. Through the buzzy wavering, a piece of the metal starts to disappear. The section of the door his hands rest on dissipates into the air. I shake my head, awed as Tiago steps away from the hole, inspecting his work. The edges of the gap are still visually wavering. Santiago laughs quietly.

"I just did that," he whispers, saddened and wistful at the same time.

A smile tugs at the corners of my lips. He ducks through the hole and waits for me as I step inside a wide, echoing loading dock.

"Yep. You did," I reply, even though he's done way more impressive things before. Then I realize we've reached the end of our plan. My momentary smile disappears.

"Santiago, what do we do now?"

All momentary confidence disappears as well.

He runs his hand through his hair, looking around the empty room. (My heart speeds up. I wish it wouldn't.)

"We... um, go down that hallway." He randomly points to the biggest hall to the left.

"Why is it so empty?" I ask as we jog to his chosen passage. Our footsteps echo. He stops in the entrance, like he's about to say something, but he doesn't. He continues to walk, shaking his head. The hall is white. It smells like cleaning products. Like lavender with sinister undertones. I shudder, trying not to think of what other smells this place is trying to hide.

Ester

As I look down from the observation balcony, where all my computers are, I think it is finally working on Ezra. The pain−induced simulations my machine creates make sure he is in constant discomfort. Or in agony. I cannot always tell. He looks so peaceful inside that tall, wide tube, floating in the blue−ish gel that gives him the minimum nutrients he needs to survive. If I strain my eyes, I can see the quick rise and fall of his chest. The breaths are sharp and uneven, moving his oxygen tube slowly through the gel.

The grey light of today streams through the planetarium dome that we replaced with glass, onto his seemingly serene face, causing pretty shadows that dance and tremble. They catch on his jutting cheekbones and the sharp angles of his face. I think I recall his face looking softer before all of these experiments and cures, but I may be wrong.

All the needles and sensors in his arms and legs do ruin the effect of calm, but that is how my creation has access to his thoughts, senses, and pain receptors, and they are, therefore, absolutely necessary. Sometimes, he will twitch, his face contorting slightly. How satisfying... how sick. That is how he looks. Sick. His face is hollow. His hair is dull, even though it is wet. His head sways ever so gently, ever so limply. There is no way he always looked like this. I cannot tell if it is the unusual light that is making his skin seem so ashen. I clench my jaw. I will not feel pity. *This will fix him.*

I will fix him, whatever it takes.

I turn away from Ezra to look at the many computer screens on the back wall. The machine has a direct feed to the lab computers through the metal caps on the top and bottom of the tube. What the artificial intelligence comes up with is deliciously horrific, making up for whatever worry his appearance caused me before. The pain comes as the machine determines.

His gift shall be gone after living in his fears for eighteen hours a day, will it not? Yes. Indeed it will.

"Madam Ester?" a tentative voice calls.

"What do you want?"

"First, I'd like to inform you that this *is not* my fault—"

I sigh. "The invisible girl has escaped. Am I right?"

The assistant looks at me in shock. "Um... why, yes."

"Well, do not fret. Her friends are on their way here at the moment. She will not be leaving without them."

He gives me a curt nod and descends the stairs.

Tiago

Rosemary's upset. I feel bad for hurting her. Although, I don't know if it could have been avoided, no matter what I said or did. Unless I had lied. And that just feels wrong.

Footsteps approach. Rosemary and I make frantic eye contact and dart into a room, closing the door behind us, as quietly as possible. The steps get louder, then fade away. She opens the door and peers out. I'm about to follow when I see a dark grey lump in the middle of the floor.

"Wait," I whisper, walking over and bending down beside the grey thing.

The thing is a sweater. I frown, picking it up. Something balled up inside the sweater, because that's what it is, clatters to the ground. Glasses. And it's *my* sweater. It has dark stains on the cuffs. Ezra's here. My hands start to tremble. Now, all I have to hope is that he's still alive. I bring the sweater to my face, using it to block the rush of tears that threaten to fall. It smells like smoke... and cloves. Him.

I wish I could take it, but I fold it, standing and placing it on the bed. But wait. I *can* take it. It's mine, so it fits me. I put it on over my other sweater. I swallow thickly. Hopefully, it won't be the only thing I have to remember him by. Rosemary stoops down, picking up Ezra's glasses. She hands them to me and I shove them in my pocket, turning to go.

"Santiago," Rosemary says. "What does that say?"

I turn around. She's pointing at the floor. There are black smudges, like someone tried to clean permanent marker off the linoleum and gave up halfway through. I kneel down, squinting. My eyes go wide.

"It's Ezra's writing."

She shuts the door again, and crouches beside me.

darling Wishes cAnnot save You nowDarling they will nOt remember When you've falleNbut will someone follow me all the way down?

It's all messy, but the last line is inexplicably neater. Like someone else wrote it.

Rosemary jumps up. "Those two lines, starting with darling, were passwords we didn't use." She looks confused. "Ezra knew Madame Ester's passwords. But he wrote them here? Why–"

"Let's go," I say abruptly, heart pounding. "We can figure it out when we find Ezra."

We have to find him. The sooner the better. I yank the door open. The hall is still empty. I see two more doors. One's at the end and the other is on the right side. I look at Rosemary.

"One on the right?" she asks.

I nod, my lungs threatening to burst out of my mouth.

Ester

Finally, the security camera in Ezra's room alerts me. Rosemary and Santiago, the dynamic duo, are almost here in the main lab. Rosemary Mae–Anderson will be my second test subject and Santiago Grey will be my... leverage against Ezra. I think they both have too much adrenaline pumping to be suspicious about the ease of their break in. I was impressed, though, when Santiago dispersed that part of the bay door.

The stairs down to the main floor where Ezra is are so steep. My knees ache too much. I will stay up here, on the observation balcony. According to the hallway cameras, Santiago is almost in the stairwell. I take a deep breath. My life's work is about to come to fruition.

Rosemary

There are no guards in the hallway, or anybody at all. Ezra was here, in that room. But he's not there anymore. Santiago slowly pushes open the door on the right. If anyone were near us, I'd definitely give us away. I'm sure Santiago can hear my heartbeat. It's all *I* can hear. Behind the door is a staircase. Flickering lights give the place an eerie yellowish glow, making the whole place feel infected.

"Should we try the other room?"

I jump, startled by his voice.

"Sorry." He laughs without any humor. "Let's check the other room."

I let out a shuddering breath. I can feel something climbing up my throat. And now that I think about it, I've felt off. Ever since the first day with the teeth. Maybe even before that. There's this dark, sticky feeling humming behind my eyes, begging to be noticed. I shudder as he shuts the stairwell door quietly. We creep across the hall into a different room. It's small and empty, with a large window looking into a lab. A drain sits innocently in the center of the floor. Santiago sharply rakes his hand through his hair. I wonder, again, how many times he does that each day. He walks over to the door leading into what looks like an observation lab. Surprisingly, it's unlocked. Out of instinct, I look behind me before I follow.

Then someone crashes into me. I gasp and start to panic, but Genevieve appears. Out of the air. Relief swamps me. I wrap my arms around her without much thought. She buries her face in my shoulder. Hot tears stream down my face. I hide my face in her hair. She's okay. She's okay.

"I'm so," she says into my sweater, "so sorry I spoke through you. I swear it wasn't supposed to go like that."

It takes me a second to form words. "It's–it's okay. I'm okay. Are you okay?"

She lets go of me, her eyes a bit wet. I get a good look at her. She's wearing a hospital gown that's way too big. I think she's thinner than before. But somehow bigger too. She looks more alive.

"Yeah," she says, wiping her nose with the back of her hand. "Yeah, I'm fine."

"Rosemary?" Santiago whisper–shouts from the other doorway. "Are you coming?"

I turn around to face him. Genevieve peeks out from behind me. A smile breaks across his worried face. He rushes towards her, sweeping her into a tight hug.

"Hey, Tiago," she says, her voice muffled. I can tell she's beaming. But I'm not jealous.

He lets her go, but holds her shoulders, looking her up and down.

"I'm fine," she says quietly.

Santiago swallows, his happiness turned inside out to reveal his distress. "You don't look very fine. But I trust you," he says as he lets her go and turns back to the observational lab.

Genevieve

She looks so... hurt and she's only been here, what? One and a half, two days? There's no way Ezra's okay. No way.

I feel awful for him. Santiago is doing what he does. Worries on the inside and acts like he's fine on the outside. Except he isn't fine. At all.

Rosemary's mind is doing much better. She's glad I'm back. My cheeks heat up. She keeps looking at me. I keep looking at the ground.

"You don't have any shoes," she says softly.

We stop in the doorway. Santiago's poking around, but turning up nothing of significance. To be honest, I wouldn't be surprised if we found Ezra stuffed into a Rubbermaid bin. This place is... awful. Okay, maybe not messed up in that way, but still. He's alive, at least. I can hear his mind, screaming underneath everything else.

"No. They took all my stuff." I pause. "Or your stuff in the case of the shoes. I really am sorry about that. And I'm sorry that you thought I was lying to you."

"Aah." She looks at me sheepishly. "Yeahhh, I'm sorry for avoiding you. I. Knew I was wrong pretty soon after but. I guess I was scared. Not that it's a good excuse. It wasn't fair of me. I treated you so badly and you definitely don't deserve that."

"No, I didn't. But I forgive you, this time. People are stupid." That earns a precious, but breakable smile from her.

"And," Rosemary adds, "thank you so much for hiking the shoes."

I look sheepishly at the ground. "Hah. Yeah. Anything for—"

Oh shit oh no what is this.

My head snaps over to Tiago as his mind goes out of control. Rosemary's face is red as she follows my gaze.

"Guys?" His voice breaks.

CHAPTER 20

chapter 20

July 20th, 4:25pm
Location: The Lab

Ezra

This
is
falling.
It's
not
that
bad.
He
isn't
here.
As soon
as
the
pain
comes,
he'll
show up.

and so   will.

The agony.

Tiago

There are computer screens all along the left wall. One is lit up, which was my reason for coming in here. Now, I wish I hadn't. It's so horrible. It's Ezra, pale and gaunt, twitching on the linoleum floor. Silent screams rip from his frail body. And I can't breathe. I clench my jaw, unable to look away, but wanting nothing more than to do so.

Genevieve is already by my side, her expression stony. Rosemary joins us. Her eyes get wider and wider. A muscle twitches in her jaw. I finally tear my watery eyes away, then grab Rosemary's hand and pull her out of the lab.

"What was wrong with him?" she asks in a low, trembling voice.

I shake my head, wishing I hadn't looked. I'm still gripping her hand. She lets go and I drop it, feeling bad.

"That happened to me too," Genevieve mutters. "They use some kind of injection to make you feel like you shouldn't be alive."

Rosemary's eyes go so wide she looks like a cartoon character. Not quite human. "They did that to you?" she whispers, horrified.

I stare hard, thinking at Genevieve. *We need to get moving-—I can't do this any more. Please. Let's go.*

She winces, like she just heard something explode, then nods to Rosemary.

"Yeah. They did." She glares at me.

"Come on," I insist, starting towards the door.

"Up?" Her eyes are still huge. I'm glad she dropped her argument or whatever it was with Genevieve. A little twinge of guilt hits me, because I remember Genevieve can hear me. *Sorry, Genevieve. It's nothing personal.*

She snorts.

"That's the only other place to go. So yes. Up." I'm on edge, but I instantly regret being so sarcastic to Rosemary. She doesn't even have to be here. Instead of looking at her pained expression, I'm about to yank open the door to the stairs, not caring whether anyone hears us or not. But then Genevieve just walks *right through the wall.*

Rosemary's eyebrows bunch together, her eyes now the size of dinner plates. (Not actually, but it's really weird to look at.) She stutters, looking for words, when Genevieve opens the door from the inside. Since I'm still holding the handle, I nearly fly right into her.

"Are you coming or not?" Genevieve demands in a half friendly, half annoyed way.

"Um... yeah?" Rosemary sounds like she might cry, but she walks, dazed, through the open door.

A little shocked myself, I wait for Rosemary to pass me before letting go of the handle and entering the stairwell. Genevieve shuts the door after me. Her face softens when she sees Rosemary's concerningly huge eyes. She wraps her arm around her shoulders, looking guilty.

"So, I forgot to tell you, but I may be sort of..." She struggles for a word. "Sort of incorporeal. Sometimes. I learned I could do that here."

Rosemary blinks. Then she nods. "Okay... okay that's... impressive. Cool. Okay."

I start up the stairs, with my fair share of confusion, but it's fine. I'll talk to her about her... incorporeal–ness another time. I'm about halfway up the first flight when Rosemary whispers, "Tiago." She brings her finger up to her lips. Genevieve slides her arm off Rosemary's shoulders and looks between us.

Loud, synchronized footfalls are very near the door. I freeze. Rosemary darts under the stairs. Genevieve follows, but she doesn't turn invisible. I wonder why.

And the stomping stops in front of the door.

"What are you waiting for?!" Rosemary hisses, panicked.

I creep down the steps, lunging down the last few and darting under the stairs just as the door bangs open. Rosemary's pressed into my side and I'm leaning awkwardly against the wall, holding my breath. Heavy footsteps clomp up the stairs. My heart rattles and fights to get out of my chest. *We're going to die,* is all I can think, my palms clammy and cold. Apparently Rosemary isn't thinking the same thing, because before I understand what she's doing, she peers out around the bottom of the stairwell.

Rosemary

I don't think the guards saw me. They *were* up there, but Santiago made sure they didn't seem me when he yanked me back by the hood of my sweater and nearly choked me to death. Wouldn't that be an untimely demise. Fucking stupid. Now we're sitting with our backs against the wall. His arm is pressed against mine again. I feel like I'm going to burst into flames, like Ezra. Even though I know it's impossible to be with Santiago, there's no way my feelings are going to disappear. I should have guessed he's gay, but I was just too caught up in assumptions. All my lies were for nothing.

He's looking up at where the guards were a moment ago. Genevieve crouches on my other side. It seems like he's just looking at solid concrete, although I'll bet he's actually seeing through to the top of the stairs. He gets up, ducking as he walks out. "We're clear."

He doesn't look at me. I know he expects me to follow him. Blindly. We have no idea where we are or what's ahead. (Or, at least, I don't.) I walk after him. The stairs are steep and I can hardly see the top. I want to leave. I want to go *home*. (But what is home anyways?)

"C'mon Rosemary. Let's finish this," Genevieve says gently.

Sometimes I wonder if she can read my mind. Or if she just always knows the right thing to say. With Tiago in front of us, Genevieve and I walk side by side. She shivers a little bit as the sound of our shoes echo through the concrete shaft. Her steps are silent. I wonder if her feet are freezing, because it's cold in here and stone sometimes feels more like ice than anything else.

I want to stop and give her her shoes back, but Tiago will freak out again. Genevieve's mouth quirks into the smallest hint of a smile I've ever seen. She's trying not to let it show, but her face is betraying her. An odd little laugh starts to come up my throat.

"Rosemary," someone whispers. And the laughter dies a quiet death.

I whip around. No one's there. Just like last time. And the time before. The voice is back. It's oozing its poison through my body. Humming and restless. I've been ignoring it. *Suppressing it... because god knows I can't deal with this—*

And now it doesn't *want* to be ignored. It won't be ignored. It demands my attention.

"What?" Genevieve turns around. "What's wrong?"

My eyes bulge. It's like what happened in the forest. And the day when Ezra killed the monster. I know what's coming.

"Rosemary?" Santiago asks, fear sewn into his voice. "What are you doing?"

I cover my mouth, turning to face them.

"What the...?" Genevieve meets my eyes.

I shake my head violently. A white panel above me opens slowly. The stairs behind me start making noise. Like they're being chipped apart with an axe. Santiago's head snaps up just as the teeth flood out of panels, which are everywhere. A rushing sound picks up, roaring behind me.

Genevieve

What the actual fuck.

There are teeth. Spilling out of the ceiling.

"Don't turn around," Santiago whispers evenly to Rosemary. "Just walk up to me."

The idiot turns around. The stairs are falling, one at a time, crashing down like thunder, onto the floor below. Everything is shaking. My breath catches. Teeth are falling, like a waterfall off the collapsing staircase. (What's next, lightning?) I have *never* experienced something like this before. What is happening?

Rosemary.

There's this voice in her head. Not the normal one. This voice is gravelly. Thick. Malicious. It's like Rosemary's talking to someone who only exists in her mind. Some kind of parasite. I can feel it. My neck starts to twitch. It's like snakes crawling up the inside of my throat.

Rosemary's mind: *I'm coming. I want to be closer to you.*

She starts walking down the steps.

"Rosemary!" That's Santiago.

The voice in Rosemary's mind: *Come. Rosemary, come here. I need Santiago. I need him to follow you.*

Rosemary's mind: *I'm coming.*

And then, Ezra's mind starts screaming. It drowns out the voices of Rosemary in a blood curdling shriek. I don't have time to think about the voice and what it wants with Tiago. Ezra's letting out a haunting, heaving cry that goes on and on and on. He's begging for reprieve.

Ezra's mind: *please stop hurting. me. i'mdone i'mdonei'mdone Ican'tdo. thisanymore pleasepleaseplease...* it fades in and out of the screaming so I can only hear fragments.

Even though it won't help, I cover my ears with my hands. My knees buckle. My head is full of pain. When my knees hit the floor, the teeth should hurt me, but they don't. The teeth go right through me, just like the darts.

Rosemary

I'm about to step off the edge. Santiago grabs my waist as the stair falls. The voice wants him. Even the things in my head don't want me. I'm going insane. I'm losing my mind, and I'm going to throw up. But my stomach is empty. My body heaves, but I swallow, coughing stomach acid onto the stairs.

"What are you doing?!" he practically yells as he tries to run through the teeth.

"There's a voice..." I trail off, realizing that I must sound insane. I am. I'm insane.

"Do you remember Stevie McBride? That girl from a few years ago?" Tiago shouts, incredulous. "She heard a voice because her gift drove her mad!"

I choose to ignore him, but the blood drains from my face. Why didn't I think of that? Stumbling up the stairs with teeth falling is horrible, but we're almost at the top. I slip. The teeth are trying to carry me away. I think

I want them to. I exhale, frustrated as he catches me. Maybe we can fall together. Gripping the railing, we fight forwards. (Well, he's actually the only one fighting. I'm *literally* being dragged into it.)

Genevieve is crouching on the landing, with her hands over her ears. Santiago stops beside her. He's bleeding, from cuts the teeth make. I squint at Genevieve. The teeth are just falling *through* her. Incorporeal right now.

But something is wrong. What can she hear that we can't?

CHAPTER 21

chapter 21

July 20th, 4:59pm
Location: The Lab

Tiago

I'm not letting go of Rosemary, because if I do, she'll walk off the rapidly shortening staircase.

"Genevieve!" I yell.

I have no idea how I'm so calm right now. This is such a shit–show of a rescue mission. Genevieve's eyes open slowly, but I can only see the whites. I shudder, swallowing bile. She takes her hands off her ears, her whole body tense.

"Genevieve, can you—"

She cuts me off in a hoarse whisper. "It's Ezra. I can hear him. Talk to me. I need someone to talk to me."

"What's wrong with him?" My stomach does a nose dive.

Genevieve's face scrunches in what looks like pain. Or suppressed laughter. I shudder.

"Can you even hear me?" I demand, having to yell over the noise.

She nods after an apprehensive moment.

Rosemary surprises me by taking Genevieve's arm and hauling her up. Me, dragging Rosemary, dragging Genevieve. We all stumble at different times. Genevieve's irises return after a few minutes, but her pupils are really small. That can't be a good thing. She's breathing heavily, her steps uneven.

"We're almost there," I say, two stairs from the top.

I make it, pulling Rosemary up. We're about to drag Genevieve over the last stair, but it crashes out from under her. The sound of the falling stair hitting the ground reverberates through the now empty stairwell. Rosemary gasps as Genevieve becomes a dead weight, dangling over the ledge. I leap forward, seizing her other arm. Rosemary's face is drenched with sweat, as she makes eye contact with me. Genevieve is hyperventilating, her legs scrambling in the empty air. I clench my jaw. We both pull as hard as we can. As we haul her over the ledge, she becomes coherent again.

"I'm—so sorry," she wheezes, crawling to her hands and knees.

I crouch in front of her. "What's wrong with Ezra?"

"I... I'm not sure." She looks at the single door in front of us, then at me. "I think we might find out. Soon."

Rosemary is quiet, gazing off of the ledge where the stairs used to be. Our heavy breath fills the air with exhaustion and fear.

"Ready?" I ask them, swallowing any kind of thoughts.

Neither of them responds. Rosemary turns, her chin quivering. Genevieve looks up at the door and struggles to stand up.

"I don't want to go in there." Rosemary looks at the ground.

Teeth fall from her knotted hair. Sweat and dirt leave tracks down her freckled face.

"We're not giving up now." Genevieve's voice is hoarse. "Okay?"

Rosemary is shaking her head, refusing. But then Genevieve grabs her hand.

The three of us stare at the door.

Ezra's in there and he's not okay. Ezra's in there and he's not okay. Ezra's in there and he's not okay.

"Shall we?" I gesture toward the door.

They nod.

Genevieve

Tiago's mind: *Ezraezraezraezraezraezra*

Rosemary's mind: *I don't want to go through that door, but Genevieve is holding my hand? I don't want to be here. I don't want to leave. I don't understand. I'm so confused. I don't want to exist. I don't want to go in that room.*

Ezra's mind: *what'shisname.*(scream) *i'mnot. gonnaloseit.*(scream) *tiagotiagotiago*

My mind: So full of everyone's thoughts that I can't concentrate on my own.

Ester

Mr. Grey was right. I heard their conversation in the stairwell with my hearing aids. Quite handy. Rosemary's gift is driving her insane. Or rather, something is *using* her gift to drive her insane. I was not sure why teeth were falling on the day of evacuation, but it was the perfect distraction.

And now I know where the teeth came from. Our dear friend Rosemary Mae-Anderson has a rogue gift. The teeth are manifestations of her grief, loneliness, frustration, guilt, and humiliation. Each part of the body has a metaphorical meaning. The teeth symbolize these emotions. Stevie was another case like this, though not remotely as bad. She heard voices and ended up dead. Rosemary must have had many, extremely strong feelings surfacing over the last two weeks to cause her gift to become so wildly unpredictable. Those feelings have attracted something—that *thing* inside her head.

Tiago

I move first. Rosemary is ashen as I turn the doorknob and yank. It won't budge. (Not a pull door? Sometimes it's impossible to tell.) I push on the door with all my strength. I'm panicking. Common sense doesn't make sense anymore. Rosemary stands beside me and pushes as well. Genevieve takes a running leap at the door in the space between Rosemary and me, throwing her shoulder into the metal. (I did the same thing when I tried to get out of my room during the lock down. It didn't work.)

The door swings open. (I guess it *does* work sometimes...) We all tumble into a huge, dome shaped room. The door slams shut behind us. I look up from the floor. There are dozens of guards, like the ones at home, surrounding us.

Rosemary's breathing is shaky, fast. My eyes dart around the room, catching fragments of the space. A tall circular tube. Armed guards everywhere. A balcony. With Madame Ester on it.

"Mr. Grey. Miss Mae–Anderson. What a pleasure. And, oh! What a lovely surprise, Miss Legend." Madame Ester's harsh voice rings across the room.

Rosemary freezes. Genevieve glares at Madame Ester with such intense hatred that I have to look away. I scan the guards, counting, sort of. The tube behind them is so strange. It's filled with a weird bluish liquid. There's a body suspended in it. Is she putting corpses in liquid...? That's fucked up.

I step closer. The guards raise their weapons. Guns. Tranquilizers. Means to sedate us and lock us away. I swallow thickly. Wait—no, the corpse is breathing. Twitching, I think. So, not a corpse. I squint. (Do I need glasses?) Is that ...? No. My mind must be playing tricks on me. (Great, I'm going insane too. I'll be insane with glasses.) I step forward again.

My stomach plunges into an endless, icy pool.

Madame Ester laughs coldly. "Correct, Mr. Grey."

It takes me a moment to realize what she's saying. *Correct.* No. *No.*

But it is. It's Ezra. I think I might be sick. (But I can't be sick.) *He* looks sick. The hospital scrubs hug his body. There are needles in his arms, neck, and legs. He's so thin. He looks so... breakable.

"Sedate them!"

The guards move in a synchronized wave.

"Ezra!" I scream.

Ezra

Darkness.

Failure.

Socold.

Pain.

"Ezra!" it's muffled.

What?

"Ezra! Ezra! You need to fight!"

Fight?
How?

"Please! Fight!" Clear, but faint.

Heat.
It's there.
Isn't it?

"Ezra!"

Whoever you are,
Don't be in so much pain for me.
I hear the pain in your voice.

Heat.
There
it is.
I'll fight.
Some for you.
Mostly for him. Because   when he's real...
he   won't hurt me

like he does here.

CHAPTER 22

chapter 22

July 20th, 5:12pm

Location: The Lab

Tiago

I fight. I won't stop until I get to him. I need to get to him. The guards are trying to stop me. Someone hits me with a tranquilizer dart. Cold spreads through my leg. *No.* I won't let them. I need him to fight. I keep screaming. Rosemary's throwing wild punches, half crazed with terror. Beside me, one of the guards falls to the ground like they've been punched for no apparent reason. Another one falls in the same way. It must be Genevieve. She's being invisible.

I need to get to him. *"Ezra!"*

I can't get to him. I'm dizzy. World spinning... someone's got my arm wrenched behind my back. My shoulder feels like it's ripping. *We failed.*

Suddenly, the glass around Ezra shatters. The liquid rushes out onto the floor, creating a thick, blue tinted pool. Everyone freezes. Did I do that? No, I don't think so. It was him. For a moment, he hovers in mid–air, surrounded by the shards, his eyes peacefully closed. Time is frozen. Everything is frozen, except for the brilliantly bright flames that dance around him. Like a fucking phoenix.

It's the most beautiful thing I've ever seen.

Then, he falls. The needles in his arms, neck, and legs rip out. He slumps to the right. It's so high for him to fall. His feet slide off the bottom of the tube, as the top crashes down. No one's moving. No one makes a sound. No one's breathing. Somehow, time stays frozen. And in that pause, I run to him, the glass crunching beneath my feet. I'm so fucking dizzy but—he's the only thing that matters. The guards react. I don't pay attention to them. He's the only thing that matters. I drop to my knees, the gel splashing me as I pull his limp head onto my lap.

"Ezra." I shake him. "It's gonna be okay. Ezra. Ezra, Ezra."

He doesn't move. His face is so hollow. How could she do this to him? I move his wet hair off his forehead. Is he even breathing? Tears flood down my face. I don't try to stop them. This can't... no. This can't be it.

I scream. All anger, sadness, fear. My regret. It all wants to escape. The last thing I said to him was that I hated him.

How could she take him from me? I'll never know what it's like to laugh with him. I'll never know how he *saw* the world. He'll never know what it's like to see the world. The *actual* world. Not our small world of broken people. And he'll never know that he means everything to me. He'll never know I figured it out. I'll have to live without seeing his smile. His eyes. His questions. All of the everything. The everything that's gone.

It's gone.

Genevieve

One second I'm fighting. The next second, I'm... not. The person I was trying to choke crumbles to the ground as his helmet crunches in on him. Muffled screams fill the room. Rosemary stumbles away from some of the guards in horror, as the armor that protected them jerks, folds, screeches, encasing them in horrible cocoons of suffocation. A cacophony of voices bounce around the inside of my skull, but one is rising above the rest in a wretched lament of the bitterest anguish I've ever felt.

Santiago Grey, how did you come to love him so much?

Tiago

My scream stops. It doesn't feel like my scream. It's like it belongs to someone else.

I drop my forehead so it rests on his.

He's so cold.

Ester

I have never seen a gift do something like this. I did not expect what just happened. It was like a bomb.

Santiago caring about Ezra? What is this? All the guards below me have gone silent now, their armor scrunched around their mangled bodies like crumpled paper. Santiago is not supposed to be able to hurt people. He could not hurt my creatures because they were partly human. And yet, he has just killed seventy-two people. And I killed Stevie McBride. It was all I could do to help her suffering end.

Rosemary has both hands clapped over her mouth, staring, terror-stricken at the bodies. Blood is beginning to leech from the corpses.

"Bravo, Mr. Grey," I say, clapping slowly. "That was so very dramatic. And all for the one you hated the most."

He does not move. Neither of them do. I do not know if Ezra is even alive. Santiago holds him, rocking. Rosemary slowly descends to her knees on the other side of the room while Genevieve appears next to her.

Rosemary

One second, I was trying to fight. The next, I was watching people be put through... a garbage crusher. Alive. There are bodies everywhere. Blood. Things that should *not* be on the ground. Everywhere. I'm nauseous. And I can feel the voice stirring in my head. I hate it. I hate everything. I'm so confused. My stomach is trying to heave again. Genevieve stands next to me. (Good. She doesn't look hurt.)

"Miss Mae–Anderson. Miss Legend. I am glad you are alive and well."

I jolt my head to look up at Madame Ester. Fear spikes in my gut. Out of the corner of my eye, I see Genevieve's hands curl into fists.

"We were just having a lovely conversation," Madam Ester says, gesturing down at Santiago. What is he doing? He's holding someone. Ezra. Santiago looks up at me. It feels like being stabbed in the stomach. Eyes tell you everything. Looking at him now, I feel his despair. We sit there, drowning in his heartbreak, for a silent eternity. Waves crashing against a feeble coastline.

"Help."

Tiago's whisper echoes. I start to crawl over. He's willing to do anything for Ezra. Everyone is. I should be too. I need to get this guilt off my chest. I manipulated him and used him to get attention. I need to tell Ezra that I am so, so sorry. Madam Ester's footsteps clang down the metal stairs. I go faster. The glass cuts my knees. There's blood on my hands. (The healer has the bloodiest hands.) Tears leak down my face. My jealousy rises. I thought I had stuffed it down enough for it to be gone, but it won't leave. Santiago is in love with *him*. Tears burn my eyes. *I'll do this for Santiago, because I don't want to do it for anyone else.* I grab Ezra's arm. God, his face is so hollow. Little bloody tears cover his arms, neck, and legs. The needles left marks. Like the ones I healed him of when he was eight. He's so lost...

I'm crushed by the weight of his suffering. It's so heavy I can hardly breathe. How can he possibly live like this? Santiago keeps his arms tight around Ezra's limp torso. He's talking, but I can't hear what he's saying. Genevieve is blocking Madame Ester from us. The pain is too much. Would Ezra even notice if I added some of my burden to his? I don't think so. But I couldn't. Because even if I was using him, we *are* friends. He was there for me. I won't put this on him.

I can't. It's mine. I need to heal him, for him. Not for Santiago. Because I have so many memories of us. We were best friends, Ezra and I. The agony is everywhere, like walking through a room full of angry wasps, with a floor covered in burning knives. I can't focus. Ezra's pain radiates, getting bigger and bigger. I try to stop it. I don't think I could, even if I wanted to. The voice in my head cackles, screaming Santiago's name. Screaming of his power. His potential.

But then I do what I know I shouldn't—I can't help myself. I wish I could say the fortress inside me broke on its own accord, but I'm the one who burnt it down. All of my wolfish envy and ravenous fury spill into his frail form. *(I'm sorry.)* All the times I was in his shadow. *(I'm so sorry.)* I could've had people like Genevieve and Tiago all along. But I didn't. I wish I hadn't been *Ezra Colton's best friend.* But I was. *(I love you Ezra. This wasn't meant to happen. I'm so, so, so sorry.)* I wasted my life. *(I don't mean it, Ezra. I love you.)*

It's all. His. Fault.

Ezra

This

is   worse.

T h a n

any

s i m ul ation.

By

f a r.

Genevieve

His mind. His mind is screaming again. I didn't think it was possible for it
to get worse. But it is. Nails on a chalkboard, needles in my eyes, and above
all, absolute agony.

Tiago

He's trembling in my arms. He's alive. Thank everything in this broken
world.

But *why* is he trembling? What is she doing?

Genevieve screams, collapsing to the floor. A nightmarish, hair–raising
scream. I look from her writhing body to an alarmed Madam Ester, to
Rosemary's tight grip on Ezra's arm, to his face. He jerks slightly to the
left. So does Genevieve. Her scream gets louder as Ezra's mouth opens. He
screams silently, convulsing at the same time as her. All of their muscles
twitch and strain in unison. I don't know what's happening.

CHAPTER 23

chapter 23

July 20th, 5:26pm

Location: The Lab

Rosemary

It's all his fault. I was his fucking sidekick.

(I'm sorry. I'm sorry I'm sorry I'M SORRY I'M SO so SORRY.)

Ezra

Th o us an ds

  of

  n e e dl es.

  A ll

  th e   p ai n.

Co m b i ne d.

Tiago

I grab Rosemary's hands, trying to pry her off. Ezra slumps to the floor, twitching. Genevieve goes limp.

Ester

It appears that Rosemary is trying to kill Ezra.

On purpose? I do not know.

Tiago

Rosemary's grip finally breaks, but Ezra keeps twitching. I pull him to me again, woozy. The fucking tranquilizer. I need to keep my eyes open. Genevieve gasps painfully, rolling into a fetal position.

Rosemary

"What are you *doing*?" Tiago asks, his words slurring together a little.

I open my eyes. Santiago is holding Ezra again. His eyes are full of confusion. There's a burn on Ezra's arm in the shape of my hands. Genevieve is on the floor too, her breathing rapid. They look so weak.

What am I doing? Hysteria spread through me. *(I'm sorry.)* I hurt him. *(I'm sorry.)* I hurt her. *(I'm so sorry.)*

My hands shake violently. My teeth chatter. The weight is too much. I cover my face with my hands. A rasping cry escapes my lips. I hurt him. I don't want him gone.

I don't *want this*

The voice in my head laughs.

Ester

Her rogue gift. It ran away from her. It brought her feelings to the surface. I have seen it before. Once in the girl, Stevie. Once in a woman. The woman killed people. By accident. And on purpose. Then she ran away from her life, and the husband she loved, when she realized that she was cursed.

Genevieve

A rogue gift. That's what the voice was. Or... that's what Ester calls the voice. It's not something wrong with Rosemary at all. There's a being. According to Ester, there's living entity inside her fucking head.

And that was hurting Ezra. It was playing with Rosemary's emotions. So it wasn't her fault. I check myself. Tired, but there's no pain. What do I do if Rosemary is possessed? Fuck. Santiago is so confused. Ester is mildly entertained, which is disgusting. Rosemary is feverishly distraught. And Ezra... is just silent.

I sit up. And turn around. I almost laugh because Tiago looks so protective. He's holding on to Ezra like a drowning man would clutch a log as he entered the rapids. But then there's Rosemary. She's kneeling with her face in her hands, her shoulders heaving. Her grief is so different from Tiago's. His was loud and passionate. Hers is like a slow trickle of freezing water. Chilling to the bone, leaving me drenched and miserable.

Rosemary's mind: *what have i done. i hurt him. i hurt her. all i do is hurt people. i hurt her. i need to leave. why did i come in the first place?*

My throat clogs for a moment, thick with pity. If only she could see herself the way I see her. And there's a dark undertone to it too, like syrup that burns my throat. It's nauseating.

Ester's mind: *Pathetic girl. Stupid little girl. Broken little pathetic stupid girl.*

I stand up. Tiago and Rosemary don't notice. Ester does. I clench my jaw. My nails dig into my palms.

Ester's mind: *Oh! I see we are going to have... a conversation, dearest Genevieve. For what do I owe this pleasure?*

Ester's face: The sardonic grin of someone who knows the game they're playing.

My face: Probably just really angry.

"Talk to me out loud," I say.

Ester's mind: *Oh dear, you are so naive. Just like your dimwitted friend, Rosemary.*

"Don't." A muscle in my neck spasms. "Don't talk about her like that."

Ester raises her eyebrows.

Ester's mind: *You think you can win with words, and fists? I have already won. So please do yourself a favour and concede.*

"Never."

CHAPTER 24

chapter 24

July 20th, 5:34pm

Location: The Lab

Rosemary

I don't want this. What have I done?

I scramble up. I'm going to run away. No one will see me again.

Wait.

"Never." Genevieve?

I turn away from Santiago and Ezra to the sound of her voice, pulling my hands from my face. It's Genevieve. And Madam Ester. A new possibility occurs to me.

"Madam Ester!" I sob, scrambling towards them.

Genevieve's head whips around at a breakneck speed. I don't meet her eyes. (I can't meet her eyes.) (How could I meet her eyes?)

"Rosemary!" Genevieve yells, as I collapse at Madam Ester's feet. "What are you doing?!"

She tries to help me up. I start crying again; I go limp. She can't move me. But she still tries. She still *tries.*

I force myself to meet Ester's iron gaze. There's this mad glint, shining behind her eyes. I ignore it.

"Please. I... I need you to get rid of my gift. It's... it's too much for me."

She looks down at me, disdainfully. Genevieve stops pulling and falls to her knees on the floor next to me. She grabs my face. I close my eyes. I can't I can't I can't I can't I can't—

"What," she demands, her voice breaking. "Are you doing?"

Ester

The two girls are crying at my feet. Genevieve stares intensely into Rosemary's face, her tears an afterthought. Rosemary is trying to wrench her face out of Genevieve's hands, her breathing sounding more like dry heaving than normal human oxygen intake.

She does not want her gift anymore?

I can remedy that quickly.

Rosemary

I can't live with myself.
But Genevieve hasn't given up on me.
Maybe we can fix this?

Genevieve

"Rosemary, love, you can't give up," I whisper to her.

She stops struggling, and takes a halting breath. "But, I'm such... a mess."

Her chestnut irises are full of everything. Hate, pain, regret, guilt, fear, hope.

"We're *all* a mess," I say, searching for her bright laughter, her smile, her loyalty.

She bites her trembling lip. "Are... are you sure?" She sniffs. "Because it... it seems like you've... you've really got your shit together."

I let out a shocked bark of a laugh. "Rosemary Mae–Anderson, you're a mess who's worth it."

Rosemary's mind: *Am I? Maybe I am. Maybe I can make things right.*

I pull her into a hug.

Ester

These children seem to have forgotten that I am here. I must fix that.

Genevieve

She's okay. I'm okay. We're okay. I'm holding her, and she's holding me, and we're gonna be alright.

Then there's a whisper.

Ester's mind: *Goodbye, pathetic little girl.*

Tiago's voice: "Wait—"

And the stopping of the heart that's pressed against mine.

CHAPTER 25

chapter 25

July 20th, 5:36pm
Location: The Lab

Ezra

The world's so blurry. So bright. Someone's holding me. The air hurts my lungs. Is this even real?

Rosemary

There's a sudden calm. An in–between.

Genevieve is shaking me. The world is kind of echoey, blurred into slow motion. And grey.

I wish you could hear me, I think. *I'm sorry, Genevieve.*

She's yelling at me. Her mouth is moving, panic and fear dancing in her pretty eyes. "I can hear you. I can hear you," she says, "Don't go."

But I'm slipping. *I'll miss you,* I say.

"No. No, you can't leave me...

Ester

I did what she asked. I took her gift away. I took all of her away. It took a mere touch of a finger.

I know what she was feeling, because I was her once. The woman with the rogue gift was me.

I am cursed.

Genevieve

She's so still. She just went still. I don't understand. She was talking to me inside my head. And now... she's silent.

Tiago

Why isn't Rosemary getting up? She went limp when Madam Ester touched her. Is it possible Madame Ester has a gift? I shake my head, trying to clear it.

Genevieve is shaking Rosemary. I thought everything was okay.

"Rosemary, say something," she begs. "Talk to me, please. Please. Rosemary, can you hear me? Please say something."

I'm frozen. Torn. Do I go over there? Or should I stay with Ezra? I don't get time to decide, because Madam Ester starts towards me. I squeeze my eyes shut, finding the tranquilizer molecule things inside me. I make them go away. I force them into nothingness.

"Stop." My voice is hoarse. I open my eyes, head pounding.

A small smile plays across her lips. It looks wrong on her face. Rosemary's still not moving. Genevieve's still pleading. I'm still not understanding.

"She's dead, Mr. Grey."

Just like all the crumpled heaps of metal, scattered around the door. I did that. Those were guards. I ignore the discomfort blooming in my body. I'm not supposed to... Genevieve stops. The huge space echoes with the last of her frantic cries. Then... the silence is oppressive. We're frozen in a moment of denial and creeping dread. No. I shake my head. Madam Ester nods, still smiling. Rosemary can't be dead. She was so full of... everything. Only seconds ago. Genevieve howls, shattering any illusion of calm, pulling Rosemary's head into her lap, crying over her serene face. She brushes her matted, limp curls back and puts a shaking hand on her cheek. I'm still frozen. Unsure.

"Yes. I have a gift, Santiago."

A gift of death. The *curse* of death.

Ezra

Things slide in and out of focus. A blurry face framed by blonde hair. And bright blue eyes. Tiago? *Are you really here?* My mouth is so dry. Everything is stiff. I try to say his name. Nothing. I can't really see...? Someone's walking towards us. Someone's crying. It's all so... defined. But I can't tell if it's real. It can't be real.

"She's dead, Mr. Grey."

Who's dead? Someone screams. I flinch.

I try again. "Tiago?" Something comes out this time, but it's so quiet that I don't think he'll hear me.

The footsteps stop. His head snaps down. He looks stunned. "Ezra," he breathes, holding me tighter. Tighter.

Why is he here? Who's dead? Who's crying? There are so many things I want to know. God. This is probably fake. He's about to laugh at me.

Instead, he fumbles with something for a second, then slides my glasses onto my face. My glasses. What?

"How wonderful."

I turn my head clumsily. It's Ester. Behind her are two girls. One of them is holding the other, crying quietly. The other isn't moving. Her curly hair is splayed out around her. Who is she? I feel like I know her.

"Ezra," Ester sneers. "Alive."

I think she's trying to smile. I try to think of another time she smiled. My memory is foggy, but I'm pretty sure I've never seen it. Not even when I was little.

Genevieve

Ester killed her. If I wasn't shaking so badly, I'd kill her. I'd *kill her.* She's probably going to go murder Tiago and Ezra too. But I just can't move. Rosemary looks like she's asleep. Her hair is a knotted mess. My fingers fumble as I try to untangle it. We were gonna be okay. A chunk of hair rips out, and it just makes me cry harder. I stop trying. Her face is dirty, but streaked with her tears. And mine.

She's still pretty, with the map of the night sky on her face. Rosemary looks like she's asleep, but she's not. And I'm not gonna see her eyes again. Or her smile. Or hear her laugh. Because she won't wake up, no matter how hard I shake her. No matter how loud I yell or how long I cry. I try to rub the dirt off her face, but it just smears. I wish she would wake up. Like Ezra just did. He's alive. Why can't she be?

Don't go, Rosemary. We're gonna be okay, I think into the emptiness.

There's no answer.

Ezra

"Stop," Tiago says haltingly to Ester. "Don't come any closer."

Ester's eyes dance menacingly. "Are you scared of me now that you know I have a gift?"

I blink. She *does* have a gift. I saw her use it once. She explained how it worked once, when she thought I couldn't hear. She can kill. Just by focusing. Like any other gift. She thinks about a light going out. A heartbeat ceasing to exist. And then, it does.

She'll kill him. Not me, though. She'll keep trying to fix me. She'll keep pushing me to the edge of sanity. (This isn't real.) (But at least I'll lose myself knowing I had the courage to say something.) (I stood up for myself.) (I did.)

"Mother." I've only called her that twice before in my life, once when I sat outside her door at the home, crying because a group of people had ganged up on me yet again, and the other time was when I was ten. I'd been begging her to stop hurting me.

"My gift isn't going to go away. Nothing will make *any* of it go away. You've done nothing but hurt people. Hurt me. I'm tired of this. Of you controlling me. Of you trying to fix me—" My voice cracks. It won't keep going. Even my voice has given up.

I'm so tired…

I look up at him. Horror slowly dawns on his face. She's my mother. I used to think I made that up. I didn't. Tiago's eyes go steely and his jaw clenches. Then it occurs to me that maybe, he's trying to protect me. His nostrils flare. I'd give my life for him. And I will, if it means saving him from this torture my mother created. Even if he's fake. Maybe I can live in a pretty simulation for a while, where everything is okay. I'd go through what I've gone through a thousand times over if it meant he could be free.

I'd give up my heart; I'd sell my soul; I'd burn the whole world to ashes for him. Always him.

Ester

I did not want Ezra. Especially after I learned he was cursed, like me. After everything I have done to him, how can he still be so gentle?

CHAPTER 26

chapter 26

July 20th, 5:48pm

Location: The Lab

Tiago

All the threat drops from Ester's face. Ezra keeps looking at her. What is *happening*?

Genevieve is still crying. My eyes fill with saltwater.

Rosemary.

Ester

I was too old to have a child. When he lit himself on fire at the hospital, at just one day old, I decided he would not live like me. I would free him. It is not a blessing to have a gift. It is the worst curse you could possibly have. The voice in my head disagreed, until I found a way to get rid of it. I gave it to someone else. Someone more powerful than me. A gifted infant. It died. The voice kills people. It twists their gifts and their emotions, and it follows me. It is always near. The mistakes I have made are inexcusable. Looking down at Ezra, I feel remorse. Or, I say it is remorse, because I do not know how to describe this feeling. It is sort of a tightening at the throat, a stabbing in the chest and a difficulty breathing. I have had this feeling before, but I still believed that I could help him. I could cure him.

But maybe I cannot. Maybe this has all been a huge waste of a life. His *and* mine. Before, I would not give up. Now, I do not think I can continue to put this boy, one I do not know, through hell. Maybe I will find someone else to help me cure these gifts. Someone who is not my own son. A volunteer, perhaps. I do not know if I have the energy to continue this research. Or perhaps, I will give it up entirely.

Ezra does not look like me. He looks more like Colton, my husband. My perfect husband. Corporate genius who quit to drive a taxi. He said he loved getting to know people's stories. Their opinions and views. He was always happy, always curious, always bright, no matter what.

But when I found out about the home for unusually gifted children, from the men who came into our hospital room after Ezra was born, I pleaded to work there. The government officials in charge of the operation found me trustworthy. I left my Colton and began to find a cure. I fell into disarray without him. I could not let anyone know that Ezra was my child, so I changed his last name to Colton. And I tried to change him.

I wish I could have... wanted him. Wanted them both.

Santiago Grey is unreadable, except for the look of disgust shadowing his features. He is realizing what an awful person I am. I did that to my own child. I tried to make him normal, but I ended up breaking him by chipping him down to a skinny, hollow, grey shell of the person he used to be.

Tiago

"You're his... mother?" I whisper, beyond appalled. How could anyone do this to their own child?

Ezra lets out a pained breath.

Is it possible for somebody as beautiful as Ezra to come from a mother who literally turns people into monsters? I need to protect him from her. Why didn't he tell anyone? (I don't *understand*.)

Family is something the kids at the home had to make. We got used to not having parents. But Ezra lived with a parent who didn't want him. Everyone made fun of him for being small and giftless, but he was only giftless because of the things his mother did to him. No wonder he always left. Ran away for a few hours just to escape. He just had to get away.

Now I see—he didn't make friends because he was afraid of getting hurt. I definitely didn't help either. How could I have said those things to him?

"I did not want to be," she answers quietly.

"No one wants me," Ezra whispers, almost inaudibly. He's laughing a bit. It makes me feel sick.

The things that have been programmed into his head. Hearing him say that fills me with pure anger. How can he possibly believe no one wants him? Kindness has been his way of compensating for all the bad.

"*For nothing, I slowly stole you away,*" she whispers. "I did. *It was as simple as can be.* I did not know it would be so easy. Why did you not fight? *Although it's over, I'll remember your light.* You always burned so bright." She grows louder, with her eyes shut tight. "*Time will not heal you anymore.* I thought you were cured."

"Stop," I say forcefully.

Ezra's laughing silently, tears streaming from his closed eyes. I can't let her hurt him anymore.

Genevieve

Tiago's crying. Ezra's crying. I'm crying. Rosemary is... not crying anymore.

Ester has a way of breaking people. I'd try to help Tiago, except I'm rooted to this spot. Rosemary's dead. I let her ask for her gift to be taken away. I should've taken her with me. We would be free from Ester. We could've left.

We could've run away.

Ezra

My poem. I wrote it for her. And I used to write it on my wall or floor every day. Someone always washed it off. Someone took my marker away. So I yelled the poem at the security camera when I had the strength to speak. I wrote it so she'd know she was breaking me. She made it the passwords on her computer when I was eight. The year I wrote it. Maybe it was because she wanted to have a reminder of her son. Maybe she did it to torment me. She told me that she used it for her passwords when she thought I was sedated. That's how I came to know anything about her. I don't really understand her reasons behind making it her passwords. I thought I made it up, that Ester used my poetry. I remember showing someone... a girl with red hair, and she laughed at me when I gave her the piece of paper with the passwords on it, surprised that I knew Madame Ester's passwords. Eventually, I laughed too and it was forgotten.

"*Darling, wishes cannot save you now,*" I continue quietly through the tears. "You used to say that to me when I screamed. *Darling, they will not remember you when you've fallen.* You told me no one would care. I always had a spark of hope, though. *But will someone follow me all the way down?* That part wasn't for you. That part kept me going."

My throat hurts so bad. I still can't tell if this is fake. If it is, it's crueler than anything I've experienced. My glasses are pressing into the side of my face. Tiago's arms around me feel so *real*. Fingers brush my hair off my forehead, over and over. This is definitely fake. Something is about to happen. I'll fall or drown or something like that. Or Tiago will kill me. Or Ester will kill me. Someone will kill me in the worst way possible and I'll be holding on to this fake memory that felt so *real*. My skin burns where Tiago's fingers brush. I love him. But he only ever hurts me.

I focus on the feeling anyways. I'll probably never experience it for real.

Tiago

It's his poem. He finishes it for Madam Ester. I stroke his hair, anger slashing through my body like knives.

"You can't keep doing this," I spit at her.

She ignores me. "Ezra." Her eyes are wide. "Why did you not fight?"

"Because fighting didn't stop you from hurting me."

He says it like it's just a fact of life. It breaks my heart.

Ester

Regret is growing inside me. I broke my son. He could have been happy. Just because I could not always control my gift does not mean he could not either. He could have been happy. He could have had a family. But I would not let him. I broke him. I should have stopped. I should not have even started. Why did I choose to break my son? The only place I acknowledged him was here, while he was screaming. There are no photographs or evidence that he is even mine. Except for my passwords. His poem. Mine.

He is not mine.

He does not belong to me. People do not belong to each other. At least, they should not. I treated Ezra like a toy I was unafraid of breaking. But he is breakable, and he is not mine. People should belong *with* each other. I took that away from him too. Nobody wanted to be near him.

One night, when he was barely four years old and we had just come back to the home from the lab, he cried outside my bedroom, but I would not let him in. The fact that he even called me Mother...

I broke him. Over and over and over. I do not deserve the title of mother. Not said in his weak *weak* voice.

Maybe he has a chance at life, if I get out of the way. If I am in his life, I will keep breaking him. I will keep trying to fix him. It has been my life's purpose to change this boy, and if I am near him, I will not stop until he is dead. Yes, it will be better if I am out of his life. That is what I will do.

I tear my eyes off the two of them. My knees protest, as I run up the stairs to my lab. I do not have a plan. But I know I need to leave. My computer screens are all lit up, and I yank out a little USB from the far end of the console. My work. Research. Blueprints and ideas. As I draw the stick out of the computer, I knock a glass of water across the keyboards. Panicking, I try to clean the mess up with shaking hands, as the glass rolls off the desk in a series of clattering bumps. The electricity shocks me. A shooting pain, through my arm. I stumble backwards as things start to spark.

"Wait!" Ezra's hoarse yell startles me. I step on something round. The glass. I launch backwards. Stumbling, I feel the railing below my waist.

CHAPTER 27

chapter 27

July 20th, 5:52pm
Location: The Lab

Ezra

She trips. I scared her. Electricity and water don't mix well. I don't want her to get hurt. Nothing is right in her mind. There must be a way to help—and she's falling.

Over the railing.

Ester

Maybe it is better this way—

Ezra

She hits the floor with a sickeningly dull thud.

"No!" escapes my lips.

After everything. She's dead. What happened? *Is* she dead?

I look at the girls again. I don't recognize the dark–skinned girl with the faded blue tipped coils of hair. She's bent over a pale girl with wild curls. No. She's not breathing. *No.*

"Rosemary?" I ask feebly, remembering now. Remembering and wishing I didn't. Why am I remembering things? "No. No. No. Not her too."

The girl who's alive looks up at the sound of my voice. Cold, hard pain is displayed so sharply across her face that it feels like being slapped. There's a dark glint of satisfaction when her multi–coloured eyes drift to Ester's body, sprawled out on the floor. I don't know who this girl is. None of them should even be here. No one should have died.

This has to be a cruel simulation. My teeth chatter—from cold or grief—I can't tell. My throat closes up. Panic. I... lurch forwards. Everything hurts. Tiago starts, but I'm dragging myself across the floor, towards the two of them and I ignore the glass digging into my arms. Because... Rosemary. I'm at her side and the other girl is just staring at her face.

Oh god. My hand trails itself down her freckled cheek, trembling, smearing blood...

Oh god.

"Rosemary. She's..." I can't finish the sentence.

"Gone," the girl rasps, meeting my gaze. Then she looks over my shoulder to... Tiago. I tear my eyes away from Rosemary's still face, not believing, not understanding... only to get trapped in Tiago's sorrowful pity. Bright, watery blue eyes.

"Are you real?" I ask him, so overwhelmed and numb at the same fucking time.

I can't bring myself to look back. At Rosemary. My only friend. How can I possibly live without her? It's hard to breathe. Too fast. I'm dizzy.

"I'm real, Ezra," he whispers.

Doubt crowds my mind. He's lying. He's wrong. What if he thinks he's real? But he isn't? Countless Tiagos in the simulations said that to me. So many times.

"Tiago wouldn't be here. He hates me. What are you going to do to me?"

I shudder. He's been holding me for so long. I want him to let me go. But I also don't. I bite my lip. Pain. Anchor.

"I'm here," he says again, eyebrows scrunched together in concern. "I'm *real.*"

My heart speeds up. Lies. He's lying. He wipes tears off my cheek with his thumb. I flinch away. It's all a lie. The girl behind us takes a shuddering breath. Tiago must share his glance with her, because it's full of fear that evaporates when I catch his gaze.

"Ezra, what have they done to you?"

I close my eyes. No. I feel my insides burning. Any moment. More pain. So much pain. It's coming.

"I'm gonna go, Tiago," the girl whispers.

We both look back a her. She looks exhausted. Tiago's shaking his head, about to say something.

"Shh," she says, voice trembling. "I need to go."

Tiago furrows his brow at her.

She flashes him a quick, dead smile. "But I'll find you, yeah? Still gotta show you the telescope."

"Genevi—" He doesn't finish her name, because she... disappears. Fuck. What? Then, Rosemary's body starts rising. I let out a strangled cry but as I lurch forwards, Tiago puts a hand on my shoulder.

"It's... okay," he says, almost regretfully.

I turn to him, mouth open. He looks so... small. Docile. Tired.

"Prove that you're real," I find myself whispering. Because I have no self control.

He pauses. A long awkward pause. And then: "Can I... can I kiss you?"

I let out a burst of shocked laughter. Tiago tenses. I don't believe it. This is fake. I nod anyway. There's another long, long, long pause. Every second is an eternity where I expect torture. Pain. Oblivion.

And then he kisses me. Gently, tenderly, softly.

He tastes like mint. Like wind in trees. Like the moment before it rains. He tastes like poetry. It's so stupidly ironic. Tastes like a fucking concept.

No he doesn't. It's a bit sour. I laugh into his mouth.

Harsh. It grates my throat. Tastes like blood.

Tiago

He's laughing. And his mouth is cold. I kiss him again. One, two, three times, quickly. I want him. And I want him to stop laughing. I want to bite his lip, but it's so dry. I pull away, heart racing. He's got his eyes closed, his mouth open. He runs his teeth across his bottom lip and oh fuck, I want him. I want him to be okay. I want him to wake up next to me. I want him to love me like I love him—

Ezra

"Ezra, I want you," he whispers in my ear, almost desperately. No one has said that to me. Ever. I can't stop. This is so funny to me for no reason. The iron in my throat... the fact that Tiago is here... god. I must be dead.

I don't know if this is heaven or hell.

Tiago

For a moment, I'm scared he's going to catch on fire. He went from freezing to almost burning hot in seconds.

"Don't worry." He's still laughing, smirking, kind of crying. "I'm not going to light on fire. I don't even know if I can."

"Thanks for the reassurance," I whisper as he opens his eyes. They're still so green, in a world of grey. Even behind the dirty lenses of his glasses.

He runs his hand gently through my hair. A shiver runs up my spine. Oh god.

Ezra

I've wanted to do that for way too long. His eyes are bright. Brighter than they used to be. So he's fake. This is a lie.

"Do you believe me now?" he asks, so earnestly that I almost doubt myself.

I hide the doubt. I raise my eyebrows. "I think I'm dead."

He doesn't know how to reply to that. I don't know why I said it. But when I laugh, he laughs too.

Genevieve

Ester is dead. Good. Tiago has Ezra in his arms. Even better. Rosemary is in mine. But not in the same way. Ezra's so confused. I'm standing on the observation deck now, the computers still sparking. There's a door up here. I couldn't bring myself to jump off the staircase Rosemary destroyed, so when I push the emergency exit open, wind gusts against my face. Stirs Rosemary's hair. I stand there, eyes closed against the world.

Ezra's mind: *Did he just kiss me? This can't possibly be real. But what if it is? He just kissed me. I'm dead. Lies. We're going to die. This is...*

Tiago's mind: *Uhhh...*

I'm happy for them. I feel like I'm invading. But I can't move. I don't have the energy. I feel hollow. Empty.

I'm so fucking sorry, Rosemary. I wish you would wake up. Tell me you're okay. Or tell me you're not. I just want to know that you're here. I want to see you look at me with your eyebrows raised and hear you thinking about how I'm such a liar. Anything. I don't care if you're mad at me. As long as you're here. As long as you're in the world. I wish I were with you, wherever you are. It doesn't matter if we're just friends or even enemies. I want you here.

What if she's stuck in the in–between? Maybe there's a way to get her back.

But that's what everyone wishes for. Rosemary's head shifts as my arm jerks on its own accord. For a second, my heart leaps into my throat, ready to soar. I think: *She's waking up!*

Then it crashes, breaking all over again, like a china vase thrown from an airplane. Not her. It's just my stupid human limbs.

Tiago's mind: *I want you.*

And I want you, I think to Rosemary. *But he's not thinking about you, is he? He found Ezra, if you were wondering. He's happy. They both are. Sort of. They're happy they found each other. They'll miss you. Just not as much as I will.*

Tiago

Ezra's eyelids are swollen and purple. He looks horrible. I guess that makes sense. His hand drops from my hair. He's sitting cross from me when he drags a red, dry hand over his face. When he lets the hand fall, he winces.

"Oh..." His face is scrunched up and one of his eyes is closed. "I'm dizzy."

"Is there anything I can do?" I offer gently, concerned. He thinks he's dead. I don't know how to deal with that. I shift over so I'm sitting next to him.

His head rests on my shoulder. "Is she gone?"

I don't answer. He takes my face in his hands, turning my head to look at him. I see the bewildered pain in his beautiful, innocent green eyes. They're in danger of overflowing. Again. His hands are cold, shaking slightly. Even this is so much of a struggle for him. He twitches.

"Are they dead?"

I stay silent.

Ezra's eyes harden and he clenches his jaw.

"Are they dead?" he asks again, and his grip on my face tightens.

"Yeah," I whisper.

Meeting his eyes is impossible now. His head jerks around, towards the bodies. (There are so many bodies. All the guards.) I stop breathing, then feel his head slump onto my shoulder again. I put my arm around him, holding him tightly to me. (I don't want to let him go. I never want to let him go again.)

I wish Genevieve was still here. Then we could figure out what to do. Together.

Just in case, I think: *I'm sorry, Genevieve. I wish I could bring her back. I want her back too.*

"Tiago?" Ezra's voice surprises me. "What are you going to do to me?"

"Shhh."

"But I can't help feeling like something is going to happen—"

"Nothing will happen to you."

"I—"

"I swear. I won't let anything hurt you."

"I don't understand."

"Ever."

"But—"

"Ezra."

"What?"

"I'm real."

"Really?"

"Yes."

Ezra

I don't believe him. I don't know if this is real. But the weight of his arm is comforting. Sort of.

How can she be dead? How are they both dead? Who was that girl who disappeared?

He's rocking. My heart is suddenly aware that he's here, holding me. I'm worried it's going to burst out of my chest. But it can. I'm dead or dying. Either way, it doesn't matter. None of this *matters*.

"Sorry about your sweaters," I mumble, ignoring the dread and darkness.

He laughs. "You've only ruined one."

I can't help but smile a little.

"You did mess it up pretty good, though..."

"Sorry." My smile fades. Apologies. Lies. I don't understand. My hand spasms. "Why didn't you just leave me? Forget about me? Then Rosemary wouldn't be dead." Tears rise, prickling inside my nose as I look at her still shape. If I'm dead then she can't be dead. "Tiago, *I* am dead. Not her. I'm so broken. I—"

"Ezra, you're not dead," he cuts me off. "No. When you disappeared I couldn't get you out of my head. I couldn't believe you were just ... gone. What I said... I couldn't let it be the last thing I said to you. It's taken me a long time to realize that ... well—" He stops abruptly. I look up at him. He's blushing. "Well, I'm in love with you."

Liar. I almost scream it. My mouth falls open. "I... I don't understand," I say instead, lifting my head from his shoulder. "How long—"

"Fuck, Ezra, do you always have to look so angelically confused?"

Then he's kissing me again. The whole world, everything falls away, letting me know that this is *not* real. This can't true. Our foreheads press together. His eyes are closed. I hungrily take in his face, so close to mine. I can't decide if I prefer the lies. But the lies... are maybe better than the reality.

"Just shut up, okay?"

"Okay." I have to be careful not to ignite. My skin gets so hot whenever he touches me. My gift. Is that fake too?

"Can you just accept the fact that I love you?" he asks timidly.

"You're the one asking me?" I find myself whispering. I love him. I have. For years. And maybe that's why the lie is better. Because he loves me back.

"Please, just no more questions."

I can tell he's smiling. I kiss his shoulder, ignoring the thickness in my throat.

"And also," he adds, "please don't incinerate me."

"I'll do my best."

"Good enough, I guess." He lies down, pulling me with him.

I rest my head on his chest. His heart is beating so fast. Mine matches it. Because I can't tell what's real. I might be asleep. I think I'm dying. (I'm so dizzy. What is *happening?*)

"Look." His voice is hushed. "You can see the stars."

The planetarium roof has been replaced with a glass dome. I didn't notice. Tiny little dots of light fill the dark sky. Purple, blue, black. It's breathtaking. I stop breathing. He doesn't notice.

"There's the constellation Lyra." He points it out. "It's from a Greek myth about the poet, Orpheus."

I don't really see what he's pointing at. Looking up makes me feel so small. How does he know the constellations?

"Tiago," I whisper. "I love you too."

I can't see his face, but his heart speeds up again. I think he's smiling.

I start trembling. Fight or flight. I want to run, but where would I go? I'm going to die. I want to scream. I want help. I want to stay right here. What's happening?

CHAPTER 28

chapter 28

July 20th, 6:10pm

Location: The Lab

Tiago

As we lie there, I feel right. Sort of. More right than before. This is how it's supposed to be. The grief in the pit of my stomach is easier to ignore with Ezra. He's kind of warm now. Pointing out the constellations to him ignites a spark of hope in my chest. I know Ezra isn't listening. Having him here is enough, whether he listens or not. I hear my name whispered softly.

"I love you too," Ezra says.

My heart flutters. Ezra is someone whose soul froze. And it froze to protect him, which was understandable. It probably helped for a while. He was like a sword, tempered to brittleness. If dropped, he would break. Vulnerable. Fickle. Abandoned. He starts shaking.

Ezra was falling. I jumped down after him. *"But will someone follow me all the way down?" That part isn't for you. That part kept me going,* Ezra said to Ester.

I would. I did. I always will, I think. *I will always follow you down, Ezra Colton.* I pull him closer, wrapping my arms around Ezra's frail body.

"Jesus, Tiago." He laughs. "Do you *want* to suffocate me?" he asks, sounding nervous. His voice is choked off.

"No. Sorry," I whisper, loosening my grip. "You're just... shivering."

"Sorry," he blurts back, going very still.

I swallow. I don't want him to be upset. I don't want him to be hurt, ever again. He's had enough pain for a lifetime. We both have. I twist my fingers through his hair.

"I dreamed about you," I whisper.

"Oh yeah?" His voice is full of stunted mischief. A bit of how he used to be. "Hot."

"Oh lord," I huff, laughing in an embarrassed kind of way. "Not like that. Get your head out of the gutter. I just meant I jumped into a pit after you."

He turns his head to look at me, a peculiar look on his face. "I think I remember that." He stares at me for a moment before a tentative grin spreads across my face. (And my heart melts.) "Maybe we have some sort of mental connection." He wiggles his eyebrows.

"Maybe we do."

"You never used to agree with me that easily," Ezra says nervously. He's shaking again. Twitching.

"What, do you want me to argue more? Would that make you more comfortable?" I want him to be okay. What's wrong with him? And what am I going to do about it?

Ezra lets out another laugh that sounds like he's being strangled. "Yes. Actually it would. This is all very strange."

"I don't think any of this is odd," I counter.

"What," Ezra says in a breathy way, like he's trying to pretend he's back to normal, "in the world are you talking about? First, I experience the worst pain of my life. Then, I wake up to a room full of... people." His composure dissolves. His next exhale shudders painfully. I almost sit up, but then he continues, "And then I find out you were gay or bi or whatever you are. Is there nothing strange about that?"

"Huh?"

"Huh what?"

"Gay? Bi? What does that mean?"

Ezra giggles, and once he starts, he can't stop. It's an uncomfortable, wheezing sound, but—at least he's laughing?

"Are you serious?" he manages to ask.

I laugh too, but nervously. "Yep. I'm confused." I pause. "Just please remember that I've pretty much lived under a rock for my entire life. Or in a prison, if you will. I didn't know what Wi–Fi was until a few days ago."

"Hmmm. Let's go with prison." Ezra's laugh fades. "Okay, so you like me, and I'm a guy." He pauses. "But you also liked Emeline, right? "

"Yeah… but why does it matter so much?" I ask.

"Sometimes people seem to think it does." Ezra sighs, then frowns. "Wi–Fi?"

"See what I mean?"

"No. No, Tiago, I know what Wi–Fi is. How did you *not* know what Wi–Fi is?"

I look at the top of Ezra's head. "How did you figure all this stuff out?"

Ezra looks up at me, something racing through the green of his eyes. "Being giftless has its advantages." He smiles his adorable, crooked smile. A muted version. It's more of a smirk now.

I waggle my eyebrows, causing Ezra to laugh again. "Not like that, you idiot. I just mean that I wasn't trapped in the home all the time. I saw some of the world. I learned about *Wi–Fi*."

I laugh.

"*And* I always made it back," he smiles, "in time for dinner. I didn't get locked out once in my life."

"We don't have to talk about that."

There's a silence. Ezra chokes on the air. It's an odd sound, full of grief and confusion. I tense.

"Everything is so screwed up..." he whispers, back to the hollow tone from before.

"Are you okay?" I ask softly, my stomach flipping.

Ezra doesn't respond for a moment. "No." He pauses again. "Someday. Maybe?"

"Better be someday soon. I don't want to have to deal with... no, never mind. It wouldn't be 'dealing with' you anymore. Just know that I'm here."

"Yeah. I know." He sounds like he *doesn't* know. I should have been better to him. Fuck. I can't relax. Why was I such a dick?

"I'm glad you know," I say softly, mindlessly twisting my fingers through the curls that are returning as Ezra's hair dries. He flinches. I stop, but then he starts breathing really fast, so I start again.

"It's okay," I whisper, shoving the feelings of unease down into some deep, dark place.

We lie silently for a while.

"Tiago, when you said you hated me, how much of it was true?" Ezra suddenly asks.

"All of it, Ezra." I pause. "Except for the hate."

Genevieve

I went down a staircase at the back of the building. There were a bunch of mind voices inside. My arms are getting tired now. It's colder outside. And my bare feet are sore. Walking in the dark along the gravel road, I still can't bring myself to take my shoes back. *Because they're on your feet, Rosemary. I feel like you still need them, even though you don't.*

I think my feet are bleeding. It doesn't matter. It's cold and dark out here. And quiet. There's nobody. Only my thoughts. And you. There's still you. Can you hear me? If you can, I hope I'm helping you. Calming you, maybe. When I get to the highway, I'm going to look crazy. A girl in a hospital gown, with bleeding feet. Alone and so far from anything. Carrying the body of her friend.

Did you think of me as your friend? Because you are certainly mine. I feel like you understand me. People were so mean to me when I was in school. Partially because of you, I'm ready to make friends again. Go on adventures. Come on, Rosemary, we'll get through this together. We'll laugh about the weird looks people will give us as they drive past. We'll endure the pain I'm going through together. We'll be okay, Rosemary.

We'll be okay.

CHAPTER 29

chapter 29

Abendroth

Ever since the girl died, i've been hovering near the high ceiling of this place. this planetarium. what a bizarre room. i wasn't shocked when the redhead died. everyone i inhabit dies at some point, before their time. i inhabited ester murtle kellwether, a woman who could kill with one touch. in fact, she created me, out of hatred for her gift. i did the exact opposite of what she intended. i made her stronger and i killed people without her willing them to be dead. (i am the rogue gift.) but i got bored. ester's mind wasn't pliable. i could only give her a certain amount of power. she was done with me and i was done with her, so when she performed rituals of exorcism, i went along, into the vessel she gave to me after she couldn't trap or destroy me. i learned with time, that my vessels have to die for me to move on. ester is a different case. she kills. she is like death.

but i killed each vessel she gave me. i drove them mad. people don't do well with voices in their head that they can't control. every now and then, i would leave ester be, only to circle back to her group of unusually gifted youth.

then i found the next best vessel. stevie mcbride, a girl who could levitate. i tried to give her more power. she didn't appreciate my efforts.

after stevie died, i became more powerful. i stayed by ester. her hatred for her gift made me anxious. trigger happy. silly. i went into the first vessel i saw.

and stayed dormant. fear and hate make me more alive. i found rosemary, who was angry. her anger made her easy to mess with. but again, her mind was too stiff. she liked to ignore me. i couldn't use her in the way i need my vessel to work. the invisible girl left the room with the healer girl's body. now, every one of my vessels are dead. i am more powerful because of it. free. finally. while i inhabited rosemary, i observed the youth of ester's home. finding my perfect host. today, there was a boy who killed just under one hundred people. he found a way to hurt people. manipulate their environment. he is smart. he is so powerful on his own. imagine what we could do together.

now, i watch the two boys sleeping. fire boy. not powerful enough for me to waste my time on. but malleable boy... he is the vessel i've been waiting for. i take in the sight of the two of them. quiet, holding each other, and surrounded by corpses, finally able to admit their feelings. the fire one is so broken. he thinks he's dead. and he's terrified. maybe they'll find happiness. i don't understand sweet feelings.

humans. so strange and soft.

maybe i can fix that.

Acknowledgements

Guys, I know this is super weird, but. The acknowledgements are usually one of my favourite parts of a book. (I get to write my own!!! Yay!!!)

So. First, I have to thank my family. My mom and dad have been putting up with me ranting about these characters and their exploits for at least four years now. Thank you so much. I couldn't have asked for a more supportive team, who were willing to read my work and give me honest feedback. And thank you to my brother. He read the first, handwritten draft of this book, so kudos to him for being able to decipher grade nine me's chicken scratch.

Thank you to all the other people who helped shape this book, like Ms. Strilchuk (grade nine English teacher who read pictures of the early chapters during the pandemic), the *Momlayna Fan Squad* group chat (you guys are iconic), Jess Verdi, (an awesome editor), and the few friends who managed to get through the early drafts. Also, I must thank Marin, who got the brunt of me rambling about this story. (*Screams* MARIN YOU ARE AN AMAZING FRIEND AND YOU HAVE SAVED ME SO MANY TIMES THANK YOU.)

Lastly, I thank you, the reader, because readers are awesome (and it's so satisfying when authors put this in. I'm such a nerd, y'all.). Thanks for coming on this journey with me.

(And to the queer kids, you're doing great. Life sucks sometimes. It's unfair and cruel and gross, but it can get better. It can 100% get better.

Keep fighting. And keep reading stories. Keep telling stories. Or *start* telling stories! This book was a step in the right direction for me discovering who I am, so you never know what you'll learn when you start telling stories, haha.)

(Also, you made it to the end! Are you excited to see what comes next? I *cannot* wait to share it with you. I'm literally shaking in my boots! I can't *wait.* >:)